ANCHOR MAN

ALSO BY JOHN HENDERSON

A Blind Eye

Musgrave Solution

Murder Scams & Gravy Trains

Taipan Club

ANCHOR MAN

SIMON WEBSTER'S SECOND FIASCO

JOHN HENDERSON

Anchor Man

ISBN 978-0-9875769-0-3

Publisher: J. Henderson, Canberra, Australia

❀ Created with Vellum

ACKNOWLEDGMENTS

To Jill for all her help and patience and to Fergus for his constant interruptions.

CHAPTER 1

*C*harlie 'Chick' Chambers watched from the driving seat located high on the flybridge of the fifty-five foot motor yacht, "Gemini" as his young deckhand, Adam Vance, perched on the bow of the vessel, prepared to raise the anchor. Normally this was achieved with the aid of an electric winch, but the new cruiser had suffered minor teething troubles and, unfortunately for Adam, just at the moment those troubles happened to relate to the winch. The owner of the good ship, "Gemini", Graham Lee, had invited a few of his close friends for a quiet afternoon cruising on the harbour, the first opportunity he had since completing the onerous task of selling "Chez Anne", which had served his purposes for many years, and purchasing "Gemini". Mr Lee believed the cruiser, "Chez Anne", had passed its use by date and it was time for purchasing something a bit more up-market, more modern and, more to the point, more appealing to his sense of the finer things in life. Once the anchor had been recovered, Charlie would manoeuvre the vessel from its anchorage in Rushcutters Bay of Sydney

Harbour, to the nearby marina in anticipation of the arrival of Mister Lee and his guests.

'Come on, Adam, get a move on, there can't be so much water under us that you need all day,' Charlie called down from his lofty position. Charlie enjoyed playing with his new toy, a far different cry from the old "Chez Anne" that Mr Lee liked but, according to Charlie's reckoning, didn't love as one should love a boat that kept one safe and dry. Maybe the "Gemini" would be different. Charlie, who had worked as skipper for Mr Lee for several years now, was fully aware of just where Mr Lee made the oodles of money needed to be able to afford one of life's little extravagances. In fact, every time Charlie refueled "Gemini", the thought crossed his mind that he would have to mortgage his house to pay for the two and a half thousand litres "Gemini" needed to fill the tank.

To Charlie it was a strange set-up, strange to the extent poor Charlie didn't quite know what side his bread was buttered. The tall, lean, brown eyed Mr Lee owned and ran a very successful casino, which was not quite a legal enterprise in Sydney town; in fact, it was quite illegal. Sure, a real government sanctioned legal casino had just opened up down in Tasmania, but the chance of a similar venture opening its doors in Sydney was probably some years away. As a consequence, and in order to satisfy the strong demand for gambling facilities, a host of illegal casinos had existed in the city since the days of colonization in 1888. Though Charlie was keenly aware of his boss's line of business, he was totally ambivalent to the matter as Mr Lee treated and paid him well; and Charlie did like playing around with boats. The difficulty for Charlie was that, given the nature of Mr Lee's vocation, two of his guests on this bright sunny Sunday morning happened to be police officers, though it had not been so long ago that there had been four officers on board the "Chez Anne", including a police chief superintendent.

Adam was not having any luck in his attempt to raise the anchor, which came as somewhat of a surprise to both Charlie and Adam himself as Adam normally found it a simple matter to haul an anchor in by hand. He turned and looked up to Charlie, the dripping anchor rope in his hands. 'Hey Chick, could you nudge her forward a bit? I think we're snagged on something.' The burbling sound of the engine exhausts in the water was music to Charlie's ears as he gently eased the throttle, the cruiser moving imperceptibly forward.

Again, Adam bent his back to find he was finally having success, the anchor on its way to the surface. Charlie sat back in the skipper's chair and watched as Adam worked hand over hand drawing the anchor to the surface, while at the same time managing to feed the rope through a hole in the deck into the anchor locker below. Charlie, overseeing the task from his vantage point high above, took time to daub some zinc cream on his nose, then pull an old floppy hat from his shorts pocket and slip it on his head. Unfortunately, Charlie had a pale complexion and bronzy red coloured hair making Charlie horribly susceptible to sunburn, an affliction he took great pains to minimize.

The task of hauling up the anchor was nearing completion when Adam suddenly let the anchor rope go, the anchor plummeting back to the bottom of the harbour with the rope in rapid pursuit. Adam stumbled backwards to end up sitting on the deck, his normally bright tanned face now pale, his eyes wide.

'No, no, that's not what we want,' called down Charlie, shaking his head in mystified confusion. 'For Christ sake, Adam, you know what goes where, and right at the moment we want the big metal thing with the hooks on it up here on the deck.'

Adam turned his head slowly up to Charlie and pointed to the bow of the cruiser, his mouth open to speak. Unfortunately, whatever disclosure Adam may have intended to convey to

Charlie, both his intention and capability were in dire conflict resulting in a total failure to utter a word. Nice enough bloke, but he'll never get his ticket if he keeps this up, Charlie reflected as he made his way to the deck below, aggravated by the intrusion into his idle moment. On reaching the bows, Charlie found Adam still sitting on the deck, still pointing to the bows.

'Cripes, Adam, what did you bring up, a bloody mermaid? Whatever it is, can't be as bad as all that, so let's get the pick in and see what's upsetting you so much.'

Charlie took up the slack in the anchor rope, preferring to leave Adam to suffer his pronounced state of shock by himself. It wasn't long before Charlie peered over the side in expectation of seeing the anchor break the surface of the water. He ceased his hauling in of the rope while his peering took on a more inquisitive inspection. 'So, it's a bit of an old sail, or a sheet I'd say. Whatever it is seems to be wrapped around the anchor. Really, Adam, I don't think there's anything to get yourself into a tizzy over. Come and help me get it onboard anyway.'

For the first time in several minutes Adam was capable of a response. 'Be buggered. You say it's a sail, so you go on believing it's a sail, or whatever. I don't reckon it's a sail and I don't want nothin' to do with it. And I don't want to know what it is, either. I'll go up and take the controls. I'll wait for you there.' With that, Adam struggled to his feet and made his way hesitantly to where Charlie had been relaxing just a couple of minutes earlier.

I've just gotta have a talk with that boy, Charlie mused as he decided he would have to get the job done and haul the anchor onto the deck himself. Hell, the boss and his mates will be rolling up soon and we'll look like real pillocks, stuck out here in the middle of the harbour having a debate as to what's on the end of the bloody anchor. Charlie stepped back from the gunwale and made a couple of energetic hauls on the rope; the anchor broke the surface of the water. He secured the anchor rope with a couple of turns around the broken winch leaving the shrouded, dripping anchor just above the surface of the water. Moving forward to the gunwale, he dropped onto his hands and knees, removed his hat, and peered over the side for a closer inspection.

The decision as to whether or not he would bring the anchor, along with whatever the snag was, onto the deck or try to cut it away with the anchor in its current position, depended on the inspection currently being conducted. Within a short time, Charlie had completed his scrutiny of the anchor, whereupon he shakily regained his feet and unwound the rope from the winch. The anchor splashed back into the harbour, the rope trailing hurriedly behind. Charlie Chambers sat down on the deck; he was not feeling well.

'Okay, Adam. What's this all about?' demanded Mr Lee after he had settled himself into the bow of the rubber ducky. 'I thought I had given Charlie specific instructions to have the boat alongside the marina by eleven-thirty. Here it is going on twelve, my guests arriving at any moment, and all I find is a rubber ducky where I thought "Gemini" should be.' While Mr Lee set out to give the impression he was somewhat annoyed by the situation, Adam knew the man's annoyance was feigned. Mr Lee, dressed in a pair of navy blue shorts, a white polo t-shirt and a navy blue baseball cap perched on his head, was generally imperturbable and renowned for the length of his fuse. However, if Mr Lee was annoyed after he had ascertained the facts, then it was a fair bet Mr Lee would definitely be annoyed.

'Sorry, sir, but I think you'd better ask Mr Chambers,' replied Adam from the stern of the craft where he operated the small outboard motor. 'We had a bit of trouble raising the anchor; the winch didn't work, not that that had anything to do with the problem. We were going to call you but as you'd be on your way we decided to wait until you got here. Will Mrs Porter be joining us, sir?'

'Well, let's see what the problem is first. Maybe no-one is going anywhere,' said Mr Lee as he prepared to grab the small aluminium ladder that hung from the stern of the cruiser. 'I'll go and see Charlie. You go back to the marina and wait for the guests. They shouldn't be too much longer.' With that, Mr Lee climbed over the stern and made his way forward to see just what the problem was. Any doubt as to the existence of a complication was quickly dispelled when Mr Lee saw Charlie sitting on the deck, a faraway, dreamy look in his eyes.

'Hi Charlie. Adam tells me you have a problem with the anchor. Can't be too much wrong; there isn't a lot that can go wrong with 'em.'

On hearing Mr Lee's voice, Charlie rose unsteadily to his feet. 'Sorry, Mr Lee, I didn't hear you. Yeah, it's not so much the broken winch or the anchor itself that we seem to have this little problem with. Here, I'll show you.' With that, Charlie took up the anchor rope and commenced to haul it in, turning his head away as the anchor neared the surface. 'If you'd like to take a look, sir? I won't haul it onboard just yet.' Mr Lee knelt down on hands and knees and shuffled towards the gunwale to assess the nature of the problem.

'Must be something interesting,' came a voice from behind the two preoccupied men on the bows of the cruiser. Adam had transferred Detective Chief Inspector Simon Webster and Detective Sergeant Noel Elliott to the "Gemini" and had returned to the marina to pick up the three girls, Georgie Webster, Sue Elliott, and Louisa Porter, the partner of Mr Lee, all now waiting at the marina in anticipation of a relaxing afternoon on the harbour.

'Ah, Simon,' said Graham Lee, pausing in his crawl to the gunwale to look up and greet his friends with a broad smile. 'Yes, the boys have been having some difficulty with the anchor. I'm just about to see what the problem is. I won't be a tick.' Mr Lee completed his crawl to the edge of the boat and peered over.

After a minute of close scrutiny, the silence broken only by the sound of the harbour water gently lapping the hull of the cruiser, Graham withdrew from the gunwale. 'Oh, bugger. Simon, you better come and have a look, you too Noel, but prepare yourself; it ain't a pretty sight if it's what I think it is.' Both Simon and Noel got down on all fours, crawled to the bows and looked over.

The anchor was hanging a couple of feet out of the water. The disconcerting feature was not so much the anchor, but the naked body partially draped in a dirty white sheet hanging from it. 'Bloody hell,' exclaimed Noel. 'I've never seen anything like that before. Cripes, Graham, you must be out to catch a bloody big fish using a hook and bait that size.'

'Okay, wise guy,' responded Mr Lee, obviously not overjoyed by the discovery, 'I'm not now and never have been interested in baiting a hook, so how would I know what to use for bait? It looks to me like it's either a body or a bag of dehydrated prunes. I don't know much about these things, but I reckon it will probably take the coroner to tell whether it's male or female, that's if it is a body. Irrespective of what it is, it looks like the fish or crabs have had a real good feast on whatever, or whoever, it was.'

'Well, I'm sure the sharks don't have a preference for the gender of the bait, but if you're trying to catch a man-eater, surely you'd have to use a man.'

'Oh, for God's sake, shut up Noel; it's not funny,' Simon rebuked as he sat back on the deck, closed his eyes, squeezed the bridge of his nose with his thumb and forefinger, and shook his head. 'Aah, what the hell, let's just cut it away and get on with our day's outing. Georgie and I were looking forward to a quiet afternoon putting around the harbour. Bugger, Graham, who'd you upset this time?' he said in exasperation.

Detective Sergeant Elliott, considerably outranked by Chief Inspector Webster, knew very well his boss was joking. 'Okay, boss, I'll get back to the marina and make a few calls. Anyone special apart from forensics?'

'Yes, though I very much doubt we need a forensic expert to tell us whoever it was didn't die of leprosy,' replied Simon. 'I s'pose you better let the water police know, and we'll need some divers to take a look around, and CIB up at Kings Cross seeing we're in their bailiwick. Oh yes, you'd better bring back a small buoy so we can mark the spot. Look, let's put the anchor down gently for the moment so we don't drift off around the harbour. As soon as Adam and Noel get back from the marina, we'll mark the exact spot, bring the anchor up and take the boat in to the marina. Charlie, go below and find a sheet or tarp, anything we can get this thing covered with when we pull it up. I daresay some people might get a tad upset at the sight of a half-eaten corps hanging off the pick. We may as well go back and explain the problem to the girls as they'll be wondering what all the kafuffle's about. Cripes, Noel, I could go a stiff drink right now, but I guess the situation calls for us to be on duty. Sorry, Charlie, but you and Adam had better stick around until we get this mess sorted. And, much as I hate to say it, Graham, I think today has just been cancelled.'

CHAPTER 2

$\mathcal{D}$etective Sergeant Noel Elliott sat back on an office chair in Sydney's Day Street Police Station. He rolled up a piece of paper into a ball and had a three point shot into the waste paper basket located at the other end of the office; and missed, which was not unusual. Newly promoted Detective Chief Inspector Simon Webster, given the option of moving to the office of his predecessor, who had unexpectedly passed away as a result of a fatal heart attack, had preferred to remain in the old office he had shared with his sergeant for several years.

The office was not palatial, its linoleum floor and one window fitted with a string operated roll-up blind giving the room a frosty atmosphere. The blind was nearly always pulled down for two reasons; the window gave an excellent panoramic view of an adjacent building's windowless brick facade, and the blind rarely worked as it should. Notwithstanding the disparity in ranks and the ancient adage "rank has its privileges", the detective's work areas were identical. The office furnishings, all consistent with the office entitlements for the rank of an inspector, included two work desks fitted with two drawers on either side and both supporting a book-keepers reading lamp, which always reminded Noel of the lamp used by Dickens's Mr Scrooge, the obligatory bookcase containing a number of lever-arch binders, and the essential two drawer metal filing cabinet, of which there were two, one located beside each desk. The only modernisation to the office within the last few years had been when the station's administration lashed out and replaced the antiquated blackboard and easel with a new shiny example of modern technology; a whiteboard. Needless to say, having received as much use as the blackboard had, the whiteboard had been unceremoniously abandoned to behind the office door, its sole purpose to gather dust; just another shining example bureaucratic spending on gizmos that were neither needed, nor wanted.

Noel stretched back from the table and clasped his hands behind his head. He was a short, stocky man, his physique far from lending itself to the sport of basket ball, which he frequently practiced while totally ignoring his obvious lack of natural talent for the game. Noel had lived the majority of his life on the coastal strip north of the city, primarily at Mona Vale on the northern beaches of Sydney where he now resided with his wife, Sue. In his younger days, and having the physique of what could be euphemistically known as a brick outhouse, Noel had played rugby union for the Manly Marlins. It was during this period that his facial features had undergone radical trans-formation, his pugnacious countenance attributed to a nose broken on more than one occasion.

'Hey, boss, who's the investigating officer into the anchor case? Someone from The Cross CIB I'd expect.'

The question was directed to Chief Inspector Simon Webster, a man a couple of inches over six feet tall with the physical attributes of a swimmer, notably a narrow waste and broad shoulders. His thinning blond hair and olive complexion tended to suggest Simon had spent a lot of time on the beach, as was the case being a member of the Collaroy Surf Club, a beachside suburb about eight kilometers south of Mona Vale.

'I don't really know what's going on at the moment. I know Superintendent Hayes has been talking to Chief Superintendent Paxton about it, and I think Paxton has been talking to Kings Cross. I'm sort of ambivalent as to who runs with it. It's in their regional area, but it could be seen that we're already involved. Anyway, it won't be us making the decision. By the way, have you seen our new boss yet, Superintendent Hayes?'

'No. Why?' replied Noel as if the matter was of little consequence.

Simon gave a wry smile. 'Nothing. I dare say we'll be introduced sometime in the future.'

'Anyway, getting back to the anchor man. You're pretty sure it's a murder case we're looking at?' asked Noel, who was rather looking forward to investigating a good grisly murder.

'Well, I think we'll have to wait for the forensic report, but I wouldn't be surprised. I s'pose it would be a pretty easy way to commit suicide as all you'd have to do is pull up the anchor, hook yourself up and jump overboard, having swum out to the boat in the first place, that is. There's little you could do if you changed your mind halfway to the bottom of the harbour.'

'So, what evidence did you notice to suggest it might be murder?' enquired Noel, hoping there would be enough evidence to confirm a macabre murder had been perpetrated by some odious villain.

Simon sat back on his chair and folded his arms. 'There are a few things that spring to mind, and I'd be surprised if you hadn't notice some of them yourself. To begin with, the body was naked, apart from the sheet wrapped around him. So where are his clothes? Did he swim out to the "Gemini" already naked

11

and with a sheet so he could wrap himself up in it then attach himself to the anchor? I think that would be pretty tricky. No, I think someone had to get the victim to the "Gemini" by boat. Also, I'm not sure as to the extent of damage, but it looked like the victim had sustained a bump on the head, which could have happened at any time.

'Quite apart from the body aspect, there are a zillion boats in Rushcutters Bay, so why choose the "Gemini"? There's a hell of a lot more bigger boats to choose from. No, I think it's a definite case of murder, but until the investigating officer, whoever that may be, gets the forensic report, there isn't much that can be done. Poor old Graham Lee was invited to take a look at the body, which is reasonable I suppose, seeing it was attached to his anchor. The story is he threw up, and that is surprising, he being a gangster and all.'

'And you say Graham couldn't recognize whoever it was?' queried Noel. 'Can't say I blame him. It was a bit of a mess, the body I mean.'

'No, he didn't have a clue. I'm not sure he could tell what it was, for that matter; male, female, or even if it was human.'

'Do you think it has anything to do with his casino? After all, there seems to be a few unsavoury characters getting around at the moment, and it wouldn't take much to set off a turf war.'

'Well, it's the first thing that comes to mind, isn't it?' replied Simon as he bent down from his chair and picked up the ball of paper and completed Noel's unsuccessful shot.

'There seems to be a lot of pushing and shoving on the gambling front at the moment. I suppose everyone's getting a bit nervous the Government will legalise casinos, like they've just done down in Hobart,' commented Noel.

'Yes, there's certainly that to consider, but I think it will be a few years before it's legalised here. They're still in the process of having inquiries into gambling, and you know what politicians are like. They only hold an inquiry when they're stalling for time. First you have a meeting to determine if it's worth going to the inquiry stage. If it is considered appropriate, having addressed all the items contained within the terms of reference, which will have been compile by a committee who know bugger all about the subject in the first place, they'll report back to an independent inquiry consisting of members of both sides of the House. They'll then deliberate on the inquiry's recommendations before determining whether the proposal justifies and warrants the calling together of a senate inquiry. Should all things be considered equal, I'd say it would take a minimum of ten years, that being if everything runs smoothly, of course.'

'Cripes,' replied Noel. 'I know you don't hold politicians in high regard, but you're becoming positivity paranoid.'

'Is that so surprising, especially after that politician, Robert Porter, had his way with the Superintendent's wife?' Simon said with a scowl.

Noel frowned. 'Just a thought, boss, but moving right along from politicians. You're a lifesaver and should know the answer to my question. With all this talk about the anchor man, it made me think of all those sharks lurking around in the harbour. Whenever a pack of sharks is sighted off the beaches, the radio reports exactly what has been seen; a pack of sharks, or maybe a school of sharks. As a group of sharks is called a shiver, why do they persist in calling them schools or packs? I've never heard them referred to as a shiver.'

Simon closed his eyes and shook his head. 'Noel, a font of knowledge I may be, but I haven't a clue why the press don't call a pack of sharks a shiver. Go ask a radio station.'

Fortunately, the inspiring little discussion between Chief Inspector Webster and Sergeant Elliott was interrupted by the ring of the telephone. Simon answered and replaced the receiver after a very short conversation. 'Don't get comfortable,

Chief Superintendent Paxton would like to see us in his office. Something tells me it's to do with the anchor thing.'

'Ah, Simon, Sergeant Elliott, please take a seat,' invited Chief Superintendent Paxton. 'I take it you've already met Superintendent Michael Hayes?' he asked, nodding to the superintendent seated in front of the Chief's desk.

'Yes, briefly,' replied Simon and acknowledged the superintendent with a nod. Superintendent Hayes, the new boy at the Day Street Police Station, was not a big man. Noel had the immediate thought that here was the bloke who had sand kicked in his face at the beach by some great hulking bully, and was a definite candidate for the before example in a vitamin pill advertisement. Simon glanced at Noel and smiled, the memory of a bank teller the detectives had had occasion to do business with mutually exchanged between the two men.

Superintendent Michael Hayes was short in stature and seemed to lack sufficient skin and bones to fill a uniform that appeared to be two sizes too big. Simon assessed him to be in his late forties, maybe early fifties. Although his physical appearance tended to suggest he may be lacking in the expected police prerequisite of muscle power, Simon fully appreciated that this superintendent must be endowed with some other valuable attribute, and that was most likely brain power. He had a mop of graying wavy hair that emphasized his dark eyes and black bushy eyebrows. Noel couldn't restrain himself from staring at the eyebrows in an effort to determine if, in fact, there were two eyebrows at all, or just one long one. Fortunately, the disconcerting eyebrow was partially obscured by a pair of tortoise shell spectacles that hid most of a long sallow face, highlighted by a rather large nose. Noel eventually came to the conclusion the superintendent may well have the ability to compensate for any physical shortcomings by the power possessed in his dark penetrating eyes.

Hayes had been posted in after much speculation as to the events surrounding the previous incumbent, Superintendent Nigel Fisher. The true story, known to only a handful of senior police and Sergeant Elliott, was that Fisher had been found to be delving into the insurance business where, for the payment of a premium, either in cash or kind, he would guarantee the premises occupied by The Taipan Club would not be raided by police. The fact that The Taipan Club was an illegal gambling casino that just happened to be owned by one Mr Graham Lee, was purely coincidental in the commission of Fisher's little insurance scheme.

With Fisher blackmailing his chief inspector, Damien Rose, over a trivial case of the embezzlement of police funds, it came as somewhat of a surprise that the hierarchy was prepared to forgive Fisher for his indiscretion. Needless to say, this benevolent attitude came at a price; Fisher's agreement to become an undercover agent in the war against the drug cartels. As the alternative was four to six years in Long Bay Prison, Fisher went undercover, notwithstanding either option augured grimly for a long and happy career.

Chief Paxton sat back behind his office table and pursed his lips, a look of deep concentration on his face. 'Okay, it seems we have a bit of a problem,' he said after a deep breath. 'Mick, some of this may appear to be contrary to what the book says, but history sometime dictates both the direction and actions we are obliged to adopt. I'm sure as we progress you will appreciate the predicament, so just bear with us.'

'This wouldn't have anything to do with the body anchored on Graham Lee's boat, would it, sir?' asked Detective Chief Inspector Webster.

'See, Mick. Chief Webster is such a perceptive and astute detective. No wonder I promoted him,' said the Chief Superintendent without offering Simon any response.

'Yes, I can see that', Hayes replied. 'I only hope we don't lose him like you did your last chief inspector. Can I take it your discussion with the CIB at The Cross has determined the investigation is to be carried out from here, in light of the history, as you put it, sir?'

'Correct,' replied Chief Paxton, pushing his chair back from the table and folding his arms. 'It seems the boys up at The Cross are up to the ears with their own problems. As you know, there is much discussion and speculation reverberating through the corridors of power following the Tasmanian casino legislation. Many people see it as the thin end of the wedge.'

'Yes, we were just talking about that,' interrupted Simon. 'But won't it take another ten years before anything happens here?'

'Absolutely,' acknowledged Chief Paxton. 'But when you put ten years on it, that's ten years for the politicians to make up their mind as to what they're going to do, which would be a novelty in itself. In the meantime, the bad guys will try and take over as many casinos in Sydney as they can. They see the introduction of legalised casinos as the end of the gravy train simply because the Government has finally realised there's a fortune to be made if they could tax the casinos. Obviously, they can't tax 'em at the moment because as they're illegal, they don't exist.

'The baddies are aware of what's going on and have decided they have to make squillions of dollars before the pollies decide to get off their collective backsides and come up with the legislation needed to legalise the casinos. Once they've done that, we'll be directed to close down all the illegal casinos. The only casinos left operating in Sydney will be those approved, and taxed, by the Government; hence it seems a turf war has erupted to see who can get control of the most casinos and make the most money before the legislation comes into effect. I think it's a pretty fair assessment that the body dished out of the harbour has something to do with illegal gaming. As a consequence, I think maybe your initial investigation should be directed along those lines.'

'Which means we will be doing the anchor investigation,' said Superintendent Hayes in acknowledgement. 'I suppose Simon and Sergeant Elliott are perfectly placed to conduct it, seeing they were present when the body was discovered. I've also read their reports on the illegal gambling business which gives them both a good insight into their operations. At least by doing the investigation from here, we won't be up for the cost of travelling and incidental expenses,' added the Superintendent, his keen insight into financial matters coming to the fore. 'You don't envisage any problems with the conflict of interest angle?'

'No, I considered that aspect but viewed the positives far outweighed the negatives,' responded Chief Paxton. 'I know they both get on well with Mr Lee and they do know The Taipan Club. I have no doubt they have a couple of people well placed to lend support, if needed. Can I suggest you get the ball rolling by getting over to Kings Cross Police Station,' Chief Paxton said, addressing Simon and Sergeant Elliott. 'Have a talk to Chief Inspector David Harris, he's expecting you. He already has the forensic report and he'll give you a rundown on the gambling issue. While it appears everything related to this case is going on in the Cross's local area, I see no reason for you to conduct the investigation from up there, so you may as well operate from here. Oh, by the way, Harris did say it is definitely a case of murder, so you boys can enjoy yourself for once. Any questions?'

'Yes' replied Simon. 'I have a quick one that won't take a

moment sir, but it's personal so if I could wait until after this meeting is over?'

'No problems. I think we've just about covered it, so that will be all for the moment. Thanks Michael, Sergeant.'

Once alone, the Chief Superintendent regarded Simon, who had remained seated as the others left the office. 'Well, Simon, you look a bit uncomfortable, so let's have it; what's on your mind, though I think I can guess?'

'Sir, in no way do I wish to appear disrespectful, but I get the idea Superintendent Hayes is like no other policeman I've come across. Is there something we should be aware of?'

Chief Paxton frowned and rocked slowly backwards and forwards on his chair, one hand on his hip, the other holding his chin. He viewed Simon without any indication as to his thoughts; a moment of stony silence prevailed before he decided how to answer such an insubordinate question. 'Simon, as you know there are two branches of policing; administrative and operational. Superintendent Hayes is of the latter. However, this operation experience has been entirely conducted in the world of white-collar crime; fraud, paper trails, business accounts, company balance sheets, graft, corruption, and embezzlement, to name just a few. After the debacle we had here not so long ago, the boffins in the police hierarchy decided Day Street needed a bit of economic monitoring, hence Hayes. It seems Hayes is highly regarded and an expert in his field. Simple enough?'

Simon shrugged. 'Yes sir, I think that says it all. But how does Superintendent Hayes view his posting here? I can't help thinking he's out to make a name for himself in the more, shall we say, the rough and tumble side of things as well now. As you are aware, sir, Noel and I may not do everything by the book and that could create a degree of enmity between us.'

Chief Paxton nodded. 'Yes, I can appreciate where you're

coming from. Superintendent Hayes isn't quite the gung-ho type like Superintendent Fisher was, and he's probably aware he has a lot to learn, despite his rank. God knows, there are times I wish Fisher was back here, even with his faults. All I can ask is for you to do the best you can under the circumstances and try not to get up Hayes's nose too often, or too far.'

'I'll pass the message on,' replied Simon with a look of apprehension. 'At least we know there won't be any sticky fingers in the slush fund.'

*S*imon, Noel, glad you could make it. Come aboard,' welcomed a smiling Graham Lee. 'I thought this would be a far better place for a quiet chat in preference to the police station or the club.' The "aboard" was on the "Gemini", now moored at one of the many marina jetties in Rushcutters Bay. 'I brought Louisa along as she's into the administrative side of the club and usually has her finger on the pulse. She's also aware of the problems confronting many of the clubs around the town at the moment.'

Louisa was now Graham Lee's partner after she had separated from her husband, Robert Porter, an influential state politician. Publicly, the circumstances relating to the marital bust-up appeared amicable, though in reality it was shrouded behind a veil of blackmail, deceit and debauchery. However, Louisa now appeared to be more than happy working for Mr Lee at the Taipan Club, and sharing his bed in what had become a warm relationship.

'Hi Louisa, bad luck about our last meeting, but I suppose it wasn't pre-arranged. No, don't get up,' Simon said as he took a seat on the lounge located on the port side of the saloon.

Louisa uncrossed her long legs and reclined back into the lounge chair on which she had been sitting. Louisa was probably in her mid thirties, a tall brunette with shoulder length hair, dark hazel eyes, and possessed an extremely well-proportioned figure. Looking very casual in dark blue jeans, yellow sneakers and a loose fitting baggy beige jumper, it was clearly to her husband's detriment that he had regarded Louisa as nothing more than a social necessity and a fashion accessory to be shown off at various political functions. Louisa had enjoyed the lifestyle of the politician's wife for a short period, but had soon realised her role in a politician's life was nothing more than that of a not-so-well paid escort.

'Simon, good to see you,' Louisa replied in her dusky voice. 'Hi Noel. Oh, I don't know. It's not every day you pull up the anchor and find a dead body. At least it gave us girls something to talk about.'

'And how do you find the "Gemini", a bit smaller than the "Chez Anne"', asked Simon as he made himself comfortable in the cruiser's plush saloon.

'I'm sorry you didn't get to have a good look at her last time you were aboard.' replied Graham Lee, 'and yes, she's a couple of feet smaller but utilizes the space far more efficiently. There's much more room than on the "Chez Anne". Anyway, shall we get down to business, because I would love to know what's going on?'

Simon sat back, crossed his legs and folded his hands on his stomach, his thumbs arched. 'Right. What we have at the moment is some brawling within the illegal gambling business. As you are aware, Graham, the police tend to turn a blind eye to these activities, unless there's a more compelling reason, other than their illegality, to close down the casinos. At the moment many of the illegal establishments are run by individuals and it's fairly easy to keep tabs on their operation. However, this increase in violence is worrying as there appears to be a link with organised crime groups.'

'Any group in particular?' asked Louisa.

'No, not at this stage. It's easy to speculate; Asian groups, of which there's a host, such as the triads, yakuza, maybe the mafia or outlaw motor cycle gangs. Who knows?' Maybe they're all having a go,' replied Simon. 'At the moment, and for want of a better theory, we are assuming the body on the anchor is connected to this turmoil. And yes, I know you should never assume anything. Graham, is there anything to suggest The Taipan Club may be targeted by corrupt individuals, forgetting of course The Taipan Club is illegal and you yourself are considered a gangster?'

Graham Lee sat on a bar stool in front of a well stocked bar and folded his arms, a look of concentration on his thin face. 'To tell the truth, Simon, lately we've had a couple of visits to the club by a Mr Paul Stack. He's the owner of a club called The Spinning Wheel. Mr Stack made it quite clear he wants The Taipan Club, but we have declined his very paltry offers, so far.'

'And do you think he may have something to do with the body on the anchor, something of a warning perhaps, or an incentive for you to change your mind?' asked Noel.

'Well, yes, I suppose he could have as he's not the sort of person you'd take home to meet your mother. In fact, I'd call him a little weed, definitely not someone you'd do a Gulliver on. But if it was meant to be a warning or threat, surely there would have been some form of communication, a note, or phone call issuing the threat. And if it was supposed to be a tacit threat, one would have thought whoever planted the body would have used a body we would have recognized. As it is, neither Louisa nor I have a clue as to who the poor sod was,' said Graham, mystified. 'Did the forensic report provide any info on who it might be?'

'No, none at this stage. The thing they did come up with was that the victim was deceased before being anchored. Despite the condition of the body, it seems they could deduce the back of his head had been stove in by a blow that would have been fatal in the extreme. He'd been in the water about a week, so they say, so can I take it no-one had been onboard for some time before Charlie and Adam made the discovery?' Simon inquired.

'No. I'd given the boys a week off as I knew I wouldn't be using the boat for a while. I still can't understand why, if it was meant to be a threat, whoever planted the body used the body of someone I don't know. Maybe Stack is just trying to intimidate me into selling The Taipan Club and there's worse to come, presuming Stack is the guilty bugger.'

'Hey hang on,' interrupted Noel. 'Just back up a bit. Pardon my ignorance, but what's a Gulliver?'

Graham Lee turned to Simon and slowly shook his head. 'See, Simon, no-one reads books these days. Noel, when the Empress's apartment was on fire, Gulliver came to the rescue and put the fire out by peeing all over it. I can't say I'd do the same for Paul Stack if he was on fire.'

'Well, I guess that says it all,' replied Noel, suitably informed.

'Okay,' said Louisa as she leaned forward in her chair. 'There's a lot of violence going on in the city right now and it all relates back to the proposed legalisation on gambling. Organised crime is trying to muscle in on those establishments that are currently operated by individuals before any legislation is passed and the whole shebang becomes legal. Once that happens there'll be licenses, taxes, regulations, fees, unionism and God knows what to consider. No wonder everyone wants to get in on the act now. Simon, surely one of your contacts can shed some light on what's going on 'cause it's sure as hell neither Graham nor I do? Maybe Ron can throw some light on the subject as he seems to know what's going on before it happens.'

'Good point, Louisa,' replied Simon. Ron was Ron Lange, with the emphasis on the "e", and known to all onboard the "Gemini" from previous events, and to members of the police hierarchy. Ron had been a petty criminal but, after the tragic death of his wife in a bungled robbery, had turned police informer and, once kitted out with a new identity, had become a very useful source of information.

'So at this stage, and unless forensics can come up with an ID, you have no idea as to who the victim is, or any reason for the body to be attached to your anchor? The only possible motive is that someone is sending you a not so subtle threat relating to The Taipan Club.'

Graham Lee shrugged and raised his eyebrows. 'Sorry, Simon, but that's about it at the moment. Needless to say, if we receive or hear anything, we'll be in touch straight away. The Taipan Club is not now and never will be up for sale, so whoever is responsible for the anchor man can get stuffed.'

CHAPTER 4

etective Chief Inspector Simon Webster sat on a park bench located near the Archibald Fountain in Hyde Park. Somehow, either by coincidence or design, the location had become a fixed meeting point for Simon and Ron Lange for the exchange of information. A cloudless, windless day in August, a seat in the sun; Simon didn't really care how late Ron was. However, all good things must come to an end and all too soon his reverie was rudely interrupted. 'Hi, Simon. I believe you wanted a chat?'

Ron Lange was a smallish, balding man and, for a man in his early forties, devoid of the middle age spread, or maybe with a hint of a paunch; Ron did like the occasional ale or two. 'Ron, pull up a pew, or would you prefer a coffee over in Macquarie Street?'

'No, here's lovely. A sunny day in winter, who could ask for more? Now, what's on your mind, though I think I have a pretty good idea? Our Mr Lee hauled in a body and no-one wants to claim it.'

Simon pursed his lips and nodded. 'That's about it. It seems a total waste of a perfectly good cadaver, especially as there was no message or ultimatum to go with it. There's not even a threat, though I suppose a corpse on the end of your anchor may be a tad intimidating. There just hasn't been anything to go with it.'

'Yes, I know,' replied Ron. 'It must be terribly disconcerting to find a corpse on the end of your anchor every time you pull it in.'

'Come on, Ron. This isn't meant to be funny,' responded Simon in a brave effort to conceal a snigger.

'Sorry, Simon, I'll try to be serious. It's just that at the moment there's so much going on, it's ludicrous. Seems like the heavy weight gangland boys are trying to bust into the gambling scene. Apart from the gambling, they're into drugs, prostitution, extortion and a host of other activities you'd never find at the Sunday school picnic. I suppose you heard about Andy Crawford? You know, the bloke who runs the casino on Palmer Street, the Red Ruby? He had some visitors call in the other night. They told him they were happy to hear his place was for sale, which of course, it isn't. Andy told them to go to blazes, so they took him literally and torched his Ferrari.'

'Hell, they do play rough, don't they?' I s'pose it's a fair assumption to connect the anchor man to Lee's casino then?' Simon asked, sensing it was a pretty lame question.

'Wouldn't surprise me in the least. As I said, these boys are moving in and they have three things going for them; organization and money. And they believe these small casinos are raking in big money, which they are, and now they want it. They have their grubby little fingers into so many illegal enterprises and schemes it would make your head spin.'

Simon sighed and stretched. 'Ron, you mentioned three things going for them?'

'Yes. The third is what they haven't got, and that's scruples, or conscience.'

Simon slowly nodded his head in acknowledgement of Ron's revelations. He accepted the gangs weren't overly endowed with integrity or moral principles, and were probably blessed with more vicious than friendly bones in their body. But to bash a person's brains in then leave the body on the bottom of the harbour to feed the fish seemed just a little bit over the top.

'You know Paul Stack has been to see Graham Lee?' asked Simon, trying to think of something more appealing than a dead body. 'Apparently he's in the market for the Taipan Club, not that it's for sale, but that's beside the point.'

'You mean the bloke who runs The Spinning Wheel? Yes, I did hear though I haven't heard anything to suggest he's responsible for the anchor man. Still, I wouldn't put it passed him to pull a stunt like that, on the competition, I mean. He's a real little weasel. And let's face it, the Spinning Wheel is a dive compared to the Taipan Club. No wonder he wants it.'

'Seems not too many people like Mr Stack. I have the idea that if the anchor man was a gang related victim, whoever was responsible for the killing would have made his motives known by this stage. Like, what's the good of tying a body to an anchor if no-one knows who the body is, or was? I don't know if that's grammatically correct, but you know what I mean,' said Simon as he scratched his ear lobe.

Ron nodded. 'Yes. There's nothing subtle about the gangland boys. They work on the philosophy that the greater the carnage, the greater the reputation. It's like the torching of the Ferrari. Everyone knows who's responsible, except the police, and the reputation of the gang that did the torching has skyrocketed. See, it's all a bit of a game of who's the toughest, or at least who appears to be the toughest. Now, take a dead body attached to an anchor, for instance. The gangs would consider such a method of disposal as being different, classy or maybe even sophisticated, if they knew what the word meant.'

'So it's pointless for one of the gangs to have perpetrated the dastardly deed, even if the anchor man did have the back of his head stove in before he was dropped to the bottom of the harbour. It's becoming a bit of ancient history now and I'd say it's unlikely for a specific group to acknowledged responsibility at this late stage,' said Simon, a look of boredom on his face. 'Maybe I should go and have a chat with this bloke Stack as he seems the most likely person to be involved. It could be his way of letting Lee know he's serious in his attempt to take over the Taipan Club, albeit in a manner as subtle as a train smash.'

*M*aking no attempt to hurry even if he was already late for his little chat, DCI Simon Webster walked slowly along Darlinghurst Road from Kings Cross railway station towards the Kings Cross police station. The fact that his friend, Graham Lee, had found a body attached to the anchor of his cruiser in Rushcutters Bay should have inspired Simon into a state of eager anticipation. It wasn't every day such a heinous murder mystery, a murder case all detectives hoped to investigate at least once in their lifetime, should fall into his lap. But Simon just couldn't get excited about it. Obviously someone had sent Mr Lee a message and, despite its grisly nature, no-one had any idea as to what the message was meant to convey. The only single clue was that Mr Lee had been approached by a shady character wanting to purchase Mr Lee's gambling casino. So What?

Having finally reached his destination, Chief Inspector Webster opened the door to a dingy office located at the rear of the building where he found his sergeant already in conversation with Chief Inspector David Harris. A man nearing his fifties, white thinning hair, and a friendly face with kind blue eyes, Harris's greeting of Simon was loaded with good natured sarcasm. 'Ah, Simon, glad you could make it,' he said with an air of feigned facetiousness.

'Yeah, okay. The traffic's a real bugger today,' Simon lied. 'I'll be with you in a tick, I need my morning coffee. Anyone else for a brew?'

'No thanks. Sergeant Elliott and I had one earlier,' came Chief Harris's pointed reply.

Within two minutes Simon returned with his mug of coffee and sat down at a desk cleared of all papers. The office was rarely used and, when it was, all desks were cleared at the end of each day. 'Right, Dave,' said Simon, 'what startling pieces of info have you for us this morning? Unfortunately I can't say we're making vast inroads with our investigation into this anchor man case but someone, somewhere, has to know something. You say the forensic report confirmed that whoever the anchor man is, or was, didn't commit suicide. By the way, best we take a copy of the report for our file.'

'Sure, no problems. I'll copy it on your way out. Now as this is your case, I haven't put anyone onto it, so the answer to the startling piece of info question is, we have sweet bugger all for you,' said Chief Inspector Harris. 'There's a bit of a difference between Day Street and The Cross where we probably know a little more about the street wise individuals. And that's the strange thing. Every man and his dog has heard about the anchor man but, even with our ear close to the ground, it seems no-one knows anything about it, apart from the fact a body has been hauled out of the harbour. And if someone does know anything, no-one's saying.'

'And what do you know about Paul Stack, apart from the fact he's not winning any popularity contest?' asked Simon. 'It seems he's a very unlikeable person.'

'Ah, yes,' replied Chief Harris with a smile. 'Our old friend Sticky Stack. Have you ever met him?'

'No, can't say I've had the privilege, yet,' replied Simon. 'Why, is there something about the man I should be aware of?'

'No, not really. He's a dead ringer for Danny Di Vito physically, but that's where the similarity ends,' replied Chief Harris as he pushed his chair back, stretched his legs and folded his arms. 'He usually has one or two henchmen in attendance and, though there's not much of him physically, what he does have he likes to throw around, when he has his support close handy that is, which is most of the time. The man does think nasty and can be ruthless at times, though he's never been convicted of any violence.'

'And he wants The Taipan Club,' put in Sergeant Elliott. 'Do you think Mr Stack would think nasty enough to send Mr Lee such a grotesque message?'

'Well, if I was in Graham Lee's position and someone attached a corps to my anchor, I might have second thoughts about not selling up. Let's face it, why else would anyone send a message like that if not to encourage Lee to sell. Hell, it's not like we're over endowed with motives. Come to think of it, it's the only motive we have, or should I say, you have.'

Simon sighed, pursed his lips and raised his eyebrows at Noel. 'Looks like there's nothing else we can do except pay Mr Stack a visit. I'll drive you over to the Spinning Wheel, Noel. You go in and have a little chat with the gentleman. Just ask him what he knows about bashing someone's brains in. You know the story, anyway, so just ask him the routine questions and follow up on anything he may be able to provide.'

'I'm sorry, boss,' replied Sergeant Elliott without any hesitation, 'but with all due respect for rank, you can get well and truly stuffed. If what Chief Harris says is true, and I have no reason to doubt him, I'm not going anywhere near The Spinning

Wheel by myself. If Stack is involved with the anchor man, and is as ruthless as the Chief says he is, I may end up strapped to an anchor and feeding the fish with my head bashed in. No thanks.'

CI Webster's face took on a hostile look for a moment before caving in to a whimsical smile. 'Come on, Noel, only joking. We'll both go over and ask our Mr Sticky Stack what he has to say for himself.'

The Spinning Wheel was located on the western side of Palmer Street, a cross-street off William Street, the main thoroughfare from the city to Kings Cross. While Mr Lee went to great lengths to ensure discretion in all matters relating to the nearby Forbes Street Taipan Club, including the lack of visible promotion of the club, the Spinning Wheel, by contrast, went to great length to advertise their existence by establishing a garish red neon sign depicting a spinning wheel that didn't. Simon and Noel decided to call in on the club at around seven in the evening, a time when management would, hopefully, be preparing for the night's business. As the establishment didn't open until nine o'clock, Simon pressed a button located on the side of the entrance door, which was promptly opened. Standing menacingly in front of Simon was a giant of a man wearing a blue bib and brace and a red checked flannel shirt, a dead ringer for the popular concept of a Canadian lumberjack.

'Yeah, who are you and what d' ya want?'

'Good God, it's Jacko. It is Jacko, isn't it?' Chief Webster asked with a look of pleasant surprise on his face.

'Okay, so my name's Jacko. What's that to ya? You look like coppers to me so I ain't lettin' you in.'

'Ah, come on, Jacko. I did you a favour once, now you can

return the favour. We just want to have a bit of a chat with Mr Stack.'

Jacko frowned as he looked searchingly at Simon. 'Oh yeah,' he said, his countenance softening as he recognized the chief inspector. 'Aah yeah. Now I remember you. It was at that pub down near Circular Quay. We sorta messed up that night and you let us go. Yeah, that was real nice of you. Me and Benny were just startin' out and we didn't know too much about robbin' a pub.'

'No, but think nothing of it, Jacko,' said Simon, obviously delighted to renew his acquaintance with the man mountain. 'Anyway, we would like to see Mr Stack, Jacko, so if you can be a good chap and take us to him, it would be appreciated.'

'Sure. No problem at all. I'm not supposed to let just anyone in the place, but you're different,' responded Jacko, proud with himself for his display of initiative.

On entering The Spinning Wheel, both Noel and Simon recognized the functional similarities between the club they had just entered and The Taipan Club, both being illegal gambling casinos. But that's where any resemblance ended. The Spinning Wheel was a dive. Cripes, thought Chief Webster, no wonder Stack wants The Taipan Club; you could end up with botulism just being in the place.

'I never thought I'd end up workin' in such a swanky place as this,' said Jacko as he led the two detectives across a large room fitted out with a very basic drinks bar, two roulette wheels and numerous tables where games such as blackjack, poker and baccarat were played. 'Mr Stack has been really good to me and he looks after all his workers,' Jacko continued. 'I was really lucky to get the job as head doorman. Here we are,' he said as he came to a door located in the extreme corner of the casino. Jacko knocked twice and waited.

'Come in if you're female, stay out if you're not,' came the voice from within.

'That's Mr Stack. He's always jokin' and playin' around,' Jacko said as he opened the door. 'Some coppers here would like to have a word with you, Mr Stack. They're good blokes, so I thought it would be all right.'

The small, rotund, balding man, half hidden behind a large office table removed a cigar from his mouth, held his forehead with a hand and slowly shook his head. 'Jacko, how many times have I gotta tell you, no policeman is a good bloke, believe me. God help me, I wonder where his other six mates are 'cause this bloke just has to be Dopey,' Mr Stack added, more to himself than to anyone in particular. 'Thanks, Jacko, it's okay, you can get back to whatever you were doing.' With that, Mr Stack stood up and pushed his chair back from the table with the back of his legs, replaced the cigar in his mouth and took a firm grip on both lapels of his coat collar. Without removing the cigar, Mr Stack stood there. 'Well?'

Simon and Noel looked at each other; this was definitely not a social visit. 'Yes, thank you, but I'm sure you're not overly concerned about our health. You don't mind if we sit?' asked Chief Webster as he drew up two plastic chairs in front of the desk before Mr Stack could reply. Once settled, Simon crossed his legs, clasped his hands on his lap and commenced to do nothing but stare at Mr Stack as he retook his seat.

'Don't you know it's rude to stare,' said Mr Stack, noticeably disconcerted.

'Yes, I do. It's just that I'm trying to figure you out,' replied Chief Webster. 'My Sergeant and I come here to have a quiet chat and we're met with belligerence and antagonism; definitely not conducive to a successful meeting, wouldn't you say?'

'No, but then I didn't invite you, did, I?'

'Okay, Mr Stack, have it your way. We can cuff you and take

you back to the station forcibly, you can accompany us back to the station freely, or we can have a little chat here. Now, what's it to be?'

Beaten, Mr Stack slumped back down in his chair. Chief Harris had been right; Mr Stack looked very much like Danny Di Vito, just older, and definitely a lot more cantankerous, mused Simon. 'Now, Mr Stack, do you have any idea as to why we are here?' Chief Webster asked.

'How the hell would I know? Maybe I jaywalked somewhere. Christ, haven't you coppers anything better to do than go 'round pesterin' law abidin' citizens?'

'Okay Mr Stack. We won't beat around the bush,' said Chief Webster, having decided the direct confrontational approach may prove more successful. 'We are aware of your approach to Mr Graham Lee for the purchase of the Taipan Club which is, apparently, not for sale.'

'So what?' replied Mr Stack indignantly. 'There's nothing illegal about that, even if it isn't for sale. Everything has its price.'

'Yes, we're well aware of that little fact,' replied Chief Webster. 'But, you see, we've come up with a little problem. Mr Lee has recently received what could be considered an inducement for him to, shall we say, review his options and possibly reconsider your offer.'

'What little inducement? Mr Lee and I have had discussions and he has made it perfectly clear that he's not interested in my current offer. And I certainly haven't sent him any "inducements". Whatever develops in the future is strictly between Mr Lee and myself and has nothing to do with you,' responded Mr Stack, now beginning to enjoy the little chat with the two detectives as he knew he was on firm ground.

Detective Chief Inspector Simon Webster looked at Detective Sergeant Noel Elliott, pursed his lips and gave a shrug.

'Okay, Mr Stack, let's forget about the commercial aspects for the moment and consider the nature of the little inducement received by Mr Lee. We couldn't give a rat's proverbial about your real estate ventures, but bashing someone's brains in, securing the body to the anchor of a boat, specifically one owned by Mr Lee, and dropping the anchor to the bottom of the harbour, does tend to rouse police interest. I don't know about you, but it would be one hell of an incentive for me to change my mind if I owned the Taipan Club. Apart from that, we are investigating a clear case of homicide and, strangely enough, you seem to be the only person on the planet out to upset Mr Lee.'

'You're joking?' replied Mr Stack, a sudden look of bewilderment etched on his face.

'It's no joke,' broke in Sergeant Elliott. 'The body is over in the morgue now, if you'd like to come and have a look.'

'And it was attached to Lee's boat?'

'Yep, well, to the anchor attached to his boat,' corrected Sergeant Elliott.

'And you think I'm responsible?' challenged Mr Stack without too much confidence and in the process of breaking into a cold sweat. He discarded the half smoked cigar into an ash tray, withdrew a handkerchief from his trouser pocket and mopped his brow. 'This is the first time I've heard of someone's body being fished out of the harbour.'

Chief Webster shrugged and pursed his lips. 'That's strange, because the news we have is it's common knowledge. Everyone seems to know about it.'

'Yeah, well, I don't.'

'That's okay, Mr Stack. As I said at the outset, we only wanted to have a little chat. Maybe you have negated the requirement for any further investigation of your involvement, provided you have been truthful, that is. By the same token, you could save us a lot of trouble and admit you are responsible for sending Mr Lee a little message,' replied Chief Webster.

'Ah, for Christ sake, get off the grass. I don't know nothin' about someone's body being on Mr Lee's anchor. I hate boats and I get sea sick in the bathtub. The whole thing is just ludicrous. Why don't you go pick on someone else for a change?' Mr Stack had abandoned his previous self-assured attitude and was now getting angry. 'Good grief, the very thought I could do such a revolting thing. No, I know nothin' about it, and I want to keep it that way. So there.'

For some reason, Detective Chief Inspector Simon Webster believed him.

CHAPTER 6

*S*imon Webster tossed his briefcase onto the lounge and collapsed into his favourite lounge chair after another long day at the office. He loosened his tie and undid the top button of his shirt before prizing each shoe off with the other foot. 'Georgie, my sweet, would you pour us a wine, please? I'm stuffed.'

'What, another bad day in Paradise?' came Georgie's voice from the kitchen. The kitchen was in the neat bungalow located at number 24 West Bank Lane in the seaside suburb of Collaroy where Simon and Georgie had now lived for several years. 'And don't bother to ask about my day, sweetheart' called out Georgie. 'Whatever peace and quiet we had around here has been shot to the proverbial.' Georgie entered the lounge room with two glasses of wine, handed one to Simon, removed the briefcase and sank down on the lounge, drawing her legs up underneath herself.

Georgie was tall, just an inch or two shorter than Simon who stood over six feet. Whereas it was the popular perception that the majority of girls on the coast were blue eyed blonds,

Georgie was dark, olive complexion, brown eyes and short black hair. It was Georgie's dark eyes that had initially captivated Simon during their commuting days on the Manly ferry, "South Steyne", between Circular Quay in the city and the northern seaside suburb of Manly. With the couple now in their thirties, the idea of a family had been the subject of a brief conversation that resulted in a unanimous decision; no kids.

Simon shrugged and sighed. 'You go first. What was so catastrophic about your day?'

'Well, the whole thing's getting a bit complicated. It seems dear old Dorothy died intestate.'

'Well, she should have thought about that before you did away her, not that her dying intestate should concern you. Maybe you should have suggested she make a will before she carked. It's the way things are usually done; make a will then die,' chided Simon.

'Look, Simon, don't be so obtuse. The thing is, will or no will, Rodger Beaton, the husband of dead Dorothy, has now occupied the house. And if we thought Dorothy was hard to get on with, wait till you meet Rodger the Dodger. I was having a nice quiet day writing my book when these two women drove up to see our interloping neighbour. I could hear raised voices so I went outside, just to bring in the washing; okay, to listen. It seems the ladies, using the term very loosely, were Dotty's sister and Rodger's ex girlfriend. The girlfriend didn't say much, but the sister was screaming that Dotty had promised her the house should anything happen to her.'

'Fat lot of good a promise does if there's no will. If they were married, the spouse get the first bight of the cherry, even if there's more than one spouse. Maybe the girlfriend does have some claim, but I'd say the sister can forget it,' said Simon trying to lick the inside of his wineglass in a patently clear message to

Georgie, who was just as patently ignoring him. 'Don't get up, I'll get it. S'pose you'd like another while I'm at it?'

'Love one,' replied Georgie and handed Simon her glass. 'And now you can tell me about your day.'

Simon returned from the kitchen with another two Chardonnays. 'This anchor man has us tossed at the moment. No-one knows who he is, or was, or why he was where he was, though I suppose the poor bugger didn't have too much to say in the matter. The forensic report stated he was dead before being anchored, which isn't surprising by the mess his head was in. And why it was attached to Graham's anchor is anyone's guess. We initially thought Paul Stack might have had something to do with it as he was negotiating, if you can call it that, with Graham for the sale of The Taipan Club, which isn't for sale in any case. However, after our little chat with Stack, I'm inclined to believe he had nothing to do with it. On top of that, none of the organised crime groups have claimed responsibility, so it's anybody's guess as to what's going on.'

'So, now you'll be working up at The Cross for a while?' asked Georgie.

'No, we thought that might be the case as Rushcutters Bay is in The Cross's bailiwick. Fortunately that idea never really got off the ground, but as all the people we've talked to know nothing about anything, we may as well conduct the investigation from Timbuktu. We'll conduct the investigation from Day Street, though we've already been up to The Cross for a chat with Dave Harris. No-one around The Cross or Darlinghurst can, or won't, provide any info, not that I think anyone in those precincts knows anything anyway.'

'And Graham has no idea who the man was?'

'None whatsoever. Naturally he thought it had to have something to do with the casino and, as Stack was the only interested party, he had the idea Stack must be involved.'

'And you believe Stack?'

Simon shrugged. 'Yes. I think he was genuine in his surprise to hear what had happened. And no, I don't think he's involved. Anyway, let's get back to your problem. You say this Rodger isn't a very nice bloke?'

'Funny, isn't it? They say opposites attract. Dorothy must have been nuts to have married this turkey in the first place because they're so much alike; both with bloody big chips on their shoulders. Okay, we're pretty much alike. But they both appear to have had the same hostile attitude towards life, both of them being capable of picking a fight with anyone unfortunate enough to run into them. And he may even be worse than she was. I daresay Dorothy, the cantankerous old bitch, is having a right royal punch-up with Saint Peter right at the moment, or more likely whining her head off to someone about it being too damned hot,' said Georgie as an afterthought.

Simon smiled and said dryly, 'Well, if he's as bad as Dorothy was, I'd say his tenure at number twenty six will be short lived. I suppose you've already sussed out any aversions you may be able to exploit to do away with him. After all, you certainly gave old Dorothy the old heave-ho.'

'Her death was totally accidental, and you know that, so don't go there,' replied an indignant Georgie. That Dorothy had had a morbid fear of spiders, and the fact that Georgie had placed a huntsman spider, albeit a harmless giant of the arachnid specie, in her peg basket was, according to Georgie, totally inconsequential to the sudden passing of Dorothy, albeit by massive coronary conclusion. Still, Georgie was viewed by her friends as Collaroy's answer to Lucrezia Borgia.

'And you say Dorothy's family is now circling?' Simon asked, getting right off the subject of doing away with Rodger.

'No, not so much the family. Just this woman who claims she's Dorothy's sister, and Rodger's ex-girlfriend. I get the idea the ex doesn't want to buy into the problem. I suppose if I was in her position, I wouldn't be bothered either. I don't know the legal aspects, but as she lived with Dorothy's husband in a de facto relationship for a couple of years, she might have some legal claim on part of his estate, that's if he should snuff it. And the way things are going, that may well be on the cards. I just think it's all terribly complicated and not worth the trouble. Anyway, I'm getting bored. How about we ask Noel and Sue over on the weekend, and Ron, too? We can run a sweep on who's likely to get the chop next door, and Sue and I will solve your anchor man murder.'

CHAPTER 7

*T*he rain was just heavy enough to make you wet, but didn't seem quite heavy enough to make you get in out of it. However, after much deliberation the decision for a congenial afternoon on the back lawn of the bungalow at 24 West Bank Lane had been amended to a congenial afternoon in the lounge room of the bungalow at 24 West Bank Lane. The small gathering of visitors consisted of Noel and Sue Elliott, Graham Lee and Louisa Porter, and the expectation of the imminent arrival of Ron Lange to complete the group. To facilitate the seating arrangements, Simon, with Georgie's help, had moved a two-seater lounge from the room Georgie used as her office into the lounge room, which now made the room slightly confined, but nevertheless cosy.

'And how's the book going, Georgie?' asked Graham as he and Louisa settled themselves onto the two-seater lounge. Georgie had worked as a secretary in a legal firm in Phillip Street before deciding to become a successful author of crime novels. Having had one book published, she was well into the next literary masterpiece, ably assisted by Simon who was well placed to provide all the gruesome technical details, not always without the odd touch of cynicism.

'Slowly,' replied Georgie as she placed a plate of crackers and dip on the coffee table in the centre of the room. 'I was planning to use a plot where there was no actual murder committed, just where the antagonist increases the chances of someone dying.'

'Seems like I've heard the story before somewhere,' broke in Noel. 'Didn't something like that happen to Dorothy? That would make for a little confusion as to who the antagonist and who the protagonist were, not that you could ever be considered either.'

'Look, let's just forget about Dorothy, there's more exciting things happening around here at the moment. It seems the three of them next door are making sure the pot, with all the ingredients needed for a bit of homicidal mayhem, continues to bubble away nicely,' remarked Georgie as she settled herself into a lounge chair.

'Sounds like a slant on Macbeth with the three witches dancing round the cauldron as it bubbled,' commented Simon flippantly.

It was Louisa who saved Simon from some vitriolic banter from the other guests as she paused in her pouring of a glass of Chardonnay. 'Oh, do tell. You mean to say you're about to have a murder committed here in Collaroy? And right next door? My, how exciting.'

Georgie shrugged. 'Certainly looks like it, and Simon wants to run a sweep on who actually gets themselves murdered. It's a real lottery at the moment between the three of them, though I somehow think Rodger must be favoured to get the chop followed by Dotty's sister. You see, the bloke living there now, Rodger, Dorothy's husband, is a real plonker and Dorothy's sister sounds no better. She's been out to see him a couple of times and it always ends in a screaming match. For the life of me, he seems to be totally wacko, not that she seems overly endowed with intellectual insight.'

'And the sister has to drag Rodger's girl friend, or ex girl-friend, into the brawl. I almost feel sorry for her, the girlfriend I mean, and I haven't even met her. But having put up with Rodger for a couple of years, she probably hasn't a very good idea of what life is all about,' Noel remarked as he took a can of beer from Simon who had just re-entered the room with a six pack.

At that moment there was a knock on the front door, followed a few seconds later by Ron standing in the doorway to the lounge room. 'Sorry if I'm a bit late; took me a little longer than I thought. Must be the weather. And thanks, Simon, I'd love one,' he said as he entered the room and took a can of beer from the six pack. 'Have I missed anything?'

'No,' replied Graham. 'I was just about to say that while there's speculation of a possible homicide here in West Bank Lane, we have a very real homicide at Rushcutters Bay, along with a real live dead body reposing in the morgue waiting for someone to come along and give it a name. Now, that has to be more exciting than a murder that might or might not happen, even if it is next door.'

Simon opened another bottle of Chardonnay, poured three wines and handed them to the girls. After settling back into his favourite lounge chair with his tinny of beer, he looked at Graham and raised his eyebrows. 'I had a talk with both Super-intendent Hayes and Chief Superintendent Paxton yesterday. It seems we're no further advanced in identifying the anchor man than we were when we pulled him out of the water. Having spoken to Paul Stack, I have my doubts as to the body being connected to The Taipan Club at all. Have you anything new to tell us, Graham?'

'Not a thing. I agree with you when you say you don't think Stack is involved. He came to see me after you spoke with him and I really found him quite reasonable, for a change. He wondered if it might be organised crime gangs getting involved, but if they are, they're being awfully quiet about it.'

'Maybe I've got the bull by the horns,' remarked Sue from the lounge she was sharing with Noel and Ron, 'but from what I gather, you're stuck with a dead body. No-one has a clue to its identity, and there appears to be no reason why it was found where it was.'

'I think I know where you're coming from and where you're headed, Sue,' said Louisa. How about you Georgie, are you with us simple minded females?'

'I'm way ahead of you,' replied Georgie as she reached forward for a Jatz and onion dip from the coffee table. 'I just can't understand why these geniuses, or is it genii, well these mere males, can't work it out.'

Simon heaved a sigh and shrugged. 'Okay, you Einsteins. What have we missed? Everything always seems so simple and clear cut to you females. What's your explanation this time?'

'Simple,' replied Georgie. 'The body was anchored to the wrong boat.'

Simon looked at Noel, and then Ron before all three looked at Graham. 'Don't look at me like that. You're the bloody police,' said Graham with a distinct suggestion of indignation in his voice. 'If you ask me, I think the whole idea is crazy, and that's being polite. No-one would go to the trouble of bumping off some poor bugger, and then make the mistake of dumping the body onto some poor innocent sod who hasn't a clue as to what's going on. And I just happen to be the poor innocent sod.'

Noel gave a quick nod and said, 'Well, that would certainly explain why there hasn't been a message to go with the body.'

Simon shook his head. 'No, I agree with Graham. The whole

idea of getting rid of a body in the manner this body was suggests that some thought had gone into the scheme. To actually go and murder someone, most normal people would just chuck the body over a cliff, or dig a grave, not go to the difficult task of rowing it out to a cruiser in the busiest boat parking station in Sydney, getting onboard the boat with the body, pulling up the anchor, attaching the body, dropping the anchor back overboard then decamping the area without being seen. Whoever did it must have done it pretty late at night. No, no-one would make such a blunder after going to all the trouble of breaking the poor bugger's head in the first instance.'

'Now, come on Simon. When you say "most normal people would chuck the body over a cliff", most normal people I know wouldn't go around chucking any body over any cliff. Well, at least I don't think they would. But that's okay, Simon, you men have your ideas and we girls will have our ideas,' pronounced Georgie as she returned from the kitchen with another bottle of Chardonnay. 'Absolutely nothing has happened since you recovered the body; all you have now is a body lying idle in the morgue, nothing else. The only theory you had, that it had something to do with The Taipan Club, seems to have been given the flick, especially after your little chat with Paul Stack.' After refilling the three empty wine glasses, Georgie settled herself back in a lounge chair. 'Louisa, just a quick question. What do you consider the major differences between the "Chez Anne" and Graham's new boat; in looks, I mean?'

'God, I don't know. His new boat is smaller, I think. To tell the truth, I can't really say. It's not that I'm not interested in boats, I love them, but they all look the same to me, except for those that have a big pole sticking up, they're different,' replied Louisa, somewhat surprised at her own lack of observational expertise.

Graham shook his head in disappointment. 'Louisa, those

51

boats with a big pole are called yachts and the pole is actually called a mast on which those white things called sails go up and down. Someday I really must explain things to you.'

Georgie said apologetically, 'I'm sorry, Louisa, I didn't mean to embarrass you. I just wanted to make a point that not everyone is so well-informed about boats. There must be, what, a couple of hundred boats in Rushcutters Bay and to the uninitiated they probably all look the same.'

'Totally agree,' chimed in Sue who, up to this point, had been listening intently to the discussion. 'If you were to ask me to attach a body to the anchor of a boat, the first thing I would have to ask is what the name of the boat is.'

Simon got up from his chair and picked up the empty cans of beer left on the coffee table. He paused at the door to the kitchen then turned. 'Well, I totally disagree, Sue. No-one with half a brain in his head would attach a body to the wrong boat. Ron, you've been very quiet on the subject.'

'Now, don't get me wrong, Simon, but I place a lot of credence in women's intuition. You should know that from past history,' Ron said as he peeled off the top of another can of beer. 'I think that to discount the girl's theory, you'd be doing so at your own peril. I can't see that a bit of a stickybeak in that direction would be too difficult before discarding the idea as a load of hogwash. Who knows? No, I think the idea has some merit and needs to be looked at. And let's face it; it's not as though you're endowed with so many leads you have something better to pursue.'

'Just a tick,' said Simon, returning from dumping the empty cans in the kitchen garbage bin. 'Graham, this new boat of yours, did you buy it from the builders or from a broker?'

'I see what you're driving at, Simon, but no, the "Gemini" is brand spanking new off the shelf. It didn't belong to anyone previously so it can't be a case of mistaken identity, though the thought did cross my mind.'

Simon looked at Noel and shrugged. 'Okay, Noel, I'll leave you to start digging around the boat scene and see what you can come up with. I daresay it will prove to be a waste of time, but we'll humour the girls, just to make a point.'

CHAPTER 8

$\mathcal{H}$aving declared the visit to the police station at Kings Cross a complete waste of time, apart from picking up the forensic report, both Simon and Noel were happy to conduct the investigation from their office at Day Street. Also content with the arrangement was Detective Superintendent Michael Hayes who now had his two subordinates in close vicinity where he could keep an eye on the progress of the investigation. More importantly, to Hayes it meant the expenditure of incidental allowances for the officers while working away from their posted station, was negated.

While happy with the way things had panned out, Detective Superintendent Michael Hayes was a little perturbed that the investigation into the death of The Anchor Man, as the body was now alluded to, seemed to have made little progress. Appearing to have the successful outcome of the investigation as his priority, purely for the reputation of the force, Superintendent Hayes undoubtedly had a far more intimate motive for the successful conclusion to the Anchor Man murder case. Being the new boy at the station, he viewed the current investigation, which had received wide publicity throughout the force, as the perfect opportunity to establish his credentials while at the same time promoting his credibility as a successful operational detective within the precinct.

'So, what line do you propose to take with your investigation now?' asked the Superintendent as he half sat, half leaned against a two drawer filing cabinet, his arms folded. The fact that Superintendent Hayes had taken the step to visit the two detectives in their own office was a new experience for Detective Chief Inspector Webster and Detective Sergeant Elliott. In fact it was a first, the detectives having previously being required to visit their superior's office; but they considered it a nice change of protocol anyway.

In an effort to at least sound as if he knew what was going on, Noel said, 'Forensics has established the body was killed by a blow to the back of the head with a blunt instrument before being dumped in the harbour. Divers failed to recover any potential murder weapon from around the anchorage so we're assuming he was dead before being moved to Rushcutters Bay.' All in all, Noel was quite pleased with his revealing oration of the facts and the brownie points he, no doubt, just earned.

Notwithstanding, Noel was somewhat bewildered as he noticed Simon fail in his attempt to suppress a wry smile; until the Superintendent, whose eyebrows were now drawn into one dark and menacing line, posed the next question.

'Well, Sergeant Elliott, that was all very enlightening. We're well aware that the Anchor Man, as you now like to call your cadaver, was well and truly murdered. But to say the body was killed by a blow to the head suggests the Anchor Man was dead before getting his brains bashed in. Am I missing something? Perhaps he was poisoned or shot or murdered a few times before being belted on the head?'

Sergeant Elliott's face turned a brighter shade of pink with embarrassment. 'No sir, a poor choice of words. Maybe I should have clarified that by saying that forensics established that the live body, or person, was killed by a blow to the head.' Noel looked at Simon who was supporting his slowly shaking head in his hand, his elbow on the table.

Superintendent Hayes was not impressed. 'Excuse me Sergeant, but I appreciate that this must be a learning curve for you. Notwithstanding my limited experience in investigating cases involving homicide and the dead, I find the use of the English language when dealing with such matters can be a bit misleading. Let me explain. When we use the term "body", we in the police force are usually referring to someone who is already dead, deceased, lifeless, extinct. You know, the state a person usually becomes susceptible to contracting rigormortis, as opposed to the living who don't usually suffer from the complaint.' The Superintendent paused in deep thought for a moment before adding, 'I s'pose there are a few exceptions to that rule, like some government employees and politicians. But to come across a live body would be quite unique and something I would dearly love to see. With me being a qualified and certified skeptic, Sergeant Elliott, I doubt the existence of the living dead, despite what Hollywood would have us believe.'

'Sorry sir. Chief, maybe you'd like to explain the situation?'

'No, not at all. I think you're doing remarkably well,' replied Simon. 'But I don't think you've told the Superintendent anything he didn't know already. It's not where we've been he's interested in, but where we intend going.'

'Ah, yes. Sorry sir,' said Noel addressing the Superintendent. 'With no-one having any idea what this case is all about, we've decided the body may have been anchored on the wrong boat.'

'Well, that's a novel approach. Who dreamt that one up?' asked Superintendent Hayes who was now pacing the office, hands in his pockets.

Before Simon could intervene, Noel gave the answer. 'Oh, the girls thought it was the obvious solution.'

Superintendent Hayes stopped his pacing and looked at Chief Webster with a very concerned look on his face. 'Might I ask who "the girls" are, or don't I need to know?'

Simon took a deep breath and raised his eyebrows. 'Sir, so far the investigation has gone absolutely nowhere. With nothing to explain the whys or wherefores, it seemed appropriate that we view the situation from a totally different perspective. To this end, we believe there could be a case of mistaken boat identity; after all, there are hundreds of them in the Bay. We propose to check the names of all the boats moored in Rushcutters Bay as we believe there must be a few with the same name as Gemini. It won't be such a difficult task; it'll just take a bit of time. We think it's far better to pursue that line of investigation than to sit on our bums with no plan of action hoping something turns up.'

Superintendent Hayes took a deep breath and then a long sigh. 'Couldn't agree more. Look, while I'm glad the investigation is being conducted from here and not up at The Cross, I think it's probably wise, and far less stressful, if the less I know, the better, for me anyway. From what I've heard, you two can come up with some pretty odd methods of detective work. All I ask is that each Friday you provide me with a situation report as to your progress. Thanks gentlemen, I think you've made your point and have cleared up a few misconceptions I may have had.' With that, Superintendent Hayes abruptly left the two detectives and returned to his office.

'Well, he seems a pretty decent bloke, bit of a change from Fisher though he does seem a bit of a cynical bugger,' commented Noel after the Superintendent was no longer in earshot. 'And thanks a million, pal. You really left me to dig a hole for myself; I felt like a real idiot.'

Simon smiled and sat back on his battered old swivel chair. 'Part of your education, Noel. Never volunteer for anything, especially comments to a senior officer. If he asks you a direct question, of course you're obliged to answer. But in this case Hayes didn't nominate a respondent to his question; you jumped in. As they say, you can let a person think you're an idiot without confirming it by opening your mouth.'

'Okay, lesson learnt,' reflected Noel. 'But let's get on with the Anchor Man. Where do we go to from here now we've announced the direction we're headed?'

'First thing I want you to do is get over to the Maritime Services Board and see if they have a list of all the boats anchored in Rushcutters Bay. I think they're responsible for many of the anchorages over there. In the meantime, I propose to have a chat to the people who run the marina. I also want to ask Graham Lee if I can have a lend of Adam and do a cruise around the Bay in his ducky, just to see what's there. One other thing. I'll ask forensics to see if they can come up with either a photo, or a diagram of the victim, or what they think the victim probably looked like. We need something for people to have a look at. For what it's worth, at least I feel we're starting to do something positive.'

CHAPTER 9

'Hello sweetheart, you're home early,' called Georgie as she closed the door to the study and followed Simon into the lounge room.

'Yes, I thought we'd have a Friday afternoon on a Wednesday and knock off early. It's been a busy week already and I didn't like the sound of the weather forecast. Apparently there's a major thunderstorm on the way and it's bad enough being a passenger in Noel's car when conditions are perfect,' Simon said. He took off his coat and tie, threw them onto the sofa and flopped down into his favourite lounge chair.

'Yes, strange isn't it? We've had some bad thunderstorms already and it's not even springtime,' said Georgie as she picked up the discarded clothing, neatly folded them and placed them on the end of the sofa. She then sat down, tucking her bare feet up underneath her. 'Apart from the weather, how's the Anchor Man going?'

'Well, for want of anything better to do, we've decided your suggestion is the only course of action open to us, unless someone comes forward with some better idea,' replied Simon, as he worked each shoe off with the other foot.

'Gee, thanks a million,' said Georgie with scorn. 'I'll pass on your apology to Louisa and Sue, after you crack this case by finding the body was attached to the wrong boat.'

'Yeah, well you could have been a bit more specific. There are only fifty zillion other boats on Sydney Harbour and, if what you say is correct, it could have been anchored to any one of them. What are we supposed to do; go 'round and ask everyone if they just happen to have lost a waterlogged corpse?' chided Simon. 'Anyway, tell me all about the dramas going on next door.'

'Oh yes. I had a visitor today. Well, she didn't pay me a visit specifically. The girl, well, lady who had been living with Dorothy's husband came to see him. He wasn't home, or at least didn't appear to be, and I ran into her just as she was leaving. Her name's Judy. We got chatting and I invited her in for a coffee; she's a nice girl and I feel she may be getting the thin end of the wedge, so to speak.'

Simon shook his head and pursed his lips. 'I tell you, Georgie, you don't want to get involved.'

'I'm not getting involved at all,' said Georgie belligerently. 'I was just being neighbourly. Somehow I think our impressions of Mr Rodger are spot on, going by what Judy has told me. Seems they were living together for about twenty months before Rodger gave her the flick for no obvious reason; just told her to get out, and that was just after she'd bought him a very expensive high tech fishing rod, not that she knows anything about fishing. Apparently he's mad about drowning worms and for him to get the chance to live on the coast is like being in a fisherman's paradise. Anyway, Judy believes she got the old heave-ho because he didn't want the relationship to be legally recognized, which it may have been if they had lived together for two years, at least I think it's two years. Like I said, he's a rare fruitcake.'

'And have you seen anything of Dorothy's sister, whatsaname?' Simon asked without any interest whatsoever.

'Oh, you mean Claudia. Yes, she's a regular caller, but he never seems to be home whenever she does drop by. Maybe he just doesn't want to answer the door. Despite the fact that he's a real pillock, I can understand why he wouldn't, answer the door, that is. Talk about a raving battleaxe, and the language when the two do get together would make you cringe. All in all, it seems our Mr Rodger Beaton is one unpopular person at the moment, and not just with Claudia.'

'And are you planning on doing a Dorothy on Rodger?' asked Simon, his interest rising, 'maybe another plot for your book?'

'Look, Dorothy was a glitch that shouldn't have happened. How could anyone have predicted she would drop dead over one little spider that was practically dead itself? And apart from that, my book needs a case where you just increase the chances of someone dying, not a sudden death by going out and sticking a knife into some poor bugger; that's too easy for the sleuths. No, my way is to create a situation where the proposed victim might or might not die. However, it just happens that you up the ante on the chances the proposed victim will snuff it. It might take a little longer than a simple case of murder, but if the chances are increased, the intended quarry will eventually satisfy the necessary requirement and do the appropriate thing; pop off that is.'

'God Almighty, I'm glad you come up with these ideas for your book and not in real life. You could tell Rodger the blue ringed octopus is harmless, or that he should take up rock fishing with his new rod, or never swim between the flags. They all have wonderfully deadly potential.'

'Gee, I didn't think of that one,' exclaimed Georgie. Simon didn't bother to ask which one she hadn't thought of.

'And how does this girl Judy feel about Rodger now? Hopefully she will have come to her senses and can see Rodger for what he is, a real little twerp,' said Simon trying to divert the discussion away from fortuitous non-murdering scenarios.

'Well, the way Judy's been treated by that degenerate, if she does bump him off it would have to be considered justified homicide. As I said, she's the one I feel sorry for. As for Claudia, she appears just as moronic and difficult to get on with as Dorothy was. Trouble is, even if Judy did do away with Rodger, she'll end up with nothing, apart from the self satisfaction she may derive in ridding the community of such a horrible little man.'

'Georgie, I didn't ask how you felt about Rodger; I asked how Judy felt about Rodger,'

'She feels hard done by him, of course. I've suggested she seek some legal advice as to her position, but I'm not confident she has any grounds for legal action. I've no doubt if Rodger were to be hit by a truck, she would consider it to be rather serendipitous and be overjoyed by the occasion.'

'And have you told Judy of your murder strategy, just on the off chance she might be interested in helping Rodger move on? I suppose she could hire a truck to get things moving, so to speak.'

'Good God, no. Well, not exactly. I may have mentioned the theme for my book and the idea of increasing the odds of having the proposed victim snuff it. But that's totally irrelevant. Judy is a good-looking lady in her early forties and has a life to look forward to, despite her miserable past. The last thing she would want is to spend it in Long Bay Jail.'

'Now let me get this straight,' said Simon, a look of frustrated concentration on his face. 'Rodger is free to go off with his high-tech fishing rod and do his fishing thing. Obviously he couldn't give a stuff about either Claudia or Judy and doesn't care two hoots what they think of him, even if both of them would like to blow his brains out.

'Claudia, on the other hand, is all bitter and twisted because Dorothy, despite the rhetoric, didn't leave her the house in a will because she never made one. On top of that, she's not overly impressed with Rodger because he's living in the house she believes is hers. I suppose she might fear Judy as she might have some legal claim on the property. Next, we have Judy who is resentful because Rodger did the dirty on her. She doesn't like Claudia because she sees Claudia as an interfering bitch who's out after everything she can get, irrespective of anyone else's legal claims. And all this because dear old Dorothy died intestate. So, who's going to be the victim and who'll be the murderer?' Simon asked as he got up from his chair and made his way to the kitchen fridge for refreshments.

CHAPTER 10

*C*hief Inspector Webster turned on his desk lamp and spread the papers on the table of his Day Street office. 'Here are the names of boats provided by the Rushcutters Bay marina. Have you the list from the Maritime Services Board, Noel?'

'Sure thing, boss,' replied Sergeant Elliott and withdrew a large envelope from his coat pocket and handed it to Simon. 'I thought it would have been longer, but it seems the MSB don't have that many anchorages in the Bay.'

'No, I didn't think there would be too many. After speaking to the people from the marina, it seems they've got the game sewn up with nearly every boat in the Bay moored to a marina mooring. And here I am thinking the expensive bit of owning a boat was the initial cost. After having a reality check, I don't think I could even afford the rubber ducky we putted around in,' replied Simon.

'And did your exhausting day cruising around the harbour reveal anything startling, or did you decide it was the Anchor

Man who shot the albatross?' Noel asked with a touch of cynicism.

'Just let me have a look at the names of these boats, including the yachts. Maybe Georgie's right when she says some people wouldn't know the difference between a row boat and a battleship. There didn't appear to be anything obvious apart from the fact that quite a few boats have the name of a star sign. Like this one here, the "Taurus". Who in their right mind would ever want to call a boat "Taurus"? I thought all boats and ships were referred to in the feminine gender, so where does a boat come off with the name of a bull?' Simon asked shaking his head.

Noel replied, 'Well, at least whoever owns it is has a boat to call "Taurus" which makes it a hell of a lot better boat than mine. Yes, there's another one, "Aquarius",' he said, looking over Simon's shoulder and pointing. 'You think someone may have got the names confused, or there's more than one "Gemini"?'

'I'd say there's at least a dozen boats with the name of a star sign, which is about the number I counted in the Bay. I think I counted three "Geminis", including Graham's, and it looks like they're the only ones, according to the lists. Let's check on them first before we go onto other star signs,' said Simon as he set about recording the details of the owners in his notebook.

'Before we start running off and questioning people about a dead corpse, can we speculate on what we think could have happened, or should have happened. I'd like to get it clear in my mind just what angle we're pursuing,' said Noel, a little bit short on just what they were actually looking for, apart from the owner of the cadaver.

Simon nodded his agreement and pushed his chair back from the table. 'Good grief, Noel, there you go again with your tautology. I've yet to see a corpse that wasn't dead, but I get the message. Due to the lack of information, other than that provided by forensics, we're working on the assumption the

Anchor Man was attached to the wrong boat. With the number of boats in the Bay, the best place to start looking for our potential owner of the dead corpse, as you so delightfully refer to our corpse, are the boats with the same name as Graham Lee's boat which is, of course, "Gemini". Should this little exercise prove fruitless, I daresay we would need to start on the other boats with a star sign name. Of course, it may be that the star sign angle is a total waste of time. However, until we have a more realistic and credible scenario to pursue, you'd better start reading the astrology pages.'

'Okay boss. At least as far as murder investigations go, the Anchor Man appears to have set us a pretty good case to solve,' said Noel with a sigh and a shrug of the shoulders.

Detective Chief Inspector Webster and Detective Sergeant Noel Elliott made themselves as comfortable as they could in light of the circumstances. In accordance with the Superintendent's instruction to provide a Friday situation report on the progress of the Anchor Man murder, the two detectives found themselves seated in front of the Superintendent's desk without too much to report. In fact, the course of the investigation had resulted in nothing new since forensics had determined the body, currently reposing in the cool-room of the city morgue, had been killed by a blow to the head and was definitely dead before entering the water.

'Well?' asked the Superintendent with an enquiring look on his face. 'Your reputation precedes you so I take it you have solved the case and have the suspect under arrest?'

'Ah, no, not quite, sir. There are a couple of loose ends we have to clear up first,' replied Simon awkwardly. 'We have completed our preliminary evaluation and analysis of the original data collated following the investigation into the circumstances relating to the recovery of the body at Rushcutters Bay. This analysis has clearly indicated that such lines of enquiries, predicated on the information available to us at that time the body was recovered, such as the sheet the body was wrapped in, together with subsequent information obtained during the course of our investigation, have proved to be both unproductive and, not to put a finer point on it, sir, a total waste of time.'

Noel looked at Simon with a look of bemusement, quite at a loss as to just when they had completed an analysis; he couldn't recall having ever started an analysis. In fact, Noel couldn't recall having any data to analyse.

Superintendent Hayes rested his elbow on the table, held his chin with his thumb and absently tapped his lips with his forefinger. After a few seconds it appeared he had completed his interpretation of Simon's recently delivered, and somewhat convoluted, exposé of progress in the matter of The Anchor Man investigation. 'So, I take it that's a sort of a roundabout admission that the investigation is no further advanced than the day the body was pulled from the harbour?'

'No, that's not quite correct, sir,' replied Simon who was by now feeling a bit more uncomfortable. 'We have undertaken enquiries that have led us to believe our prime suspect has absolutely no knowledge of the case and is unable to provide any information. Unfortunately, sir, there has been surprisingly little forthcoming in the way of evidence or information, which can only be expected until the body is positively identified. As a consequence, we anticipate some delay to the expeditious and successful conclusion to this investigation. Naturally, the course of our further investigation will be contingent upon the receipt of additional information as it comes to hand. At this point in time, there is a severe lack of basic intelligence needed to give us precise direction in which our investigation should follow.

So, in essence, sir, you could say we'll be running around in ever diminishing circles, at least until we get something to point us in right direction.'

During Simon's brief, but nonetheless tortuous presentation of the case, the Superintendent had given the impression he had been listening intently. It came as somewhat of a surprise to both Simon and Noel when Superintendent Hayes, apparently choosing to ignore Simon's load of linguistic twaddle, asked, 'Now, after you've fed me all that crap, how about we get on with the whole idea of this meeting, like, what's the name of the victim and what do we know about him? And this time, let's cut the pretentious claptrap.'

'Yes, sir, well sir, that's one of the loose ends. We haven't actually been able to positively establish the identity of the body, beyond any doubt that is, and we know very little about him. But I suppose that's only to be expected at this stage of the investigation.'

'So, you at least have some idea as to the name of the victim?'

'When I say we haven't established the identity beyond doubt, sir, it's probably more correct to say that, at the moment, we don't know anything about him; we haven't a clue as to who he is, or was.'

'So, I suppose it would be a bit ambitious to ask about possible suspects?'

'That's another loose end, sir.'

'No, don't tell me. You haven't got a suspect?'

'No sir. We did have one, but now we don't although we are working on it. After all, sir, that is the whole aim of our investigation.'

Superintendent Hayes's erect posture behind his desk collapsed as he dropped his head and shoulders, slumped back in his chair, almost disappearing from the view of the two detectives, then rested his chin on the palm of his hand and gently tapped his cheek in contemplation. 'And I was led to believe you two were the Sherlock and Watson of the force. So, just what have you achieved as this investigation now happens to appear very similar to the body you recovered; dead in the water and going nowhere? If I remember correctly you've decided the body was on the wrong boat.'

Simon took a deep breath before answering. 'Well sir, there is nothing to suggest Mr Lee is involved in any way, apart from his boat "Gemini" having provided a convenient and accessible anchorage for the body. There are three cruisers moored in the Bay with the same name and we have interviewed the owners of the other two boats without result, positive result, that is. Obviously, any interview produces some sort of result, positive or otherwise, as you are, no doubt, aware. There is at least a further dozen boats in the Bay with names of other zodiacal star signs and we believe it possible there might have been some confusion in selecting the correct sign.'

'Well at least your thinking is innovative, I'll give you that. I'm not going to ask if you're armed with a Ouija board as I don't want to know. I suppose you're going to pursue the idea that the body belongs to someone else and not Mr Lee?' enquired the Superintendent. With a touch of both despondency and sarcasm, Superintendent Hayes had managed to convey the fact that he now considered the investigation, destined to establish his credibility at Day Street, may not be achieving the results he had so hoped for.

'Yes sir. I have no doubt Graham Lee knows nothing about the Anchor Man and that it has nothing to do with The Taipan Club. I still can't help thinking the name Gemini is significant. When you think about it, it's the only confirmed piece of evidence we have and I feel sure it must have some relevance to the case. While it's the most obscure, vague and cryptic clue I've ever come across, I'm sure we'll be kicking ourselves with its simplicity once we've nutted it out,' replied Simon, pleased for the opportunity to at least sound if he was on top of the case.

'Well, I'll leave you to get on with it. Forget about the Friday updates as I fear they would be a waste of time for both of us. If, just if, on the rare chance the unforeseen should eventuate and you come across something of interest, or something of significance comes up and bites you on the bum, I'd love to be informed,' said the Superintendent as he folded his arms, a look of disappointment etched across his face. Bloody Ouija boards and crystal balls.

CHAPTER 11

'*T*wo cappuccinos please, Linda', Simon requested as Linda took the order and returned to the counter. Simon and Georgie had strolled down to the Eleven Fifteen Coffee Shop located on Pittwater Road in Collaroy, just passed the ridiculous Alexander Street where a car could burn out its brakes coming down and its engine going up. The Saturday was dry and sultry, the temperature climbing into the high twenties with the possibility of late afternoon thunderstorms predicted.

Georgie asked, 'So, you think the new superintendent isn't overly impressed with the way your investigation is going?'

Simon shrugged. 'No, to say he's not overly impressed is somewhat of an understatement, and I can't say I blame him. In fact, I'd even go so far as to say our investigation is rocketing along with all the speed of a tectonic plate. Now we've had a good think about it, I somehow feel your idea about the body being on the wrong boat is probably right; it's just we have the small problem of trying to find which was the right boat. We've checked out all the boats in the Bay named "Gemini" without any luck. Look, here's a list of all the boats that have the same name as a star sign. See what you can make of it, if anything.' Simon took a crumpled sheet of paper from his pocket and handed it to Georgie.

'Just before we start. Have you considered Graham's "Gemini" might be the right boat and the baddies have attached the wrong body?'

'Holy hell, just when did you come up with that ridiculous idea, or are you trying to throw a bloody great spanner in the works? I s'pose it's possible, but crikey, Georgie, the thought that there's a bunch of dead bodies piled up somewhere to be used to intimidate people...No, forget it. Let's get on with our simple case of homicide.'

The coffees were soon delivered with a friendly smile from Linda and, after spreading the paper on the table, Georgie settled herself into some intense scrutiny of the names of boats moored in Rushcutters Bay. 'So, we have three Geminis, a Taurus, two Virgos – must be the last two in Sydney, four Capricorns – all owned by old goats no doubt, two Scorpios, one Sagittarius – must be a bloody big boat to be able to write that across the stern, and one Aquarius.' Georgie raised her eyebrows and looked at Simon inquiringly. 'And you still think the name Gemini is significant to the investigation?'

'It must be,' replied Simon, a touch exasperated. 'I don't know anything about star signs, but as we haven't anything else to go on, I'm hoping it is significant, somehow.'

'Okay, let's not throw in the towel just yet. Do you have the list of all the boats moored in the Bay back at the house, not just those with a star sign, I mean?' Georgie asked with an air of confidence in an effort to boost Simon's flagging morale.

'Yes. It's in my brief case. Why?'

'Well, let's just go through it and see what we come up with. Gemini can be linked with a host of names in Greek mythology. Even though they were hatched from an egg, the Gemini twins' mummy and daddy were Leda and Zeus, after Zeus took on the guise of a swan and had had his way with Leda, hence the egg bit. Oh yes, just one question. Did you ask the owners of the other two Geminis if their boats were in Rushcutters Bay around the time we found the anchor man?'

'No I didn't. I didn't think it necessary as the owners didn't know anything about the body irrespective of where their boat was parked at the time. Maybe there could have been another "Gemini" parked in the Bay.'

'I didn't think of that,' replied Georgie. 'But it's a terribly long shot to think another "Gemini" would moor there without the MSB or marina people knowing.'

'No, I suppose not. Anyway, let's change the subject for a moment, but before that, another brew?' After drawing Linda's attention and ordering two more cappuccinos, Simon turned to Georgie and asked, 'And how's everything getting on next door with Judy, Claudia and Rodger. I take it they're all still alive, so far?'

'So far, but I don't think it will be long before someone takes an axe to someone. And that's the tricky bit; just who is going to take the axe to whom? They all got stuck into each other yesterday. You'd think the two women would join forces against Rodger, but they all seem quite obsessed with having a three way battle. Judy, who appears to be a nice person and the only one with a brain in her head, would no doubt take the axe to both Rodger and Claudia, given the chance. But then again, all three of them would like to bash the other's brains in. All terribly exciting.'

'So, you don't think your ploy of just increasing the chances of someone dying will be employed?' asked Simon, sardonically.

'Hell no. If there is going to be a murder there won't be anything subtle about it. A twelve-gauge, double barrel shotgun at six feet seems more likely.'

'Well, in the words of the inimitable Ned Kelly, "such is life". Let's go home before this thunderstorm breaks because it looks like it's going to be a doozy,' Simon said as he looked out of the window at the darkening sky.

'Hey, before we do anything, go close the bedroom windows. I'll do the rest of the house before this storm hits,' yelled Simon as the constant angry rumble of thunder became angrier with the occasional flash of lightning now a continuous and relentless rip through the ominous black storm clouds above. The expected downpour hadn't quite started, but the size of the few drops already beating down with the sound of a handful of stones thrown onto the roof, heralded the approach of a major storm. 'Cripes, only September and we have a real thunder-storm. Looks like being a wet summer. Now Georgie, you're about to give me my first lesson in astrology?' said Simon, now sitting at the kitchen table awaiting enlightenment.

Georgie entered the kitchen with an encyclopedia tucked under her arm, along with pencil and a note book. 'Don't expect to become an expert 'cause I know very little about the stars, except what I read from the horoscopes.'

'Yeah, well we're only interested in Gemini and boats with that name, or something akin to it,' said Simon. Though he believed there had to be some reason why the body was attached to the "Gemini", sitting down to explore the nature of astrology and the star signs couldn't stop Simon feeling a trifle sceptical, and even a little foolish, for even entertaining the possibility of a link to a murder victim.

'Okay, let's have a look at the list of names of cruisers moored in the bay first. We've already had a look at those having the same name as a star sign without anything obvious popping out at us,' replied Georgie as she spread the list on the table. There were forty three cruisers moored in the bay and it didn't take Georgie long to pencil a circle around a boat called "Castor".

'Why "Castor"?' asked Simon.

Georgie smiled with pride, her superior knowledge of the misty realm of astrology obviously evident to Simon who had never really taken any notice of the subject. 'Because Castor is one of the Gemini twins,' Georgie replied as if expecting everyone to be aware of the simple fact. 'There's no boat with the name of Pollux, who was the other twin, but it might pay to give the owner of "Castor" a visit. At least it's something. Good Lord, is that our next door neighbour going fishing?' Georgie exclaimed as she glimpsed a car with fishing rods on the roof rack backing out of the driveway.

'People who go fishing and those who play golf are a breed apart. Maybe they like the thrill of risking their lives swinging metal golf clubs or fishing rods around in the middle of a thunder storm,' replied Simon. "Anyway, thanks sweetie. Noel and I will have a chat to this bloke who owns "Castor" and see if it's his body in the morgue.'

'Well, that was a waste of time and effort,' remarked Noel as he screwed up a piece of paper and had a long, three point shot at the office waste paper bin, and missed. 'Mr Douglas, or should I say, the wealthy Mr Douglas, knew nothing about who the body should belong to. You'd think we could palm it off onto someone as it's a perfectly good body, apart from a little water damage.'

'That's the stupid part of it. Someone is missing someone and the missing someone is our Mr Anchor Man. Check out Missing Persons and see what they can come up with. As you say, someone must own him.'

The ringing of Simon's phone interrupted his thoughts which, for once, he considered a pleasant distraction. Noel looked across at Simon in anticipation of some facial reaction that may convey the significance of the call. The call was significant. Simon reached for pen and paper, leaned forward and started taking notes, his face the epitome of concentration. Within a few minutes he hung up, threw his pen onto the table and pushed the dilapidated swivel chair back from the desk.

Noel raised his eyebrows questioningly. 'That was Jacko, you know, works for Paul Stack at The Spinning Wheel. Seems he's heard something on the grapevine about our body and would like to have a chat, I mean Jacko would like a chat, not the body. He says that as far as he knows, Stack has no involvement. I suggested we meet at the El Alamein Fountain this afternoon. Like to come along?'

'Sure, love to. They say all good things come to those who wait and we've been waiting long enough. It's good to see Jacko regards you as well as he does.'

Jacko was waiting on a bench in Fitzroy Gardens, close enough to the nearby fountain for the relaxing sounds of spraying water to be clearly heard. Despite the soothing sounds, Jacko, anxious to pass on his vital information, was tense and nervous, furtively looking around the park when Simon and Noel arrived.

'Hi boss,' said Jacko to Simon, a hint of a smile on his face before giving Noel a friendly nod. 'Shall we talk here or would you prefer somewhere a little less conspicuous?'

'No, here's fine with us,' replied Simon as he sat down. Ironic, thought Simon. Here we are about to bust the Anchor Man case wide open just ten yards away from the police station we started the investigation. Well, maybe not wide open. 'Okay Jacko, what have you got for us?'

'Well, I was talkin' to this bloke who came to the club last night. Never laid eyes on him before, but seemed friendly enough. He said he'd just been paid for a job so had a few bob to spend on the tables, not that I think he knew his way around a casino too well. Anyway, seems he has a little tinny boat he uses to go fishin.' He said he usually launches it from a ramp at

Drummoyne as that's the closest ramp to where he lives,' Jacko said with an air of importance.

'You see, everyone seems to know you have a dead body that was fished out of the harbour on your hands. Well, I got to thinkin' just maybe, so I started asking a few questions, quiet like, you know, didn't want to sound too interested. This bloke with the tinny goes by the name of Tiny Timmins, probably because he's so big, I suppose. Said he lives somewhere in the Balmain area, though didn't say exactly where. He didn't specifically say what the job was, but indicated he had to use his boat. The thing that struck me was that he commented on the fact that if he could win enough on the tables he would buy a decent boat, like the ones in Rushcutters Bay where he had been recently. Slim chance of that happenin' 'cause not too many people win at the tables, and rarely enough to buy a flamin' boat when they do.

'Seems the bloke who asked him to do the job was a Mr Glover. I don't know how Timmins knows this Glover character, and I suppose that's beside the point. I just thought it a bit funny that I should run into this bloke who happens to own a boat and has been over at Rushcutters Bay recently. Let's face it, Timmins isn't the sort of bloke you'd normally expect to see around that neck of the woods; a bit up-market for him and there are less crowded places to drop a line. I s'pose fishin' in Rushcutters would be like playin' marbles in the middle of the M5 Motorway. Like, I don't know if the info is of any value, but from what I hear, you're not doin' too well with the investigation.'

'Jacko, the way things are at the moment we'll chase up a dog's lead,' said Simon. 'And you say Paul Stack isn't involved?'

'No, not a whisper about him. But to be truthful, I wouldn't trust him as far as I could throw him, even if he is my boss.'

'Well, you're a big boy, Jacko, so I reckon you could probably throw him half way to the boundary,' chided Simon good naturedly. 'Okay, look Jacko, if your info turns out to be important, I'll buy you a few beers. In the meantime, here's my card. Feel free to give me a ring anytime. And on second thoughts, here's ten bucks; go have a couple of beers to keep you going,' said Simon and handed Jacko a crisp ten dollar note.

'Ron, sorry to drag you away, but with weather like this it's probably better out than in; early spring, best time of the year,' said Simon as he got up off the Hyde Park bench to meet his friend.

'Couldn't agree more,' Ron replied amicably. The two men unconsciously set off, hands in pockets, for a leisurely stroll around the fountain highlighted by Apollo standing atop a spray of water. 'I was hoping you'd get in touch with me as I hear you had a word with your old mate Jacko about your John Doe. I was wondering how you were getting on with your investigation.'

'Come on, Ron. If even Jacko knows we're having trouble, you must know we ain't making too much headway,' replied Simon, a little embarrassed by his admission.

'Okay, mate. Sorry I asked. And what did Jacko have for you?' asked Ron.

'It might not be anything, but he mentioned he'd had a conversation with a bloke by the name of Tiny Timmins. You know Timmins at all?' asked Simon.

'Tiny Timmins? Now there's a character for you.'

'Yes. I checked him out after we had spoken to Jacko. Seems he has some minor offences, nothing to hang for, but seems he'll do anything for a buck.'

'That's Tiny all right', said Ron with a smile and a nod. 'I've come across him a few times. He's harmless enough, but as you say, he'd kill his own mother for a few dollars. I don't think he's ever had a permanent job; just seems to get through doing odd jobs for people.'

'Have you ever come across the name Glover? That was another name Jacko mentioned.'

'Can't place it,' replied Ron. 'Leave it with us and I'll get back to you on that one. Did Jacko give you anything to suggest there's a link between the two?'

'Yes. It seems Tiny did a recent job for Glover that needed Tiny's boat, which is said to be a small tinny with an outboard motor; apparently Tiny likes fishing. Jacko says the strange thing was Tiny had talked about the boats in Rushcutters Bay, which is odd in that people don't go fishing in Rushcutters Bay. Apart from that, Tiny usually sticks to the west side of the bridge, mainly up the Parramatta River where there's less boat traffic and more boat launching ramps to choose from.'

'So, you think Tiny may have something to do with your body?'

Simon shrugged. 'Who knows? Noel and I are going to have a chat with this Tiny character, but I thought I'd sound you out first, just to be on the safe side. I'd rather have the answers to questions before I ask them.'

Ron nodded in agreement. 'Yes, it's nice to be in that position, but unfortunately it doesn't always work out that way. Tiny might not appear to be the brightest bloke on the planet and he likes to keep to himself. Really, it's quite surprising to see him provide Jacko with so much info. Whenever I've met him he appears quite taciturn and generally doesn't go flaunting his knowledge about anything. In fact, if Tiny is an accomplice in the Anchor Man case, he just might have signed his own death warrant. If you, me and Jacko know he's opened his mouth, you can bet it's now general knowledge and that could prove quite disastrous for Tiny.'

Simon stopped his strolling and looked at Ron, a look of concern on his face. 'Good point, Ron. I didn't think of that. Maybe Noel and I better get over to see our Mr Timmins as a matter of urgency.'

'Might be an idea. As I said, Tiny's harmless, but there's not much he wouldn't do for a buck. Unfortunately he's not the sort of guy who'd think about the consequences,' replied Ron. 'Look, as soon as I have anything on this bloke, Glover, I'll give you a ring. In the meantime, I hope Tiny's still alive and kicking.'

 he house in Ross Street, Balmain was a small federation style dwelling in a severe state of neglect, crying out for much needed maintenance and a lot of paint work. Before ringing the front doorbell, Simon and Noel took the small pathway along the side of the house that gave access to the back yard and a double wooden gate leading to a narrow laneway. The yard was not tidy. The aluminium boat sitting on its trailer, an ageing, silver four-wheel drive vehicle and a two wheeled box tow trailer, had obliterated any lawn that might have once been, and what was left was now overgrown with weeds. Some corrugated iron sheets were stacked against a dilapidated wooden fence, along with some rotting timber, a breeding ground for red back spiders, Noel thought.

'Well, it looks like Tiny's at home, both his boat and wanker wagon are here,' remarked Noel. Noel, who drove an EJ Holden that was now close to being regarded as a vintage car, referred to all four-wheel drive vehicles as wanker wagons.

'Yes,' replied Simon. 'Come on; let's go have a chat with him.'

The two detectives returned to the front of the house, rang the doorbell and waited. After a minute or so Simon rang the bell again with growing concern; there was nothing but silence from within. 'I have this funny feeling no-one's home,' said Simon as he tried the door only to find it locked.

'Want to try the back door?' asked Noel.

'Might be a good idea, especially in light of the position Tiny has placed himself,' replied Simon.

The two men made their way to the back of the house where Noel tried the door and, finding it unlocked, pushed it open. 'After you, boss,' he said and stepped aside for Simon to enter. The first thing that struck the two detectives was that the house smelt stale and musty, and lacked any evidence of female influence. It was clear the owner was a minimalist, but what furniture and fittings there were, were drab, dirty and not well looked after.

The house consisted of two bedrooms, one used as a storage room filled with nothing more than dusty empty cardboard boxes and other stuff that could only be considered as junk. The other bedroom had a single, unmade single bed, a small dresser, a wardrobe, and a window covered with a sheet secured by nails. The lounge room was carpeted with a worn-out beige carpet, two non-matching lounge chairs and a small TV set in a corner of the room. The kitchen smelt rancid, a lidless garbage bin stuffed with several pizza boxes containing the scraps of past banquets only adding to the unhealthy fetid odour permeating the house. The sink was stacked with unwashed dishes, while the gas stove featured a liberal coating of stale dripping. The message Noel received suggested the occupant of the house was not too concerned with creating gastronomic orgies designed to impress upper class toffs who were, no doubt, regular visitors to this humble abode.

'Not the sort of place you'd bring your girlfriend home to,' Noel remarked. 'Georgie would say this bloke was definitely increasing his chances of dying with a simple case of food poisoning. It looks like you were right, no-one home which is probably good news.'

'Could be good news, could be bad news,' replied Simon. 'If Tiny is an accessory to murder, he may be regarded as a loose end and needs to be eliminated. There are just so many ifs and buts I feel like we're running around in ever diminishing circles. He may already be dead, or he could be in hiding, especially if he realizes the situation he's in. By the same token, we could be totally wrong and he's got nothing to do with the Anchor Man.'

'So, what's our next move? Do we go and have a chat to Glover?' asked Noel as he closed the back door behind him.

'Not yet. I'd rather wait to see what Ron can come up with. The name Glover comes up in police records a couple of times, but the Glover we're looking for may not be any of them. It might be a pretty good idea to find the right Glover before we go nailing him to the wall. In the meantime, it looks like our only suspect has disappeared.'

Simon and Noel sat at a window table in the coffee shop on the corner of Bathurst and George Streets in the centre of the city, and gazed at the rain pouring down. It was not a pleasant day and, though now September, the temperature was having an uphill battle to reach the twenties. Samantha, the young waitress who had waited upon Simon and Noel for a couple of years now, nodded to the detectives in acknowledgement of their order; one cappuccino and one flat black.

'He's late again,' remarked Noel flatly.

'He'll be here. He's probably held up by the weather,' replied Simon. 'Ah, the brews. Thanks Sam, and can we have another flat black as Ron should be here any moment now?'

Sam smiled as she placed the two coffees down. 'Another flat black coming up,' she responded just as Ron entered the coffee shop, pausing to shake the water off his umbrella.

'Hi boys,' he said as he took a seat next to Noel. 'Haven't seen rain like this for years, and the experts say we're drying up. Anyway, to business. Simon, you say Tiny is missing?'

'Can't be sure he's actually missing as he probably knows where he is; it's just that we don't. We've called around to his house a couple of times, but he's never in. His wagon and boat are in the back yard, but no sign of Tiny. There could be a very logical explanation for him not being at home, but I'd just feel a little more comfortable if we knew where he was.'

'Would you like me to spread the word he's been mislaid?' Ron offered.

'No, not at this stage. That could give people the message we're looking for him, which we are. However, right at the moment I think it preferable we don't advertise the fact that the police are interested in Mr Timmins. Unfortunately, if this Mr Glover finds Tiny before we do, Tiny may not be in any condition to provide us with any answers. And while we're at it, have you found anything on this Glover character, which is probably more to the point?'

'Not much, apart from the chip on his shoulder. The bloke you're referring to is Andrew Glover and he lives in Drummoyne. Apparently he had a brother, Thomas, who was married to a Joyce Cruikshank. A few years ago Andrew and Thomas were partners in a property development company until they had a great tiff over something or other, and Andrew walked out. He was of the belief the company owed him money, but

Thomas told him to get stuffed as it was Andrew's choice to leave; nobody asked him to, so the company didn't pay him his entitlement, if he had any entitlement, that is. But that's ancient history. Glover, the Andrew one, must be in his fifties and I believe Thomas died of cancer about eighteen months ago. He left a wife and two kids who must be close to their thirties by now.'

'So we had the beginnings of a family feud and a probable motive for murder if the body had turned up a couple of years ago,' mused Simon.

'Probably, though Andrew Glover has reportedly moved on, albeit a tad bitter with the family,' replied Ron. 'He now works for a real estate agent specialising in the top end market. He's doing most of his business around the Balmain area and, as you know, that's one place that's gone from rags to riches. I don't know how he and Tiny got together, but it seems Tiny uses his wagon and trailer to cart rubbish away from houses Glover is preparing for sale. There's never any shortage of buyers and the commission he's being paid must be worth a bundle. It might pay you to have a chat with the nephews. Talk is that when Thomas died, Andrew started calling on Thomas's wife, who inherited his fortune.'

'Nice bloke. So, on face value there doesn't appear anything untoward going on apart from Tiny's unknown job for Glover. Maybe we should see both the sister-in-law and nephews before we front our Mr Andrew Glover. Have you any idea where we might find this Joyce Glover?' Simon asked.

'Not exactly, but she shouldn't be too hard to track down. She lives somewhere in Elizabeth Bay, Billyard Avenue I think,' Ron replied before finishing off the last of his coffee.

'As I said, it's good to have some information on this Glover character before we see him, so thanks, I appreciate your info,' said Simon as Ron got up and organised his brolly ready for an instant opening once outside.

'No problems. If I come across anything I'll get in touch.' With that, Ron strode from the coffee shop and made his way across Bathurst Street to soon disappear into the lunchtime crowd.

CHAPTER 14

*S*uperintendent Michael Hayes was not a big man and his desk and seating arrangements did nothing to enhance his lack of presence. Despite his physical attributes, or lack thereof, and the fact that the Superintendent appeared to be not overly endowed with operational acumen, Simon had found him to be a man of sharp intellect and friendly disposition. Whether these attributes would compensate for his perceived shortcomings in the conduct of a gruesome murder investigation was a question Simon had given some thought. It was obvious Hayes was very good at his job; it was just determining what that specific job was. 'So, what stage are we at now, Simon?' he asked.

Simon crossed his legs loosely and clasped his hands on his stomach. 'Well, unfortunately we're not about to make an arrest at this juncture of the investigation. However, we are following up significant information which I'm sure will prove very helpful. Needless to say, we are acting on this lead most strenuously, although we have run into a slight problem.'

'Oh, yes. And just what is this "slight problem"?'

'The lead has gone missing, although we're confident this will only be a short-term hiccup,' Simon replied uncomfortably, not sure if his boss would consider the overall progress report good news or bad news.

'That's handy,' replied Superintendent Hayes. 'Something like losing the Rosetta Stone, no doubt?'

'Well, I wouldn't put it quite like that, sir,' replied Simon, slightly aggrieved by the cryptic innuendo. 'Though the person in question has gone missing, we're still in the process of following up other leads. In fact, we have identified a couple of people to interview. However, we are somewhat concerned as to the whereabouts of our person of interest as someone may view him as a lose end to a murder, not that we have anything concrete to associate him with the Anchor Man.'

'So I take it you're now in a race with this "someone" who you believe to be the murderer; the "someone" looking to find his loose end so he can eliminate it, and you to find your person of interest before your person of interest, who just happens to be the loose end, gets themselves murdered by the "someone"? And I suppose there's no doubt the loose end and the person of interest are one and the same person, bearing in mind there's no evidence to suggest that the loose end and the person of interest, probably one and the same person, is involved in the Anchor Man case at all.'

Simon sat back, folded his arms and let his gaze wander the ceiling of the office as he concentrated on the Superintendent's apparent assessment of the situation. 'Well, we don't believe there's any doubt about it, sir, although there's always that possibility. However, we're working on the belief that the two are, in fact, one and the same person and, until something better comes along, we will continue our investigation accordingly. I know things haven't been progressing as well as we would have liked, but I think we are now making considerable inroads with

Sergeant Elliott and myself out this afternoon; over at Elizabeth Bay, coincidently.'

'And that's just a hop, skip and a jump from Rushcutters Bay,' said the Superintendent who, despite the "considerable headway", couldn't conceal his own conflicting thoughts on the matter. In fact, he viewed the conduct of the investigation with a degree of scepticism which only resulted in the horrible thought that the imminent closure of the case was anything but a foregone conclusion. 'I'm sorry, Simon, but despite your show of confidence, I can't get the idea out of my mind that this investigation is making as much progress as a public servant returning from a coffee break. The way things are going we might as well put it down to a case of a John Doe suicide and get on with something we can solve.'

'As I said, sir, we're off this afternoon for some interviews, which I'm sure will produce something concrete.'

'Simon, please get on with it and make an arrest, or my reputation in this place will be utterly sunk, along with the Anchor Man.'

They say location is everything in real estate, mused Simon as Noel drove the unmarked police car into the curb. The house in which Joyce Glover lived must have been a developer's dream with uninterrupted views across Elizabeth Bay and the harbour, together with a mansion obviously passed its use by date and ready for demolition. 'Now, no smart aleck wisecracks,' Simon warned as they alighted from the car. 'The butler's name is not Igor. Well, I don't think it is, so just you behave yourself.'

The house in Billyard Avenue was not so much a house as it was an imposing mansion, suitable as a location for many films of the horror genre, or Hitchcock thriller. It was an old two storied Elizabethan brick building, probably more Gothic looking than Elizabethan, with lots of shrubbery and vines hanging from a first-floor verandah that was covered with a bullnose corrugated tin roof. The number of brick chimneys protruding from the shingle rooftop suggested many rooms within the mansion were provided with an open fire place, not that any of the chimneys were emitting smoke.

The garden, which had probably been quite impressive – once, was now a sea of rampant weeds and bushes, dominated by one very large and ancient Morton Bay fig tree, along with its occupant colony of fruit bats. The large stone front fence was dilapidated and in need of major surgery, or total and permanent demolition. Considering the size of the hinges and bolt still imbedded in two sandstone blocks located on either side of a dilapidated path leading to the house, the gate, which no longer existed, must have been quite imposing.

'Well, don't think for one minute you'll ever get me to spend a night in this place. It wouldn't surprise me if Dracula lives here,' replied Noel with a doubtful look. As they approached the front door, Noel paused. 'Seems they got the name right for this place, it certainly makes me cringe,' he added, nodding to the ornate brass plaque grandly displayed above the door with "The Grovel" suitably embossed.

'Ah, come on. She's probably a very sweet old lady,' Simon said as he pulled a long chain that hung from the wall next to the door. As doorbells go, the chain system was impressive, unique and, more importantly, functional as it wasn't long before the door was opened by a young man dressed in white slacks, a pink shirt and a paisley blue cravat. Although Simon's first thought was that the man was neatly dressed, his second thought was that it was unusual to find many men dressed as this man was.

'Yes gentlemen, what can I do for you?'

'I'm Detective Chief Inspector Simon Webster and this is my Sergeant, Detective Sergeant Noel Elliott,' said Simon nodding. 'We're here to have a chat to Joyce Glover. I take it we are at the right place?'

'Oh yes. I'm Bruce, her son. I'm terribly sorry, but there must be some mistake. Mummy died nearly a year ago, not so long after daddy really. I'm living here now as Paul, my brother who did live here, is now shacked up with his girl-friend somewhere over in The Cross, or at least I think he is. Look, would you like to come in instead of chatting on the doorstep?'

'Yes, that would be lovely,' replied Noel and immediately received an admonishing scowl from Simon.

Bruce ushered the two detectives into a living room which was probably referred to in this house as the drawing room; Noel could never figure out the difference. The mansion's exterior proved to be a good indicator as to the ambience of the interior, which exuded all the atmosphere of the House of Usher. The walls appeared to be adorned with many old paintings and older looking tapestries, but as the light within the room was so dim, little of the details were discernible.

The ceiling was high, well over fifteen feet according to Noel's estimation, a large ornate chandelier hanging dimly in the centre of the room. The room itself, occupying a corner of the building, had three large windows on each of the two external walls. Simon considered himself a man of the world and had seen the living rooms of many well-to-do mansions, but the black velvet curtains were a first. It was quite clear to both Simon and Noel that someone in the house had a pronounced aversion to light, or maybe someone, Noel thought with some trepidation, must be suffering from a case of rabies. The unpleasant smell of dampness, attributed to the large mouldy looking rugs on the floor, permeated the room and only added to the oppressive atmosphere. Altogether, both detectives found the room dismal and foreboding.

'Please take a seat, gentlemen,' said Bruce indicating to an old floral settee as he settled down into a similar coloured lounge chair and crossed his legs. 'Oh, I am sorry. Pardon my rudeness, gentlemen. Can I get you anything, a sherry, glass of wine, tea, coffee?'

'No, not for me, I'm feeling a little queer at the moment.' Noel replied before he closed his eyes in consternation, realizing the crassness of his feeble attempt of dry humour.

'No, nor me, thanks,' replied Simon, eager to bypass Noel's comment and get on with the interview. 'I believe you may know a man by the name of Andrew Glover?'

'Yes, I have the unfortunate privilege of being one of his two nephews, Paul, my twin brother being the other. Uncle Andrew was daddy's brother and I'd rather not talk about him. He's a thoroughly odious creature, even if I do say so myself. But you can't pick your rellies, can you?' Bruce replied with the look of having just bitten into a clove.

'So, you and Paul are twins?' Noel asked with interest.

'Oh yes, he's a lovely man – we get on so well together.'

'But he doesn't live here with you?' enquired Simon.

'Oh no, that would never do. Just because we get on doesn't say we are alike. He lives in a flat over at Potts Point and has a girlfriend, or had one. Her name is Cheryl, but I doubt they're an item now, at least not after the brawl they had last time I saw them together. Anyway, when I last spoke to Paul, he mentioned he was looking around for a home unit over on the north side, somewhere around the Mosman area, I think. You see, Paul and I were the sole beneficiaries of mummy's will, apart from two small amounts left to two of her old friends, and that has made both of us quite wealthy. I must say, it has made a lot of difference, the money, I mean.'

'And mummy left you this, this mausoleum to you and Paul?' Simon asked, gesticulating with his arms, his eyes sweeping over the grandeur of the once stately home.

'Yes, wonderful isn't it. The first thing I did after probate was granted was to take the title deeds off to a solicitor to have the new title recorded with the Lands Department. I find this place suits me down to the ground.'

'And as there was a sizeable inheritance, what did you spend your money on?' asked Noel.

'Well, I invested the majority of it in both real estate and shares with a bit on term deposit, just to be on the safe side. I splashed out and bought myself a cruiser, something I've always wanted. That was my only extravagance,' replied Bruce with a coy smile.

'And you moor it at Rushcutters Bay?' asked Simon, expectantly.

'Why yes. It's called the "Mithuna". I'd be glad to show you aboard sometime, not that I've had the opportunity to use it much, more's the pity.'

'Getting back to your uncle,' Simon said. 'Why don't you like him?'

'Well, it all started after daddy died really. We never used to see anything of Uncle Andrew until daddy passed away following a long illness; cancer, you know. Anyway, as soon as he was in the ground, Andrew started calling on mummy, chatting her up, bringing her flowers, being overly nice in a sickening sort of a way. Mummy wasn't in the best of health after daddy's death and it appeared to both Paul and me that Andrew was trying to ingratiate himself.

'See, when daddy died, he left everything to mummy which made her a very rich lady. Now, when mummy died, she left everything to myself and Paul, apart from some money to the two friends I mentioned earlier, Vicki Agnew and Debbie

Grimes. They had been long time friends of mummy. They looked after her following daddy's death, you know, kept her company, took her shopping or out to the park. Mummy made provision for them in her will; nothing substantial mind you, but enough to make them happy.'

'And was Andrew left anything in the will?' asked Noel with raised eyebrows.

'Well, yes and no. Mummy left him what she thought he deserved and apparently, having given the matter a lot of consideration, she left him five dollars, which was a real kick in the bum, metaphorically speaking, for Andrew, I mean. I think it would have been more polite to have left him nothing at all, but five dollars, really. Andrew considered it an affront and the whole thing really got up his nose. He even had the gall to direct his solicitor to approach us, the benefactors, to ask for a donation on his behalf for all the time and effort he had put into helping mummy. Mind you, if there was any help at all, it was done so with nothing more than the hope and expectation of remuneration sometime in the future. And it's not as though Andrew is short of a few quid, the rotten sod. Anyway, we, the benefactors, got together and decided that seeing mummy hadn't provided for Andrew, no way in the world were we going to. We all sent letters of reply back to the solicitor telling him our collective response was for Andrew to get stuffed, if you'll excuse the language. We certainly didn't care if Andrew ended up without a penny. That must have really upset him as he had the nerve to call us a bunch of parsimonious bastards. No, he was very uncouth about the whole thing.'

'And when was the last time you spoke to Paul?' asked Simon.

'Well now, let's see,' mused Bruce. 'It must be nearly a month ago now. Yes, it must be that long ago. My, how time does fly. He and Andrew came over for a family chat and Cheryl, Paul's girlfriend, turned up a little later. The whole thing turned out to be a bit of a shemozzle really. You see, Andrew and Paul want to knock the place down and redevelop the land, but I don't want anything to do with the idea. Under the terms of mummy's will, both Paul and I have to agree on whatever happens to the place, and I want it left exactly as it is.

'Anyway, the proposed amicable discussion planed for the night failed dismally. In fact, it ended up in a right old punch-up, especially when Paul told Cheryl she was as useless as tits on a bull. It seems Paul finally got the message that Cheryl had no influence whatsoever on the council's decision regarding the application to redevelop the property. Andrew and Paul lodged an application with council a few weeks ago, which was rather stupid as any decision is totally irrelevant in view of my stance on the subject. Unfortunately for Cheryl, Paul's perceived notion of her influence in council was the only reason he was stringing her along. When the truth about their relationship was revealed, she stormed out of the house which was a good thing as she would probably have killed him, Paul, that is. You know what they say about a woman's wrath. Just one thing, Chief Inspector, I'm at a bit of a loss at the moment as you haven't mentioned the reason for your visit. Would you care to enlighten me?'

'Yes, by all means,' replied Simon. 'Unfortunately, we are conducting an investigation into the death of a man whose body was recovered from the harbour about three weeks ago. We have no idea as to the identity of the body, or how it came to be where it was found.'

'And whereabouts was it found?' Bruce asked. 'Surely I have nothing to do with it?'

'No, we're sure you haven't. It's just that your uncle's name came up during our investigation and we thought it a good idea to check on everything, especially now we find you have a boat moored at Rushcutters Bay; that's where the body was found. By the way, here's an artist's impression of what the dead person may have looked like, not unlike you, really,' replied Simon taking a photo from his pocket. 'It might not be exactly like the person, but it's the best he could do with what was left after the fish and crabs had had their fill.'

Bruce rose from his chair and took the artist's impression of the dead man that had been photocopied for easier dissemination to those concerned. He looked at it in silence, his face slowly transforming from the cherubic, smiling countenance to one of a mournful sadness. He slowly sat down, still staring at the photo. 'Yes, that's Paul. I'm almost certain it's him.'

'And can you think of anyone who might have had reason to kill your brother,' Noel asked with feigned sincerity.

'No, no-one I'm aware of. Paul got on with everyone. Well, obviously not quite everyone.'

Simon purser his lips and remained silent for a moment, thinking; everyone except you, eh Bruce. 'You mentioned earlier that you and Paul were twins. Are you saying you were identical twins?' Simon asked.

'Twins yes, but no, not identical. We do, did, look similar but not identical, not that there was any great difference, I suppose, in looks, I mean,' replied Bruce as the hint of a smile crossed his face.

'Yes, we can understand the point you're making. And do you know if Paul made a will?' Noel asked.

'I shouldn't think so. He was never one to take life seriously so I don't think he had dying in mind,' Bruce replied.

'No, I don't suppose any of us do. And have you made a will?' Simon asked matter of factly.

'No I haven't. I suppose I should, but it seems like it's one of those things you never get around to. And who would I name as the beneficiary? If Paul was alive, I would leave what I have to him as he's the only one left in the family, apart from Andrew and I certainly wouldn't leave anything to that twerp,' Bruce replied indignantly.

Simon looked at Noel who looked at Simon, both with the same question on their mind. 'I saw a movie about this some years ago, something about a tontine where the last person alive in the family inherits the lot,' remarked Noel.

'And you think if both Paul and Bruce are eliminated without a will, Andrew will be the last man standing?' replied Simon.

Noel gave a look of grave concern. 'But even if there are wills, it doesn't say Andrew won't. He probably doesn't know if they exist or not, which they obviously don't.'

'Won't what?' broke in Bruce who was being left behind in the conversation.

'Won't murder you and leave your body lying on the bottom of the harbour,' replied Simon. 'You see, if we positively identify the body as your brother, which we can through DNA analysis, and if it turns out Andrew is the murderer before we have sufficient evidence to arrest him, you may well be the next in line. With Andrew out to eliminate all members of the family in order to become the sole member left, he would have a very strong claim to the entire family fortune.'

'Oh, how thoroughly despicable,' Bruce said, shocked that anyone would want to kill him. 'I suppose it doesn't matter if having a will would stop me from being killed, will it?'

'Shouldn't think so. As I said, it's doubtful Andrew knows who has a will or who doesn't have a will. I suspect it's somewhat immaterial whether you do or you don't, it wouldn't stop him from killing you. This is one situation of "where there's a will there's a way" doesn't apply. The best you can do is to leave a will making sure you name a beneficiary other than Andrew. When he does, murder you that is, at least you'll have the satisfaction of knowing he won't get the family jewels without a protracted and expensive legal battle against the beneficiary you nominate. By the way, you have no objection to supplying forensics with a mouth swab just to confirm your relationship with the body?' Simon asked as an afterthought.

'No, not at all,' replied Bruce, who appeared genuinely happy to oblige.

'It seems your mother was quite a collector of antiques,' remarked Simon as he casually mooched around the room inspecting the trinkets and trash collected over many years by Joyce Glover. He paused to take a closer look at a heavy brass statue of a knight in full armour, mounted on a horse.

'Oh yes. Mummy was always going to antique sales when she was alive. She really loved the old-fashioned stuff.'

'I suppose it would have been somewhat difficult for her to go to antique sales when she was dead,' responded Simon as he replaced the knight back on the mantle shelf. 'And you have such a lovely fire place here. Why don't you use it as it seems very cold in here?' Simon asked as he continued his inspection, stopping to look at the ornate brass fire screen.

'Yes, well, though I live here, the burden of arranging for the delivery of a pile of wood and then having someone chop it up seems unjustified for the amount of time the fire would be needed. Mummy used it occasionally, but then she had Paul around to organise the wood,' replied Bruce as he casually inspected his finger nails, which Noel had noticed were painted a soft pink.

Meanwhile, Simon ceased his casual inspection of the room and turned to Bruce. 'Look, I know our visit may appear unproductive, but we do need to get an idea of the family situation. If you think of anything that may assist us in our investigation, you know where to get in touch with me or Sergeant Elliott.'

Just as they were about to exit the living room, Simon

paused. 'Just one last thing, the fire poker and the knight on the horse; we really would like forensics to have a closer look at these two items in view of Andrew having been present in the room with Paul. You never know, and it's probably a waste of time, but we'd like to eliminate all possible murder weapons. Noel here will give you a receipt for them, if you wouldn't mind?'

CHAPTER 15

'And do you think the beneficiaries got up the nose of Andrew Glover to such an extent he's started killing them off?' Noel asked as he rolled a piece of paper into a ball and had a shot at the waste paper bin at the other end of the office – and missed.

Simon stopped writing on a pad, tossed his pen onto the table, pushed his chair back and clasped his hands behind his head. 'The problem is both Andrew and Paul were for the redeveloping of the property. If anyone was in line to get killed off, I thought it would have been Bruce as he's the fly in the ointment. I'm not discounting the fact that Andrew is, or at least is said to be, totally cheesed off with the entire Glover family over Joyce's will.' A silence prevailed as Simon appeared to be in deep thought, his head now resting on his hand, his elbow on the table After a moment he added, 'I s'pose he really could be out to do away with both the twins and be the sole remaining member of the Glover dynasty.'

Noel frowned. 'Yes, but why put the body on Lee's boat? It's pretty hard to get the two names mixed up – they're not even similar. Let's assume, for argument sake, Tiny did the job of disposing the body for Andrew Glover, that's presupposing Andrew is the guilty bugger, of course. Obviously both the right boat and the wrong boat were moored in Rushcutters Bay at the time of the said disposal. Somehow I think maybe Tiny couldn't find the "Mithuna", which we believe was the right boat, so he dropped the body onto the first anchor he came across, which was the wrong boat. Maybe it wasn't meant to be attached to any particular boat at all, just any boat. I know, it sounds a little far-fetched, but I don't think even Tiny could get the names mixed up so maybe any boat would have sufficed. Or could he?'

Simon sighed, bent down, picked up Noel's ball of paper and completed the shot into the bin. 'I only wish we could find Tiny. At the moment, and not having met the man, I would be surprised if it turns out that Andrew Glover is the cold, calculating serial killer intent on inheriting the family fortune. To do so would mean murdering two members of the family, plus anyone else who happened to be in the way, like Tiny. But I s'pose I could be wrong. Maybe he's holding Tiny somewhere to help him with the next body, and that would be Bruce.

'Now that Bruce is the sole owner of "The Grovel", and opposes the redevelopment scheme, it puts him in a pretty precarious position. It would be hard for Andrew to do anything until he became the sole owner of the place, or was able to change Bruce's mind on the matter. Just a thought, Noel. Get yourself over to the local government department dealing with heritage and national trust buildings, or whatever. Just see if there's anything of interest we should know about "The Grovel" that makes it so appealing to Bruce.'

'Right boss. One quick question for my own education in police terminology. When you refer to a serial killer, which you just did, is each kill that the serial killer perpetrates referred to as an episode? Like, are there six episodes to the serial?'

Simon scowled and shook his head in disbelief. 'Noel, I really don't know and I really couldn't give a stuff what they call it.'

'Sorry, boss, I was just wondering. By the way, have you let the super know what's going on?'

'Yes, I dropped in to see him after we got back from Elizabeth Bay yesterday. I don't think he's overly impressed with our progress.'

'Well, bully for Mr Hayes. At least I think we're doing pretty good,' replied Noel derisively. 'I suppose you should be thankful you haven't a body turning up next door at Collaroy, yet. Or, at least I don't think you have.'

Simon pressed his lips together and gave a grunt. 'No, not yet. At least when it happens it'll be out of my bailiwick. That's one for the Manly CIB, or will be.'

'You seem pretty sure there is going to be a murder.'

'As sure as one can be when dealing with homicidal maniacs. Georgie and I haven't worked out who the most likely victim will be as they're all potential candidates. We'll just sit back and see what happens, though we could run that suggested sweep on it. Say we all put in five bucks. There's Graham, Louisa, Ron, the four of us and we could probably drag a couple more into it and make it winner take all. We all select our victim and see if that person ends up dead.'

Noel shook his head in wonder. 'No, I don't think so. I'm not really a betting man and if I was I could probably think of better things to bet on, like the size of the thunderstorm we're supposed to be going to get this afternoon, according to the forecast. That reminds me, Simon. When the weather bureau predicts late thunderstorms, does that mean they should have been here earlier?'

Simon folded his arms and stared blankly at Noel. 'And what sort of a stupid bloody question is that?'

'I don't know, just curious,' replied Noel with a shake of the head. 'To have two thunderstorms in the one day seems a bit much. Apparently the northern beaches received a bad one this morning, and it looks like we're in for another pounding this afternoon.'

While often the brunt of cynical comment for its forecasting ability, it seemed the weather bureau had, on this occasion, got it right. By three thirty the sky was frighteningly ominous with a huge black storm front rearing up like a giant wave about to break. Moving inexorably in over the city from the southwest, the sweet smell of the storm was already heavy in the air, the continuous low, angry rumble of distant thunder a menacing harbinger of the tempest to follow.

'Holy hell, looks like it's going to be a doozy,' remarked Noel, having just returned from making an observation from the front door of the police station. 'On the grounds of occupational health and safety, can I float the idea we knock off now, or maybe it won't be just the idea that's floating?' he suggested. 'You know how much I hate driving in the rain and the traffic will be an absolute bugger's muddle later.'

Simon didn't have to be asked twice. 'Grab your coat and let's get the hell out of here.'

The idea of leaving the city early in an attempt to avoid the deluge failed dismally on two counts. Noel, driving as carefully as he could in the deteriorating conditions, had successfully negotiated Military Road and had made the sweeping left hand curve into Spit Road at Spit Junction when the monstrous wave broke. Up to this point, Noel had been driving with the headlights on and, though very murky, there had been only a few heavy drops of rain, albeit the drops had the size and sound of bricks falling from a great height. Those conditions didn't last. A bolt of lightning appeared to be caught frozen in time as it struck a power pole on the side of the road, only to be followed by the ear- splitting crash of the associated thunder clap. Then, the enormous black wave broke and the rain came, not in drops, but in a deluge of biblical proportions.

So, in effect, by leaving work early Simon and Noel had quite unsuccessfully avoided the predicted climatic cataclysm. The second failure had been that by leaving work early, they had joined the other fifty zillion cars heading for the northern beach suburbs, their drivers having decided that they, too, would avoid the impending cataclysm by leaving the city and heading home early.

'Remind me to buy a pair of Wellies on the weekend, Noel,' remarked Simon as he tried in vain to demist the windscreen of the ageing Holden with a handkerchief. 'And if you have any more bright ideas of getting home before the next storm breaks, forget it. Christ, we don't need a car, we need a bloody ark,' he mumbled to himself cantankerously.

'Ah, stop your complaining. We'll still be home earlier than normal and I'd rather be driving now before it gets completely dark.'

In view of the calamity taking place outside the car, Noel decide to turn off Pittwater Road and deposit Simon outside his home in West Bank Avenue. 'And just what's going on here?' asked Noel as the sight of a blue flashing light of a police car came into view. 'It looks like they're outside your house, Simon, or at least the one next door. Betcha five bucks it's Rodger.'

'You're on,' said Simon with enthusiasm. 'Come on, you won't want to miss this,' he said as he slammed the car door and bolted to the front door, his briefcase held over his head in a valiant but vain attempt to keep off the bucketing rain.

On entering the lounge room, Noel had the uncomfortable

feeling he had just walked onto a movie set. The scene confronting the two detectives could have been taken directly from a myriad of detective films where the crucial scene was about to unfold. Two plain clothed gentlemen, presumably detectives thought Simon, were standing in the middle of the lounge room, with Sue and Georgie seated together on the sofa. A third woman, unknown to both Noel and Simon, sat relaxed on a lounge chair.

'Oh, hi sweetheart,' said Georgie as she stood and planted a kiss on Simon's cheek. 'You're home early, which is probably a good thing. This is Detective Inspector David Spring-Brown from Manly CIB. He's just arrived to ask a few questions. Oh yes, and this is Judy, you know, the girl Rodger dumped Dorothy for.'

Simon looked at Judy and found a middle aged woman dressed in a pair of blue Levi's and a white T-shirt. Judy, a red head with shoulder length curly hair and a pale complexion, accentuated by an outbreak of freckles over her nose and under her eyes, smiled winsomely at the two new arrivals. Both Simon and Noel nodded, Simon immediately appreciating the apparent ease with which Georgie had befriended the bright-eyed redhead with the engaging smile.

'Well Inspector, I doubt your little trip out to Collaroy in this weather is to pay us a social call. By the way, this is Detective Sergeant Noel Elliott.'

'Sergeant,' Detective Inspector Spring-Brown said, nodding. 'No, unfortunately we've had a bit of an incident and Sergeant Gaskill and I are just tying up a few loose ends. In fact, we hope you may be able to fill us in on a bit of the history leading up to the circumstances of this particularly unpleasant event.'

'Look, before we get started, how about you let me get my coat off and organise a brew,' said Simon anticipating the few loose ends may take a little longer to tie up than anticipated.

CHAPTER 16

'*R*ight,' said Simon as he settled himself back in to his favourite lounge chair with a mug of coffee. 'Now just what is this little unpleasant incident you'd like to talk about?'

Inspector David Spring-Brown sat on a dining room chair which had been relocated to the lounge room to accommodate the sudden influx of visitors. He wrapped his hands around his coffee mug, for although the weather wasn't cold, the raging storm outside gave the impression it was. 'I'll come to that later, but right at the moment we're more interested in what you can tell us of the goings on in the house next door. Miss Kemp, it is Miss Kemp, isn't it?'

'Why, yes it is, Detective Inspector,' replied Judy with all the sincerity and coyness, but without the drawl, of a southern belle.

'And what exactly was your relationship with this Rodger, er, what was his name, Sergeant?'

'Beaton, sir. Rodger Beaton,' the Sergeant replied after referring to his notebook.

'Ah yes. Rodger Beaton,' echoed the Inspector.

'I don't have any relationship with Mr Beaton, not now anyway, thank goodness. Though Rodger and I were shacked up together for nearly two years, as soon as his wife pegged out, I was sent packing. I hadn't even made it out the door and he was off like a shot to live in her house, which happens to be the house next door. He often talked of divorcing Dorothy, his wife, and marrying me, but somehow I don't think he's likely to start thinking about that now.'

'Oh yes. And why is that, Miss Kemp?' the Inspector asked with sudden interest.

'Well, while there had always been talk of getting rid of the battle-axe, there was never any action. I suspect he didn't have any long-term plans for me; I was there just to warm his bed until he found another interest. Of course, when Dorothy died the house became his interest. He's firmly convinced that, as she died intestate and as he was still married to her, the house is his. When he found out she died without a will, he had a smile like the Cheshire cat.'

'So how come we find you out here at Collaroy today?' asked the Inspector.

Judy uncrossed her legs and settled herself back into the lounge chair. 'Okay. I thought it a bit rich that he could just run out on me after I'd given him nearly two years of my time and effort. Legal opinion is sort of iffy regarding any claim I might have, but I'm not going to let Rodger get away without letting him know I'm peeved. Claudia Daintree comes out here quite often looking for any chance to hook into him as she's convinced Dorothy left her the house. I took the opportunity to come out earlier today with her in the hope I might be able to hook into Rodger as well, not that I expect hooking into him will ever achieve anything.'

'So, there's some enmity, at least on your part?'

Judy rolled her eyes in scorn. 'Yes, you could say that. I could kill the bugger. He's turned out to be a real sleaze.'

Detective Inspector Spring-Brown frowned. 'I take it Claudia is, or was, related to Dorothy?'

'Oh yes, I should have made that a bit clearer. Claudia is Dorothy's sister. She's mentioned on several occasions that Dorothy had told her the house would be hers if anything happened to her, not that Claudia, or anyone else for that matter, expected Dorothy to peg out so soon. She did have a bit of a heart problem, but it never seemed to worry her. Claudia and I came out here today to give Rodger a bit of a hard time seeing he thinks the house is his.'

'So, you were both speaking to Rodger Beaton today?' asked the Inspector as he put the empty coffee mug on the coffee table, sat back and folded his arms while Sergeant Gaskill continued to scribble madly in his notebook.

Judy cast a glance at Georgie and Sue before answering. 'I suppose we started off speaking to the cretin. You know, Inspector, there are some people who just seem to get under your skin and Rodger eventually got under mine. He was a nice bloke once, but that changed dramatically after Dorothy's death and I knew I was about to get the old heave ho. Talk about a Jekyll and Hyde. Anyway, the speaking turned a little more bois- terous and probably became a shouting match between the three of us. See, Claudia and I hate each other's guts, though we try to pretend otherwise, we both hate Rodger, for obvious reasons, and all Rodger wants to do is go fishing. His attitude is, I've got it, you get it.'

'And just how did the conversation between the three of you come to a conclusion, this morning I mean?' Inspector Spring- Brown enquired as the situation became more intriguing with each revelation.

'I'd had enough,' Judy replied, her coffee mug untouched on

the coffee table, 'so I came over to see Georgie. I needed a bit of sanity and I find Georgie's company quite refreshing. I have no doubt everyone in the street would've heard the blue going on and I suspect even Rodger eventually had had enough. It must have only been a few minutes after I arrived here that I saw his car drive down the driveway. I presumed he was going fishing as he had his fishing rods on the roof of the car. Claudia must have left soon after that.'

'So there was no discussion between just yourself and Claudia?'

'No. Why, was there something we should have discussed?'

'Not that I'm aware of. I just wanted to clarify that you and Claudia hadn't come to some sort of arrangement.'

'Arrangement? An arrangement about what?' asked Judy who was by now becoming a bit befuddled with the continuing stream of obtuse questioning.

'An arrangement involving Rodger Beaton, of course,' replied the Inspector as if the question was perfectly obvious.

'Look Inspector. If you would get to the point I might be able to answer your stupid questions. As far as I know the three of us, Rodger, Claudia and I all detest each other and the thought of two of us jacking up against the third is ludicrous. I may be wrong and Claudia might even have the hots for Rodger, but I very much doubt it. Maybe you should speak to the other two about any arrangement they may have discussed.'

Thoroughly bored with the discussion between the inspector and Judy, Simon frowned. 'This is all very stimulating, Inspector, but can we get to the crux of the matter?'

'Just a few more points, Chief. You know how it is with a possible homicide.'

A stunned silence hit the room like a cannon ball. Georgie and Sue, sitting on the sofa, just stared blankly at Inspector

Spring-Brown, the answers to questions they, no doubt, wanted to ask being so appalling no-one bothered to ask. Noel look at Simon and gave him a 'there, told you so' look while Simon pursed his lips and raised his eyebrows.

'Yes, I know,' replied Simon. 'It can get awfully tedious. Look, before we carry on and get to just who has been homicided, can I get anyone else something to drink, another brew maybe?'

'No thanks,' replied the Inspector. 'I'd love a whisky and water but Sergeant Gaskill and I are on duty. But don't let that stop you, you go right ahead.'

'Yes, I'll have a large scotch and dry if you've got one,' Judy responded. 'I have a funny feeling that whatever the Inspector has to say won't be a laughing matter, or maybe it will. Going to join me, girls?' Both Georgie and Sue declined, both more eager to cut to the chase and get to the details of the unpleasant event, irrespective of just how unpleasant the event might be, while Simon and Noel elected to join Judy in a Scotch.

Once settled, Simon gave Inspector Spring-Brown an enquiring look. 'Okay, when you say you're investigating a possible homicide, are you implying you have a victim and can't decide if it's murder, manslaughter, accidental death or death by misadventure? Or are you simply suggesting you have evidence of a conspiracy and that the homicide hasn't taken place yet?'

'Oh no, we have a body all right. In fact, we think we have two bodies,' replied the Inspector with a smile on his face. 'And, as luck would have it, we have an eyewitness to the whole grisly affair.'

'Well, just to humour us, could you start at the top and let us know who's dead and the circumstances?' asked Simon, who was getting somewhat annoyed with the Inspector's long-winded and circuitous method of getting to the point.

'Right. It's a pretty long story so please bear with me. We

received a telephone call earlier this morning from the station down in Ramsay Street here at Collaroy. They advised that an incident had been reported by one of the green keepers at the Long Reef Golf Club, a Mr Kenneth Grey. It seems Mr Gray was doing the rounds of the course on his cart, one of those three wheeled motor bike things, as they had received a weather alert warning of an impending severe electrical storm. Apart from the storm we're having now, we had another blow in from the north-west this morning, not quite so big, but quite angry enough, with a lot of lightning. On such occasions they go out and warn any golfers stupid enough to stay out on the course that they're inviting trouble.

'Anyway, he's driving down the sixteenth fairway in the pouring rain when he notices this bloke with a couple of fishing rods walking towards the cliff above the Butter Box on the southern side of Long Reef. I don't know if that's its real name, but the kids call it that as it's supposed to be a surfing spot. This bloke, who we believe was Mr Rodger Beaton, laid his fishing rods down and went closer to the edge of the cliff, probably to determine if it was worth the hike down to the bottom to do a spot of fishing, despite the weather.

'Grey was some way off and, as Beaton wasn't playing golf, he decided Beaton wasn't his problem. Just as he was about to cross back over the course, he noticed a person in a dark coat pick up one of the rods and creep up behind Beaton. Of course, with all the thunder going on and with the wind and blackness of the sky, the creeper probably didn't have to do much creeping. It's for sure Beaton didn't know anyone was behind him until the creeper poked him in the back with one of the rods, and bingo, he's headed for the rocks below like a sack of potatoes.

'It appears the creeper may have had an aversion to heights, thus using a fishing rod to nudge Beaton over. Whatever the reason, the creeper didn't go too close to the edge to make sure Beaton was dead. Whether it was remorse, contemplation of the deed or something else, the creeper just stood there for a while with the rain, thunder, wind, and lightning. I suppose it must have looked like a scene from Shakespeare with the raging storm being an accomplice to the cowardly act perpetrated by the rod-bearing assailant.

'Anyway, the creeper had already made a fatal mistake. Beaton had two fishing rods, one fibreglass, the other graphite and, as luck would have it, the creeper must have chosen the graphite rod to tap Beaton on the bum. After nudging Beaton over the cliff, the creeper just stood there waving a metal fishing pole around in an electrical storm the like we haven't seen for donkey's years. Grey took off on his bike to warn the creeper of the imminent danger but, you know the old saying, one flash and you're ash.'

Simon took a deep breath and let it out with a "phew". 'You mean the creeper was struck by lightning?'

'From the charred remains and what Grey says he saw, it would appear so. There's very little left to assist in identification of the body, which is only to be expected, I suppose. After all, fifty thousand degrees does tend to overcook the roast,' replied the Inspector in a vain attempt at some dry humour. No-one laughed.

'So you've recovered Beaton's body?' asked Noel.

'Yes, though as yet we haven't a positive identification. From details in his wallet, and the fact it was his car parked at the top of Long Reef, we're almost certain it's Beaton,' responded the Inspector, now basking in the glory of his perfect narration of an apparent brutal homicide.

'Have you any idea as to who the creeper may have been?' enquired Judy with keen interest.

'Yes, we have an idea, but identification is presenting us with a bit of a problem. We thought you may be able to help us with that complication. You see, a second car found at the top of the Reef is registered to a Claudia Daintree and that is the only piece of evidence we have, apart from a smattering of charred clothing. Could you tell us what she was wearing today?'

While a murder case usually conjures up feelings of sadness, sorrow and distress, Judy, for some unaccountable reason, had a smile on her face and a twinkle in her eye. 'Oh yes, Inspector, Claudia was wearing a dark brown lightweight coat over a pair of jeans. She was also wearing small ankle high boots made out of the same stuff gum boots are made of. Obviously I don't know what she was wearing under her coat.'

'That seems to fit, though we haven't got much to go on, but the boot we found matches with your description. I just know it must have been one hell of a flash that hit whoever the person was. I went up to the spot where it happened and, believe me, it was enough to turn you off barbecues for life,' said the Inspector shaking his head in wonder. 'We got a statement from Grey before they took him to Mona Vale Hospital for treatment, for shock, not the electrical type. And that's about it. Miss Kemp, may I offer my condolences in the loss of your partner. In view of your obvious bereavement, I'll leave getting a statement from you until later.'

With great effort, Judy managed to look doleful. 'Why, thank you Inspector, that is awfully nice of you.'

'Just one question,' interjected Simon. 'Why on earth would Claudia follow him up to Long Reef? Did she plan to do away with him or did she avail herself of an opportunity she couldn't miss?'

The Detective Inspector gave a shrug. 'Who knows? I'd hazard a guess and agree with you about an opportunity she couldn't miss. She obviously had her own motive, and that's where we'll need you all to provide statements; you know, the old motive, means and opportunity stuff.'

After Detective Inspector David Spring-Brown and Detective Sergeant Gaskill's departure, Noel turned to Simon who had already withdrawn a five dollar note from his wallet.

CHAPTER 17

'*N*ow, after yesterday's brief interruption, could we please get on with a bit of work?' Simon was not happy. The little domestic dispute next door had been something of an interesting distraction, but now, with the situation having been resolved with the death of two of the antagonists, Simon was hopeful they could proceed with the job at hand, which was clearing up the Anchor Man case.

'Well I'm sorry, but it wasn't my fault the way things turned out as they did,' came Noel's retort. 'It would've happened whether we left work early or not. And let's face it, Judy seems a nice girl and I would prefer she be the winner than either of the other two. Besides, I'd bet you'd rather her as a next door neighbour than Madam Battleaxe or rapacious Rodger.' Noel paused and reflected before continuing. 'Strange isn't it. Two fishing rods lying on the ground and Claudia has to pick the wrong one to nudge Rodger over the cliff. Not the normal way of killing off someone, but a method to file away for future reference.'

'Certainly is. And talk about retribution. You know I'm not a religious man, but crikey, talk about swift justice,' said Simon shaking his head. 'Anyway, let's forget about yesterday and get back to work. Just where were we up to before this rude interruption?'

Noel withdrew his notebook from his coat pocket and flicked through the pages until he came to what he was looking for. 'Tiny's still missing; Paul Glover has been tentatively identified as the Anchor Man, pending DNA results; Bruce Glover owns a boat called the "Mithuna", and Andrew Glover is cheesed off with the family because he was snubbed in the matriarch's will. I suppose he thinks he's been hard done by the family for a second time, the first being when he and his brother had the falling out.'

'So it's imperative we find Tiny as all we have on Andrew Glover is circumstantial,' said Simon. 'Any suggestions?'

Noel leant forward, his elbow on the table, his cheek resting in a clenched fist. 'You know, I can understand why Tiny is missing, but you'd think he'd take his wagon and boat with him, but no, they're still parked in his back yard. And I'd hate to think Andrew Glover knows where to find him. It could be that if it's Andrew Glover's intention to eliminate Bruce, he may have another job lined up for Tiny before eliminating Tiny, that's assuming Tiny is the disposer of the dead and Andrew is guilty of Paul's murder.'

Simon frowned, sat back and folded his arms. 'Well, not having his boat and wagon with him could suggest he's gone to ground somewhere in the city. It's not the easiest place to find a parking spot at the best of times, and especially if you're dragging a bloody great boat behind you. Maybe it's time for us to have a chat with Mr Glover, Andrew, I mean, sort of shake the branches and see what falls out, though I was hoping to talk to Tiny first. But before we get to Glover, let's ask Ron to put out the word and see if he can find Mr Timmins. I can't help thinking that if Timmins thinks he's in trouble, he'll gravitate to the Cross or Darlinghurst area.'

'In trouble with who?' asked Noel. 'Or should I say with whom?'

'God, I don't know and I don't really care. Tiny may think he's in trouble with Andrew Glover, the police or maybe even both.'

'Well let's face it. If he did attach Paul to the anchor of the "Gemini", he's definitely in the poo with the police, not that I think he's the murderer; that has to be Andrew Glover,' responded Noel.

'Yeah, maybe,' responded Simon doubtfully. 'There's too much we don't know about this case to go jumping to conclusions. At the moment we appear to have two motives for Paul's death. The first is the tontine idea with Andrew taking his vengeance out on the family for being excluded from Joyce's will. That suggests Andrew could be Paul's killer and Bruce is the next on his hit list.

'The second motive is the redevelopment scheme and that presents us with two possible murderers. Paul's dead because Bruce didn't want the property redeveloped, which could mean Bruce murdered his brother. If that is the case, Bruce may want to kill off Uncle Andrew as well, seeing he was on Paul's side. But on the other hand, seeing Andrew didn't get anything out of the family will, the tontine idea might come into play and he's out to get as much as he can by redeveloping "The Grovel" on his own. That would mean eliminating both twins which puts Bruce in line for joining his brother in the morgue.'

Noel shook his head; he was missing something. 'Yes, but if Andrew murdered Paul, why the hell did he murder him at the time he did? Andrew needed Paul, at least until the place was redeveloped. I don't know for sure, but I would think the application would have to be in the names of the property owners, which means both Bruce and Paul, and we know Bruce would never have signed it. Not wishing to be funny, I think there's something very fishy going on with this application. And if Andrew did knock off Paul, you would have thought he would have waited until the job was completed, the redevelopment job, I mean. After all, the whole thing is a multi-million dollar scheme and the last thing Andrew, or Paul, would have wanted would be a hiccup in the planning stages.'

'Okay,' replied Simon, 'let's assume, for argument sake, Andrew Glover murdered Paul because of Joyce Glover's will. That in itself doesn't benefit Andrew financially one iota. As I said, for Andrew to reap the family fortune he has to be the last member of the family left standing. That puts Bruce right in the firing line. And if things are complicated enough, necessity would dictate that Andrew has to eliminate the loose ends and clean up the mess he's created, which means doing away with Tiny as well. Looks like we have to find Tiny before Glover does, unless Andy has already found him, that is.'

'And what about Bruce?' Noel asked, a little confused as to who killed whom and for what reason. 'If Andrew is the guilty bugger, then Bruce may well expect to be eliminated, not that he gave me the impression he was too concerned about the whole thing. All we know is that Tiny did a job for a Mr Glover, who we suspect was Andrew Glover, and that the job needed Tiny's boat. At the moment we haven't any evidence as to the nature of that job, though we can speculate all we like. We can't very well haul Glover in just because we think he killed Paul and paid Tiny a few dollars to dump his body in the harbour, and all because he got cheesed off with the family.'

'Okay, but we can't play nursemaid to Bruce and look for Tiny at the same time. Maybe playing nursemaid to Bruce isn't quite the right phrase as he'd probably love to be nursed by a big strong policeman,' quipped Noel.

'Look, we just gotta find Tiny,' said Simon with a touch of exasperation in his voice. 'If he is responsible for putting Paul on Graham Lee's anchor, I would love to know why he chose his boat, and if it was Andrew Glover who paid him to do the job. I could understand if he put it on Bruce's boat as that's where it was probably meant to go, but the "Gemini"; I just can't see it.'

'Hell, what a mess. How about we go and have a chat with Ron. He seems to be able to come up with stuff we could never come up with,' said Noel submissively.

Ron, already at the coffee shop on the corner of Bathurst and George Streets when the two detectives arrived, had ordered the two flat blacks and a cappuccino. 'Hi Simon, Noel. I thought you'd be just about ready for a bit of a chat. Word has it that it's all getting a bit messy, even if you finally have an ID on the body.'

'Well, that is interesting,' Simon said as he sat down against the window. 'We've no confirmation yet, but the body has been tentatively identified as that of Paul Glover, a nephew of Andrew Glover. And could you be a little more specific about the messy bit?'

'Okay. If what I hear is correct, you're still looking for Tiny Timmins who seems to have vanished. Trouble is, apparently someone else is now looking for him and I believe that someone is, strangely enough, Andrew Glover,' replied Ron as Sam arrived with the coffees.

'And have you heard anything on Bruce Glover? We have this morbid idea Andrew is going to do away with the rest of the Glover family so he can inherit the family fortune. Obviously that puts Bruce's life expectancy in some sort of doubt.'

Ron nodded. 'Yes, I can appreciate that if things are as you say, Bruce could be in a bit of trouble. But let's be honest. I took a run over to Elizabeth Bay, just to have a look at the area of interest and to see where the Glovers live. Some nice houses over there, but who in their right mind would voluntarily live in that specific house? Talk about a mausoleum; sort of place you'd expect to find the Elizabeth Bay version of The Texas Chainsaw Massacre.'

'Yeah, I know what you mean. I wonder if there's a pit and a pendulum underneath the lounge room,' replied Simon. 'Still, it must be nice to live by the harbour. And you're right, he, Bruce I mean, should've joined his brother and sold up to a developer. He'd make another fortune and, if we're right about Andrew, would certainly beat the hell out of being dead, which seems to be a possibility.' Simon tried unsuccessfully to suppress a yawn so decided to go the whole hog and have a good stretch to go with the yawn. 'You know, Ron, this is all becoming quite tedious and all because Graham Lee was good enough to invite us for a day out on his boat. I'm beginning to think that now we've cleared Graham from any involvement in the matter we should just pack it in and go home.'

'Ah, come on boss,' said Noel. 'You're just as curious as all of us to find out why the "Gemini" was targeted for the disposal of a body. Presuming it was Tiny that did the disposing, and assuming it was Andrew Glover who killed the tentatively identified Paul Glover, and assuming Tiny Timmins, whenever we find him, or if we find him alive at all, will positively identify Andrew Glover as the disposer of Paul Glover, and Tiny is prepared to sign a statement to that affect... And bugger, I've lost my train of thought and have forgotten what I wanted to say. Okay, so let's just find Tiny, ask him and then pack it in.'

'Okay, Ron, you heard the man. All we have to do is go find Tiny and the case is solved. Simple. Just one thing, Ron, you don't mind if I ask you a stupid question, do you?' asked Simon as he scrapped the last of the cappuccino froth from the bottom of the cup.

'Well, that depends on the nature of the question, bearing in mind there are women present,' replied Ron as he conspicuously looked around the coffee shop.

'No, nothing like that, you idiot. I just have this idea the case of the Anchor Man may be wrapped up with the development of "The Grovel" and yet I know sweet bugger all about the hoops you have to jump through to develop a property. I thought maybe you might know?'

Ron opened his eyes wide, pouted his lips and shrugged his shoulders. 'What, property development? You have to be joking. I suppose you'd have to go to the council and ask them. The only thing I do know about property development is that you'd better have bags of money, lots of time and not be too surprised with the integrity and ethics of those with whom you have to deal. But heavens to Betsy, Simon, I had enough trouble with the local council just to get another garbage can after mine was used as a bonfire by some moronic delinquent.'

Simon pondered for a moment, then said, 'Okay, Ron, seeing we're both so ignorant of the requirements, how about we plod off to the council and find out the basics, you know, an idiots guide to redeveloping. There are a few local council offices around the city. What d'ya think?'

'Sounds good to me. A little bit of knowledge can be disastrous, but what the hell.'

～

'So, the sign says "INFORMATION". I reckon if we stand here for too much longer the only information we'll need is whether we'd prefer to be buried or cremated,' snarled Simon from in front of the counter. 'Talk about staff reductions; this is ridiculous. Apart from that pillock over there reading the paper and pretending he doesn't know we're here, you could fire a cannon through the place and not hit a sole.'

The "pillock" happened to be a man in his mid thirties dressed in a pair of ill-fitting dark trousers and what was probably a white shirt left to hang outside the trousers. Judging from the clothing, Ron had already come to the conclusion the gentleman had most likely experienced a good night out and had addressed the consequences by sleeping them off on a park bench somewhere. Quite apart from his attire, the gentleman failed dismally to display any enthusiasm or initiative for his job, and appeared to be consciously ignoring the two customers waiting patiently at the counter: no doubt in total compliance with his duty statement.

While Ron had prejudged the gentleman by his physical appearance, Simon had resolved himself to the idea that whatever cleverly concealed attributes the gentleman may possess, they clearly failed to enhance the "pillock's" work ethic. In all, Simon suspected the gentleman currently sitting idly behind a desk reading the newspaper, and wishing the two yobbos at the front counter would go away, was on the road to a successful future as a public servant.

'Hey, how does someone get some service around here?' called Simon to the uninterested gentleman.

Ron looked at Simon and gave him a "there, told you so" look. 'See, he's not dead. I saw him move,' Ron said, a feigned look of shock on his face. The gentleman, without removing his head from the paper, mumbled something that sounded like "the bloke who works the counter is out having a cigarette. You'll have to wait."

'I'm sorry, it must be my hearing, but did you say the bloke who's on the "Information Counter" is out having a cigarette?'

Simon asked, perfectly aware that that was exactly what the gentleman said, but now wanting to interrupt this inert bureaucrat's rude newspaper reading with a needless confirmation. With all the speed of a lethargic sloth, the gentleman exploded into an adrenalin rush of pulsating action. He calmly, and with great care and precision, folded the newspaper in half, nonchalantly dropped it onto the desk in front of him, and slowly turned his swivel chair ninety degrees to face the two yobbos at the counter. He sat back and folded his arms; all terribly confrontational.

'You see, it's like this. TBones is entitled to a cigarette break every forty minutes and, as I'm his supervisor, I go to great pains to ensure he complies with the rules.'

Simon, having some difficulty in understanding the situation, asked for clarification. 'You mean you make sure TBones has his cigarette break every forty minutes whether he wants a cigarette or not? And what sort of a name is TBones?'

The gentleman nodded, the atmosphere becoming more lucid. 'Yes, that's right. Once we, the workers, win these entitlements, irrespective of how trivial they may appear, you must ensure the workers take every opportunity to avail themselves of such entitlements, whether they want to, or not. Hell, if we didn't, could you imagine what would happen? There would be sheer anarchy. After all, we certainly don't rate the smoko as a privilege, but an inalienable right, a part of the Australian tradition and folklore. You just wait and see. The rights of the workers, such as the smoko, will one- day be forever encapsulated into the Australian Constitution. And TBones is really Trevor Jones but he's always been known as TBones for some reason.'

'How quaint. And I must remember to pay my union fees. And just how long is a cigarette break?' asked Simon wondering just how long he should have allowed to ask a few basic questions on redeveloping a block of land.

'Thirty minutes.'

'So, TBones comes back from a smoko, does forty minutes work then goes and has another thirty minute smoko?' asked Ron who was just as confused as Simon.

'Good God, no. We're entitled to a smoko every forty minutes and that's what it means. The clock doesn't start ticking from the time you get back from the smoko; it's from when you leave for a smoko. TBones will come back half an hour after he went. That means he'll be in the office for ten minutes before he's entitled to another smoko, irrespective of whether he wants another cigarette, or not. See, he might choose to have a cup of coffee instead, which he is obviously entitled to, so he may go across to the coffee shop over the road, or maybe go to the loo or something else, all of which doesn't count as smoko time. In reality, he might not come back to the office at all before he's entitled to another smoko. But don't think TBones is the only one. We're all entitled to a smoko every forty minutes whether you smoke or not. I suppose the non-smokers could call it a brewo, or chatto. Yeah, that's a good one. I'll have to remember that.'

Simon looked at Ron who looked at Simon. Both men didn't know whether to be appalled, angry, confused, or just accept it as par for the course. 'Look,' said Simon. 'We just called in to try and obtain some very basic knowledge on how to go about redeveloping a block of land.'

'Oh, why didn't you say so,' said the gentleman with eager enthusiasm as he jumped to his feet and tucked in his shirt. 'We have an interview room just through that door there,' he said indicating. 'If you'd like to take a seat, I'll be with you in a second.'

'Holy hell, and we haven't asked a question yet. This has to be the greatest bludge on the planet,' quipped Ron as they entered a small room furnished with a swivel chair behind a very basic table, and two vinyl chairs where the expectation was for the clients, or whoever, would be seated. Within a couple of minutes the gentleman returned, a broad smile that couldn't quite conceal the sneer on his face. Well, if that isn't an "I got something you want and you ain't getting it" look, I don't know what is, thought Ron who was beginning to think the whole idea of finding out the basics to redeveloping a property wasn't worth the trouble.

'Right gentlemen, my name's Stuart Boswell. You wish to know the basics on how to redevelop a block of land, I believe. I take it the said block of land is in the council's area?'

'Yes of course,' replied Simon, quite amused that this gentleman just had to be related to some Scottish throwback who went nuts after he banged up his girlfriend, Mary; this bloke's loopy already. 'It would be pointless to ask someone from the Warringah Council regarding the redevelopment of a block of land at Cronulla, would it not?'

'Absolutely,' returned Mr Boswell. 'Now, is there an erection on the property at the moment and what sort of development do you have in mind?'

Ron and Simon cast a glance at each other; their thoughts clashed halfway. Oh yeah, I've got my doubts about this bloke. Simon, with great effort, replied, 'Yes, there's an old two storey Elizabethan erection, er, let's make that a dwelling, that we want to knock down. Once cleared, we intend to put up some luxury townhouses in its place. But before we get ahead of ourselves, who is required to sign the application to develop the site?'

'Oh, that's easy. We check with the Lands Department to make sure the application is signed by the owner, and in the case of joint ownership, all joint owners are required to sign the application.'

Simon nodded his understanding of the situation. 'Okay, we submit the application. What then?'

'Well, you mentioned you have an old Elizabethan house you want to knock down. We would certainly hope this Elizabethan dwelling is old as we don't come across too many new Elizabethan type dwellings,' mused Mr Boswell. 'Now, is the dwelling covered by any orders under the National Trust, or State Heritage? Is there any impediment to the Local Environmental Plan, and does the construction of townhouses constitute a breach of the zoning regulations for the area? Do you foresee any protests, or demonstrations from political or environmental groups who may oppose the demolition of any property they may consider of architectural or environmental significance? You know, there are pink nosed, green eyed possums and native flying foxes in many of our areas, and the tree-huggers are very concerned with the conservation of their habitat. Just so there's no ambiguity, I mean the habitat of the animals, not the habitat of the tree huggers; they're human.'

'Woowa, just hold your horses right there. We came here to ask the questions, not be confronted with an avalanche of stupid bloody questions that I couldn't really give a stuff about. All I want to know is, if I knock the place down, can I hire a bulldozer to clear up the mess and drag a builder in to put up some townhouses?'

Mr Boswell nodded in recognition of Simon's clear and concise question. 'Ah, yes of course you can, if you like. But if you did, we'd probably tell you to knock 'em down, the townhouses, I mean. There are a million and one considerations to go through and a million and two applications to be made to various authorities. All of this takes both time and money, a lot of money.'

'And I suppose all this money has to be paid up-front?' Ron asked, having a good idea of what the answer was going to be.

'Yep. They say there are always two ways to skin a cat, but not this time. To get approval to knock down a building is hard enough, but you want approvals to knock 'em down and build 'em up again. Now, that takes time and money and the only way to do it is the long and expensive way,' said a very confident Mr Boswell. 'And if you get the approval to knock 'em down and build 'em up again, it will be done by contractors appointed by council, not just any part-time handyman. We do have building standards to maintain, you know.'

Simon shrugged, heaved a sigh and sat back on his chair and folded his arms. 'Okay, Mr Boswell. Now you've told us all the bad news, how about some good news. I hear what you say, but I've never come across a situation where there was only one way to skin the cat. I'm sure there's a host of other ways of getting things done that you haven't mentioned?'

Now it was Mr Boswell's turn to sit back, clasp his hands behind his head, and swivel his swivel chair from side to side in a most annoying manner. 'Look, I don't know the name of either of you two gentlemen, and I'm not about to ask. However, it appears you are both men of the world and are not totally ignorant of life's little follies. Though I don't propose to go into details of the decision making processes, it is incumbent upon me to disclose certain information which may not be readily available to the general public.'

'Ah yes,' Simon nodded. 'I suppose this where you tell me there are procedures in place that may precipitate the expeditious determination of applications which may, under normal process, necessitate protracted deliberation without any certainty that such application would receive favourable consideration? So, it's bribery. Okay, who do I pay, how much and how quickly is the system circumvented?'

Mr Boswell gave a look of feigned disgust that anyone would consider such a thing. 'Gentlemen, please. Perish the thought we would ever consider stooping so low as to be a party to bribery. The word itself is so abhorrent; it conjures up the perception of a wrongdoing, or at least some sort of nefarious activity. I can categorically state here and now that a specific council statute, established to cover this very contingency, emphatically prohibits the acceptance of gifts, rewards, contributions or any other form of remunerative recompense for any decision, favourable or otherwise. And that includes bribes. If I have unwittingly misled you to believe otherwise, or if I am responsible for any misconceptions you had, I humbly apologise.'

At this juncture Mr Boswell stopped his chair swiveling and folded his arms, his expression taking on a more serious look. 'However, gentlemen, be that as it may, I am led to believe there may possibly be an exception to this particular statute. In extreme cases, and on the very rare occasion, the conditions relating to the ruling may be waived, but only on the approval of a council select committee. Should a waiver of the ruling be exercised, the exalted senior functionaries within the decision making executive just might, and I stress the word "might", be amenable to offers in one form or another, including fiscal remuneration, if you get my drift.'

'Ahh, yes,' replied Simon, nodding his head as the facts became clearer. 'Yes, I quite understand now. Bucket loads of money are transferred to a specific council bureaucrat, or his totally uninformed lady and, in recognition of the benevolent nature of the said contribution, he may see his way to give a specific application favourable consideration. Of course, the nature of the recompense, or whatever, would never be considered an inducement for a preferential decision. If the circumstances relating to the said payment were ever queried, it would be submitted that it was nothing more than a gift from two philanthropists who had nothing better to do with their money. The benefactor's payment to the fortuitous councilor would be made solely because the councilor would be highly respected and whose integrity has never been questioned. Apart from that, he would be regarded as a good bloke. Right?'

'Got it in one,' came the reply.

Simon and Ron understood the drift perfectly, and didn't want to know. No wonder Mr Bruce Glover wants nothing to do with redeveloping "The Grovel".

CHAPTER 18

Simon sat at his desk his chin rested on the palm of his left hand while the right drummed out an infuriating rhythm on the desk. 'Must you do that?' questioned Noel with a hint of exasperation in his voice. 'Okay, it's only been a couple of days since you asked Ron to find Tiny and now you're as frustrated as all hell just waiting for the phone to ring.'

Simon stopped his tapping, gave a sigh, sat back and folded his arms. 'Yeah I know. But our whole case depends on finding Tiny, and with Andrew Glover looking for him, it's a race to see who finds him first. At least we now have a positive identification of the body with the DNA confirming it was related to Bruce, which means it has to be Paul. I suppose that makes Bruce twice as wealthy as he was last month, and twice as likely to get his head bashed in by Andrew.'

'Some time ago you mentioned there were now three beneficiaries of Joyce Glover's will who are likely to be targeted. Do you still hold with that idea?' Noel asked as he folded a piece of paper into the shape of an aeroplane.

'No. I think we can discount the other two beneficiaries, who were they...?

'Vicki Agnew and Debbie Grimes,' Noel broke in.

'Ah, yes. No, I don't think Andrew will go after them as they're not part of the family. And let's face it, the amount they received is inconsequential in comparison with what the other two got. If Andrew is after the family fortune, it'll be Bruce pushing up daisies, or feeding the fishes.'

'Well, all I can say is, it's a bloody mess,' remarked Noel as the flight of his paper aeroplane failed dismally. 'Poor old Graham Lee is bearing the brunt of a lot of smart comments and jibes up at the club. The staff is giving him heaps; "found any more bodies this morning, boss. Pulling your anchor will send you blind. Try using live bait, you'll catch bigger fishes". At least he has a sense of humour and can see the funny side of it, not that Paul Glover would consider the situation funny, being dead and all.'

The conversation was rudely interrupted by the ring of Simon's phone which he quickly answered in anticipation of vital news from Ron Lange. Noel, watching for the facial expressions that would to determine the importance of the call, was disappointed to see the boss, after a multitude of yeses and yeps, hang up the phone without a hint as to the significance of the conversation. Simon pushed his chair back from the table and folded his arms. 'That was Jacko. He says he has a bit of info we might be interested in. He asked if we would like to have a chat this afternoon up at The Cross. He didn't have time to say too much as he was using a phone at The Spinning Wheel and says Stack would fire him if he found out.'

'Then how about we ask Ron along as it no doubt has something to do with Tiny. Perhaps pooled resources may prove more fruitful?' suggested Noel, picking up the remains of his aerodynamic failure.

'Good idea. Get on to him and let him know, two thirty at the fountain.'

~

'Jacko, I think you've already met Ron, but if you haven't this is Ron Lange, and he's not a cop. He's been doing a bit of work for us trying to find Tiny Timmins,' Simon explained as the four men stood on the corner of Bayswater Road and Macleay Street, close to the fountain. 'Look, instead of looking like a bunch of suspect gentlemen meeting in the park, let's find a coffee shop and have a brew.'

As finding a coffee shop in Kings Cross is not a difficult task, it wasn't long before the group had settled back into an alcove of a near deserted coffee shop and the coffees served. 'Okay, Jacko, what's the info you think we may be interested in?' asked Simon.

'I had a talk with Tiny last night,' Jacko replied nonchalantly.

'Come again?' said Simon as if he hadn't quite heard.

'I had a chat with Tiny last night. He's a bit worried that things might not be all they seem.'

'Well, I'd say he's right on that score because at the moment we haven't a clue as to what he's done, if anything. Let's face it, Jacko, you know more about Tiny Timmins than we do; at least you're getting the information first hand. In view of the circumstances, and from what you've told us, it's just that we'd like to have a chat with him ourselves before it's too late,' said Noel.

'So what's worrying Tiny now?' broke in Ron. 'Every man and his dog knows Andrew Glover is looking for him for some reason, quite apart from the police, and he'd better hope the police find him first. And, more to the point, where is Tiny right now?'

Jacko put his coffee down and shifted uncomfortably in his

seat. 'Look, I might know where Tiny is, and I might not. I never expected to see him again after that first night he came to the club, but obviously he wanted someone to talk to. He turned up again last night, though this time he appeared to be a bit agitated. He said he'd heard on the grapevine that Andrew Glover is lookin' for him. Now, as you blokes know, Tiny did a small job for Mr Glover. Tiny had an idea it was probably illegal, but Glover had offered him an amount of cash that Tiny would have considered a small fortune. Tiny didn't tell me what the exact nature of the job was, but from what he told me I have a fair idea.'

'You think it has something to do with our waterlogged body?' asked Noel showing absolutely no respect for the dead. Jacko, not bothering to answer, just looked at Noel, raised his eyebrows and pursed his lips.

'So let's cut the crap,' said Simon becoming annoyed at the beating around the bush. 'Jacko, we think Tiny may have been responsible for attaching the body of Paul Glover to the anchor of a boat moored in Rushcutters Bay. From what you've told us, it's possible Tiny may have carried out this task at the request of Andrew Glover, though we haven't any evidence on that score, yet. And that's the reason we're looking for Tiny. We haven't a clue as to why Glover is looking for him, unless…'

'Unless Glover wants to tidy up the loose ends. Yes, I can see that,' replied Jacko with surprising foresight. 'See, I don't believe Tiny knew he was getting' rid of a body, if he actually did get rid of it. In fact, I don't think he would have had any idea of what he was doin' at the time. All he knew was Glover was payin' him a lot of money for him to do a little job in his tinny.'

'So, as I asked before, what's upset Tiny now?' asked Noel.

'That's what makes me think your body is involved. I get the idea Tiny now thinks he may have overstepped the mark and is a bit out of his depth, no pun intended. You see, it's only after

Tiny did this job and Andrew Glover started lookin' for him that he's become jittery. I think he must have known that what he'd done was probably illegal and that Glover was involved. As I said, it's only since he found out Glover is lookin' for him that he's gone to ground, so to speak. Tiny's a gentle giant and I would like to think he would baulk at ditchin' a flamin' body, irrespective of whose body it was, or how much he was bein' paid. But now I've got to know Tiny a bit better, I doubt there's much he wouldn't stoop to, if the price was right.

'Let's face it. If he discovered he was getting rid of a stiff after he'd already started the job of getting rid of whatever he thought he was getting rid of, there's little he could do about it but finish the job. I suppose he could have called the police but that wouldn't be Tiny,' added Jacko, more as an afterthought.

Simon sat back, clasped his hands on his stomach and steepled his index fingers. 'Now Jacko, I hope you can appreciate why we need to find Tiny before anyone else does. Everything we've spoken about is pure speculation and based on the presumption that Tiny disposed of the body belonging to Paul Glover. Okay, so Tiny did a job for Andrew Glover. So What? Until we find out exactly what that job was, we're flying kites. Obviously the nature of the job has sent Tiny into a tizzy after the event, and with Andrew Glover now looking for him, Tiny thinks he's in a spot of trouble. I don't think Tiny would have given any thought as to the consequences of doing whatever it was for Glover, initially at least, as there was nothing to give him cause for concern. And it sounds like Tiny is the sort of person who would have gone into raptures at the sight of the bundle of bucks offered. Naturally, with Tiny being Tiny, he would have done anything, well nearly anything, to get his hands on that bundle.

'So, Tiny's in trouble, but I think he's in a lot less trouble with the police than he is with Andrew Glover; at least the police don't want him dead, not that we know for certain Andrew wants him dead. Jacko, if you do know where he is, I suggest you let him know we're looking for him to try and keep him alive. If he has as much information as we hope he has on Glover, I think we could come to some arrangement that may prove beneficial to Tiny at a later date.'

'I'll see what I can do,' said Jacko. 'Tiny's a good bloke and I'd hate to see him get into any more strife than he's in already. I have your card, Chief, so when I see Tiny, I mean, if I see him, that is, I'll suggest he get in touch with you. But go easy on him.'

CHAPTER 19

*F*or a late September afternoon it was unusually warm, the sun shining, the birds singing. The small group of people sitting in a circle on the Webster's back lawn at Collaroy was enjoying the company of good friends, good conversation and the occasional drop of good wine, or beer depending on the individual preference.

Simon, not having had the chance to speak to Graham Lee for some time, thought that Graham may be interested in the direction the investigation had taken, especially as to the identities of the Anchor Man and the suspected perpetrator of the act. The girl's conversation, generally confined to topics more absorbing to girls, had ceased in order to listen to the men's discourse relating to the body found on the end of Graham's anchor. In fact, Georgie couldn't help thinking that having a body on the end of your anchor could be quite painful.

'So, you've positively identified the body?' asked Graham, grabbing a handful of potato chips to go with his can of beer.

'Yes,' Simon replied. 'DNA has revealed the samples taken

from the body and from Bruce are a match, so the Anchor Man was definitely the brother of Bruce. Seeing as Bruce tentatively identified the body as Paul Glover, we now accept the DNA as confirmation. I spoke to one of the pathologists at forensics who said they're trying to get a set of fingerprints off the body. Apparently with bodies that have been in the water for a while, that can take a bit of time, but he'll let us know the results. And no, it appears this Paul Glover hasn't, or didn't, have anything to do with illegal casinos. He recently came into some money that was part of a family estate, and once you bring money into the equation you can find all sorts of motives for murder.'

'So if he didn't have anything to do with casinos, why in the name of heaven was he stuck on Graham's anchor?' asked Louisa, sitting back on her director's chair, a glass of wine in her hand.

'Now that is a very interesting question,' responded Noel. 'To be quite honest, we haven't a clue, yet. We know, well, at least we think we know, who put the body there but the why is still unanswered, and believe me, we'd like to know just as much as you would.'

'And the forensic report indicated the body was dead before being anchored?' queried Sue, remembering the sight of the corpse being dragged onto the deck of "Gemini".

'See, Simon. I'm not the only one to suffer from tautology,' remarked Noel. Though it was unlikely others had picked up on the obvious, Noel felt the opportunity too good to miss. 'Sue, my sweet, my love and lust, for forensics to report on the state of a body would tend to suggest the body was definitely dead. In the case of Paul Glover, the answer is yes, his body was dead; in fact, he was very dead with the back of his head stove in before being anchored.'

'Well pardon my ignorance,' returned Sue haughtily as she

poured herself another very large glass of wine. 'But if the person was dead before going into the water, that would mean the person wasn't a person at all, not at that stage anyway as he would be a body, a dead body.'

Georgie winced and said, 'Oh, shut up, you punctilious pea-brains. Anyway, you still haven't figured out the whys and the wherefores?'

'You want the convoluted answer or the simple answer?' Simon replied. 'I'll give you both anyway, no and no, and that's about it. As Shultz would say, "Ve know nothink", well, next to nothing. Hey Ron, can you grab us anotherie from the esky?'

'Coming over,' he responded and lobbed another can of the amber to Simon. While Ron had been somewhat taciturn since his arrival, it had become quite apparent to both Louisa and Georgie that he was somewhat preoccupied, and the centre of that preoccupation was Judy Kemp. Since the breakup of her relationship with Rodger Beaton, and following the golf links debacle, Judy had been required to vacate the flat she and Rodger lived in at Strathfield. In view of the circumstances, and with the outcome of legal matters still pending, Judy had moved into Dorothy's old house next door to the Webster's. She had no inclination of permanent residence at Collaroy, but the situation was a convenience until the dust had settled. It was only then would she consider her options. But in the meantime, Judy appeared thoroughly happy with the afternoon's company.

'And Judy, has Inspector Spring-Brown finished his investigation?' asked Noel before washing down a handful of peanuts with a cold beer.

Judy finished off her third glass of wine and started to pour herself a fourth. 'Yes, he has and, despite all the motives the three of us had for doing each other in, there was only one murder and poor Rodger, bless his little heart, just happened to be the victim,' she replied with all the sympathy and remorse a death adder might display. 'Funny isn't it. My solicitor told me that in view of the fact that Dorothy's husband and sister were the two remaining members of the family, and the fact that Rodger and I had been in a defacto relationship, the chances are I might even get the house next door. Even more laughable is that it appears neither Dorothy nor Rodger anticipated dying as neither had made a will.'

'Now, just where have I seen something like this happen recently?' asked Simon looking directly at Noel.

'Ah yes. The old tontine trick,' replied Noel.

'Now, hang about.' It was Louisa whose interest was suddenly aroused. 'You mean to say you've identified a tontine?'

'Well, not in the strict sense of the word, but a case of where the last remaining member of the family gets to inherit the family fortune,' replied Simon in an effort to diffuse any ambiguity of the perceived tontine. 'The Anchor Man, Paul Glover, was one of the sons of a wealthy lady who died recently and left her fortune to her two sons. There's an uncle of the two sons, a Mr Andrew Glover, who seems to feel he deserves his share. With one of the two sons now out of the way, he only has to kill the other off to be the only remaining member of the family left and the family fortune is his.'

'And I bet the two sons were twins,' replied Louisa, nodding her head as the situation, to her, became painfully obvious.

'Yes, they were,' replied Simon, a look of surprise on his face. 'How'd you know?'

'So, it's now perfectly clear,' said Louisa reaching out to hold Graham's hand in an act of relief. 'What is the name of the boat and which twin owned it?'

Simon rested his elbow on the arm of his chair, held his face with his hand and shook his head. 'Well, I certainly know which one of the seven dwarfs I am. God, Louisa, you must think Noel and I are a right pair of imbeciles.'

'Hey, just back up a second 'cause I'm obviously missing something here?' said Noel as the significance of Louisa's questioning failed to register. 'Ron, do you know what they're talking about?'

'Oh yes,' Ron replied giving Louisa a big smile. 'And I'm sure Graham is very relieved now there's an explanation for the Anchor Man.' While there were four people within the circle sharing the benefits of Louisa's brilliant display of knowledge and foresight, there were four others still requiring enlightenment.

'That bit of thinking deserves another beer,' said Simon as he scrunched the empty can and tossed it into the metal garbage can used for the empties. Before he could ask, Ron had lobbed another can over. 'Come on Louisa, this is your story so you better share it with everybody,' he said as he snapped the ring pull off the can.

'Love to,' responded Louisa as she shook the remaining drops out of the bottle of wine before handing Graham a fresh bottle and a cork screw. 'Right from the beginning we girls had come to the conclusion that the body had been attached to the wrong boat as Graham didn't have a clue as to the owner of the body. By the same token, the only person interested in the Taipan Club claimed he knew nothing about the event so that, more or less, put the criminal side of the problem to rest. By the way, Simon, you didn't answer my questions; what is the name of the boat and which twin owns it?'

Simon thought for a moment. 'No, some weird name I can't recall. Noel, you any idea?'

'Something like My Tuna is all I can think of,' said Noel. 'I thought it an odd name when Bruce mentioned it.'

'Oh God. How bloody stupid,' sighed Louisa. 'Because the

body was attached to a boat named "Gemini" we all thought it had to have something to do with the twins. Naturally, you looked for boats with the same name, or boats related to Gemini, such as Castor or Pollux. Well, you were right on that score, but you didn't follow through with the idea. I'll bet a pound to a penny the name of the boat is "Mithuna". Correct?'

'Bingo,' exclaimed Simon. 'That's it, and the owner is Bruce Glover, the twin brother of Paul. But pardon my ignorance, what has Mithuna got to do with Gemini?'

While the three other girls had listened in silence as Louisa told the story of the Anchor Man's involvement with Gemini, it was Judy who threw her arm in the air like a pretentious school girl. 'Oh, ask me, ask me, I know.'

Louisa smiled. 'Okay Judy. It is an easy question if you know the answer, and I bet you know the relationship between Gemini and Mithuna.'

'Of course,' replied Judy. 'Nearly all women read their stars to see if they're about to come into a fortune or meet some tall dark handsome stranger to brighten up their lives. Even with so many women interested in what the stars have to prophesise, I'm sure only a few delve any further into astrology.'

After explaining the relationship between Gemini and Mithuna, a pregnant pause enveloped the group. 'Holy hell, so maybe we have to look at this from an entirely different angle. It looks like poor old Tiny couldn't remember the name of the boat he should have attached Paul to, that's if it was Tiny, of course,' said Simon shaking his head in wonder at the simplicity the case had become.

'Okay, and who's Tiny?' asked Graham Lee, a little confused.

'Tiny did, or does, some odd jobs for Andrew Glover who's in the real estate business. They're just small jobs, like removing garbage and cleaning up places soon to be put on the market. Glover always pays him in cash for his handy work, which suits

Tiny down to the ground. We have an idea it might have been this Tiny character who attached the body to the anchor. Until we talk to him I s'pose we can speculate all we like, but right at the moment Tiny seems to have disappeared. Even so, for the first time since we dragged the Anchor Man on board the "Gemini", and with Louisa's insight, I think our investigation is now progressing, which does makes for a nice change.'

CHAPTER 20

$\mathcal{D}$espite the apparent ease of solving the Anchor Man conundrum, back at Day Street the two detectives still had problems determining their next move. 'So what now, boss?' Noel asked as he scribbled a little stick figure hanging from a scaffold on a sheet of paper. 'There doesn't seem much we can do until we speak to Tiny; so far everything has been second hand info. We haven't actually heard it from the horse's mouth that the job Tiny did for Glover was dispose of Paul's body. And let's face it; even if he did do the disposing, there's nothing to suggest Andrew Glover killed him in the first place, apart from a pretty far-fetched motive of killing off all the family members to get the family fortune.'

'Well, if Glover did kill Paul, he hasn't many more family members left to kill off; only Bruce and the fortune will probably be his,' replied Simon. 'It's a good thing Thomas and Joyce only had two offspring. If we're right on the tontine score, things might have developed into a full scale massacre, if they had had a dozen kids. Anyway, we'd better let Bruce know our train of thought just so he can be on his guard against Uncle

Andrew. Seeing there isn't much we can do until Tiny turns up, we may as well go and see Brutus now and tell him the good news.'

'Sounds good to me,' replied Noel. 'And why Brutus?'

'I don't know. Maybe I thought of him as an oxymoron, a contradiction in terms sort of thing.'

'Well, perhaps I should buy Brutus a bunch of flowers to brighten up that mausoleum he lives in.'

'I strongly suggest you forget the flowers or you may end up having a problem you'd prefer not to have on your hands. Just grab your coat and let's get going.'

Regardless of the morbid perceptions the two detectives may have harboured following their initial visit to the Elizabeth Bay mansion, their second visit only enhanced those perceptions to new heights of uncomfortable apprehension. However, being brave police officers, neither detective was going to openly admit to the other of their discomfort. Though the day was sunny and bright, for a change, it appeared the sunshine had steadfastly refused to venture any further than the dilapidated stone front fence. Notwithstanding the lack of anything resembling a cloud in the sky, both the mansion and surrounding grounds were bathed in a cloak of dreary greyness and shadow, a phenomenon giving rise to a sense of appalling foreboding and dread.

Noel, making no attempt to get out of the car, regarded Simon with a troubled look. 'I didn't notice that last time we were here,' he said as he pointed to two large stone pillars about eight feet high and some twelve feet apart. 'It must have been a driveway at sometime or other, not that there's a gate or driveway there now. Those tyre marks, which don't appear to be that old, suggest someone has been using it lately.'

'Yes, I see what you mean,' replied Simon. 'Last time we were here I didn't think to ask Bruce if he drove a car. Come to think of it, there's a stack of questions I didn't ask. Look, you go and have a chat with him and I'll wait here in the car for you. I can't see the sense in both of us going in.'

'Sorry boss, but I ain't going anywhere near that mansion without a backup with me, and with our lack of resources, you're it,' replied Noel indignantly.

'Ah, come on then. I can't see why you're so reluctant; after all, it's just like any other house in Elizabeth Bay.'

'Yeah, well how come the only movies I've seen where gruesome murder is perpetrated and bloodsucking vampires do their thing only happens in mansions exactly like this one. And why's it so sunny out here in the car and it looks like midnight only fifty feet away. I'll bet my booties there's been murder committed in this place sometime in its history.'

'Well, there'll be a bloody murder in this car if you don't make a move, so let's get on with it,' said Simon.

Noel pulled the chain located next to the front door. As before, it was Bruce who answered, this time dressed in a cheesy yellow floral dressing gown and pink slippers, the whole ensemble appearing quite incongruous, the time being around one thirty in the afternoon.

'Ah, Sheriff Webster and his deputy, Elliott. So nice to see you again. If you had informed me of your visit I would have been attired more appropriately,' gushed Bruce.

'That's okay,' replied Simon. 'We apologise for the inconvenience, but we would like to ask you a few questions, not pass judgment on your bedtime attire.'

'No, I quite understand. Please, come in.'

The two detectives were shown into the same room as on

their first visit. Things hadn't changed, the room still managed to exude the same damp, musty smell and the same dim, somber atmosphere. Simon noticed that even with the heavy, dark purple curtains, initially thought to be black, drawn back, the pitiful amount of sunlight that had the audacity to venture through the closed windows failed dismally to soften the morbid feeling of unease he was experiencing. Bruce sat on the faded floral lounge chair that had seen better days and gestured to the faded floral settee.

'Oh, I am sorry; I've done it again, haven't I? Can I get you gentlemen a coffee, glass of cherry? No, nothing at all?' Bruce queried.

'No thanks. The quicker we get started the quicker we can be out of here,' blurted Noel without any sense of political correctness.

'By the way, I take it I will be getting the fire tools and the statue back?' Bruce asked with an air of indignation that surprised Simon.

'Of course, no question about it. As soon as the forensic boys are finished with them I'll drop them around myself,' replied Simon. 'But right at the moment I'm concerned with learning more about the family. I take it after the death of your father, Andrew Glover was around to help your mother as much as possible?'

'Yes, he was, but not to do anything physical or get his hands dirty,' replied Bruce with a twitch of his nose.

'After your mother died, how did you, Paul, and Andrew get along together? I know you don't like Andrew, but was there any other animosity between the three of you?' Simon asked.

'No, I don't think you would call it animosity. Maybe there was a little hate and bitterness, probably even a bit of hostility thrown in. Paul didn't like Andrew either and I suppose Andrew doesn't, or didn't, like either Paul or me as a result of the inheritance shambles.'

'So you think your mother's will was a bit of a shambles, do you?' asked Simon, his interest piqued.

'Au contraire, Chief Inspector. Both Paul and I believed mummy did an excellent job. Mummy hadn't seen daddy's brother for donkey's years and it wasn't until daddy died that he started to show up, just like a bad penny.'

'And now you get to inherit Paul's estate as well?' queried Noel.

'Why yes, I suppose I do,' replied Bruce with a wry smile. 'That will make me quite rich.'

'Didn't you have enough without Paul's share?' Noel asked.

'Yes of course. But as they say, every little bit helps.'

'And what sort of car do you drive, Bruce?' Simon asked.

'I don't know what that has to do with Paul's death,' replied Bruce, surprised at the nature of the question. 'At the moment I'm not driving anything. I really hate driving in the city and my boat is close handy so I can walk to Rushcutters Bay. I'll probably buy one soon enough, but I'm in no hurry at the moment.'

'Would it come as a surprise if I said we think Andrew Glover is involved in your brother's murder?' remarked Simon.

'No, not in the least. In fact, he was the first person I thought of,' responded Bruce, as if Andrew's involvement was taken for granted.

'At the moment we have no evidence to suggest he is involved. However, it seems pretty clear that Paul's body was attached to the wrong boat, the boat it should have been attached to was yours, the ...' Simon could not remember the name.

'The "Mithuna". And you are so clever. I can't think how you worked that out because there are just so many boats,' responded Bruce with admiration. 'And can I ask you how you came to that conclusion?'

'We think the person who actually disposed of Paul's body couldn't remember the name of the boat. Somewhere along the line he must have heard that the names Mithuna and Gemini had a connection. When he couldn't remember the name Mithuna, which is a pretty odd name to begin with, he must have thought Gemini was close enough so chose a "Gemini" as the boat to dump your brother. All terribly simple really, if we're correct that is,' replied Simon.

'And you think Paul's body was supposed to give me a warning of what I could expect?' replied Bruce.

'Well, the thought did cross our mind. You haven't received any threats from anyone lately have you, specifically from Uncle Andrew?' Simon asked, not really expecting a positive answer.

'No, not even from Rodney who dropped by the other night while I was entertaining a friend. Quite embarrassing it was,' replied Bruce with a coy grin.

'Look, until we get this case sorted out, I wouldn't have too much to do with Uncle Andrew,' suggested Simon. 'By the same token, I would stress that Andrew is only a suspect and the most likely person doesn't always turn out to be the murderer.'

The meeting had the air of informality, the four detectives sitting around the coffee table located in Chief Superintendent Paxton's office. Joyce, who had worked on the fourth floor of the police station for more years than she cared to remember and yet to be replaced by a mechanical coffee machine, had provided the necessary coffee and cookies, which only added to the informality.

'And how are you settling in, Michael?' asked Chief Superintendent Paxton as he added some milk to his coffee.

'Pretty well, considering, sir,' he replied, immediately regretting his qualification as soon as he said it.

Chief Paxton finished the mouthful of biscuit, raised his eyebrows and pursed his lips. 'Care to elucidate?'

Superintendent Hayes, having never conducted an investigation into anything more brutal than a paper cut sustained by an eccentric embezzler on a piece of stock market scrip, was suddenly conscious of the fact that his own stupidity had forced him into a corner where he was about to cast aspersions on the investigative competence of a chief inspector and a detective sergeant. His first thought was to back pedal, rapidly. 'Well, sir, you no doubt have heard of the Anchor Man, the body recovered from a Mr Graham Lee's boat. You are probably also aware that the person was murdered before being attached to the anchor of the said boat. All this happened at least a month ago and, unfortunately, Chief Inspector Webster has yet to arrest anyone for the murder. I must admit, sir, I was hoping a quick and successful conclusion to this case would establish my credibility here at Day Street, to some extent at least.'

Chief Paxton nodded his head indicating he appreciated the new superintendent's viewpoint. 'Simon, would you care to comment?'

Simon looked at Noel with a look of profound hurt indignation. 'Sir, I'm sure I could run out a few clichés in an attempt to explain the situation. Sergeant Elliott and I have made progress, taking into account the Anchor Man wasn't identified until sometime well after his recovery. We have endeavoured to keep Superintendent Hayes appraised of the state of affairs, but we feel it more appropriate to pass on what we know as opposed to what we think we know. At the moment we have a person of interest with whom we wish to speak to, however we believe any approach at this juncture may frighten this person off.'

'Yes, I can understand that,' remarked Chief Paxton. 'But, let's face it, you can't sit on your bum all day waiting for the right time to question this person of interest. The bloke might be dead from old age before the right time comes along. Maybe you just have to take the bull by the horns and hope you won't scare him off.'

'Yes sir,' replied Simon. 'To be honest, sir, it's not so much that we might frighten him off that we're worried about. Perhaps it's more correct to say the person we'd like to question has probably already been frightened off and has decided to go missing on his own volition. You see, sir, we believe this person has very good reason to be afraid of both the police and, probably, an even greater fear of someone else. In fact, the "bloke" to whom you refer might not make it to old age if this "someone else" finds him before we do.

'In the meantime, we are pursuing other courses of enquiries which we believe are relevant to the case. However, I think we can say, with some confidence, the prospect of an arrest can be reasonably anticipated. That expectation is based on the anticipated outcome of the interview with our person of considerable interest. Unfortunately, that person of considerable interest is the person who's gone missing.'

'Hey, hang about. Isn't this the bloke you spoke to me earlier about, the one that's already buggered off. And you still haven't a clue as to his whereabouts? Well bloody well find him. And this idea of the "prospect of an arrest". Hell, Simon, there is always the prospect of an arrest, no matter how difficult a case may be. If we didn't hold the prospect of an arrest, why ever start the investigation in the first place. And as for pursuing enquiries relevant to the case, I would hate to think you were pursuing enquiries that weren't relevant to the case,' returned Chief Paxton getting a trifle annoyed that Simon had resorted to the use of clichés.

As the three detectives prepared to leave Chief Superintendent Paxton's office, the Chief nodded to Simon. 'Simon, if you have a moment, I'd like a word.' Once alone in the office and Chief Superintendent Paxton had resumed his seat, he motioned to Simon to take a chair. 'Okay, Simon. What's this all about?'

'Sir?' responded Simon with a confused look.

'Ah, come on. Something smells fishy and it's not the bloke on the end of an anchor,' replied Chief Paxton. 'Something's amiss here and I want to know what it is. Has it anything to do with Superintendent Hayes?'

'He's a new bloke in town, sir, and we just have to get adjusted to his method of operating, as he is to ours. You have to expect a few bumps along the way.'

'Yes, I appreciate that, and having you two wild cats working for him from day one doesn't make things any easier.'

'Sir, you are aware that Sergeant Elliott and I work well together. That we do get along so well is probably attributed to the fact that we tend to look outside the square and don't always apply the accepted methods of investigation. Superintendent Hayes probably doesn't appreciate our investigative methodology. And to be honest, sir, the superintendent isn't overly endowed with experience in homicidal investigations. I appreciate he might be a whiz at financial fraud, but murder is another thing. I know he's anxious for an arrest to show his metal at Day Street, and to be honest, sir, I can't argue with that; we'd all like to make an arrest as soon as possible.'

'And is there anything you haven't told the superintendent that you feel might be relevant?'

'Well, you know we are looking for a person whom we believe may be able to shed some light on the problem. As mentioned, we do have a suspect at the moment. But it's as you say, sir, something smells fishy and we're in no hurry to make an arrest without knowing the full details, and currently it's more the motive details we're after.'

'And as you haven't told the Super of your theories, he's getting the idea you're just being slack?'

'Sir, we have absolutely no desire to get things off on a bad footing with the Superintendent and we'll do everything we can to bring this investigation to a successful conclusion. But that's just it. We want a successful conclusion, not one where we make gigs of ourselves by fixing someone up for murder just to make the statistics look good.'

'I should hope not,' replied Chief Paxton, horrified that any policeman, let alone a detective chief inspector, should even contemplate such a thing. 'Look, Simon, just get on with it. I'll see what I can do to placate the waters with the Superintendent Hayes.'

Having found a parking spot some distance from their destination, Simon and Noel made their way along Palmer Street until they reached The Spinning Wheel. At two twenty in the afternoon the club was closed, but persistent pressing of a door button eventually aroused someone's ire inside to the extent they were oblige to answer.

It was Jacko who opened the door and now stood looking at the two detectives with a look of frustration. 'Oh no, not you again? 'Look, I'm only too willin' to talk to you boys on mutual ground, so to speak, but Mr Stack would not be please if he knew you were here talkin' to me right at the moment.'

'It's okay, Jacko. We won't take up too much of your time; we just thought we might do you a bit of a favour,' explained Simon.

'Yeah, I appreciate the fact you did me a favour once, but I can't believe you'd want to do me another,' Jacko grumbled.

'Now Jacko, it's very simple really. You know we're looking for Tiny Timmins. You also know exactly where he is and we want you to tell us. See Jacko, the favour is, you tell us where Tiny is and we won't haul you in for perverting the course of justice, failing to answer a policeman's lawful questioning, obstructing a police officer in the performance of his duties, failing to display the name of the licensee at the entrance of the club. Can you think of any more, Noel?'

'Not off the top of the head, but I'm sure there's a host of health and safety issues that could close the place down, and I reckon if we have a look around there'll be a dozen or so local council bi-laws being breached. I thing we could come up with enough to upset Mr Stack quite considerably. What do you think, Jacko?' Noel asked amiably.

'Christ. You don't give a bloke much of an option, do you? Look,' said Jacko with frustration, 'Tiny's shacked up at my place and says he doesn't want anythin' to do with the cops. He knows he's done wrong so he's layin' low at the moment, especially as the word is out that that bloke Andrew Glover is lookin' for him as well as you blokes. Tiny thinks the cops will do him for murder and lock him away for the rest of his life, or Andrew Glover will just pop him for what he knows.'

'And where's your place?' Simon asked.

'I have a flat in Underwood Street, over in Paddington, just opposite Vic Barracks.'

'And would Tiny be there now?'

'Should be. If he's not he'll probably be over at the Paddo Green.'

'See, there you go, Jacko, that wasn't too hard was it? And we just did you a big favour,' said Noel smiling.

'Yeah, some favour. Tiny's a good bloke, but he's goin' to rip my bloody arms off when he finds out I told you blokes where he is.'

'Don't worry, Jacko. We'll explain it all and I'm sure he'll understand,' responded Noel in a placatory manner.

Noel looked troubled as the two detectives walked back to their car. 'Something's worrying you, Noel?' Simon asked.

'Yeah, boss. It seems Tiny is a bit concerned about this bloke Andrew Glover. From what Jacko says, I think Tiny has the idea Andrew did away with Paul Glover. Problem is, as I see it, we haven't established the motive, means or opportunity bits which leaves us a long way short of arresting anybody, let alone this Andrew Glover.'

'Yes, I'm well aware of that, and so is Superintendent Hayes, unfortunately,' replied Simon. 'By the same token, just because Andrew Glover may have supplied Tiny with a body to dispose of doesn't mean to say he's the murderer. Hell, we don't even know where he got the body from. Glover may have used Tiny as a sub-contractor with Glover himself being paid by someone to dispose of Paul after the someone else had bashed his head in.'

'Well, I don't know,' said Noel as he unlocked the car door. 'Let's hope Tiny can help as we seem to have placed all our bets on him to provide the answers. And if you're right about the sub-contracting, I s'pose the supply and demand principle comes into play; if you've got the body, we can do the disposing. Hey, remember Graham Lee and Louisa's little discussion about body disposal and the costs involved?'

Simon smiled. 'Yes, but that was very different. That incident was all class.'

Having established that he was not at Jacko's flat in Underwood Street, it didn't take Detective Chief Inspector Simon Webster and Detective Sergeant Noel Elliott long to locate Tiny Timmins. After all, Jacko had told them where Tiny would be, if not at Underwood Street. With the time just after three in the afternoon, the Paddington Green Hotel appeared deserted, the lunchtime drinkers having departed, and it just a little too early for the after work drinkers to arrive. As a consequence, the large man sitting at the bar with his back to the door opening onto Oxford Street was hard to miss, quite apart from the fact that he appeared to be the only patron in the pub.

After taking a seat at the bar and ordering two middies of beer from a bored looking barmaid, Simon looked at the man who was preoccupied in reading the horse racing section of the Telegraph. The man was big, horribly big, but not fat. The fact that he appeared not to have been near a razor for a few days gave Simon the uncomfortable feeling the man was either a gangster or a bloke down on his luck. Hell, if ever I want my phone book ripped in half, I'll know who to see, thought Simon. 'Tiny Timmins?' he asked very politely.

The man's reaction confirmed his identity as he closed the paper, slowly and deliberately folded it in half, and laid it on the bar next to a half empty schooner of beer. He then rested his head on his left hand, his elbow on the bar and looked at Simon with a look of resignation. 'Yes, I'm Tiny Timmins and I s'pose you're the cops. I knew you'd turn up sooner or later, and I probably have Jacko to thank for that.'

'Yes, Tiny, we're the cops. But don't blame Jacko as we sort of coerced him into telling us where to find you. I'm Detective Chief Inspector Simon Webster and this is Detective Sergeant Noel Elliott.'

'And I suppose you want to ask me about a little job I did for Mr Glover?'

Simon nodded. 'Before we get down to the nitty gritty, can I get you another beer?'

'Yeah, thanks. All of a sudden my mouth's gone very dry. And if you don't mind, can we go sit over there in the corner where it's a little more private?' Tiny asked rather sheepishly. 'If I'm going to have a chat with you blokes, I'd prefer if we didn't let the whole bloody world know.'

The table in the corner was circular with bar stools on which the three men now perched. The lighting in the Paddington Green's lounge was always subdued and a person, on entering from the sunshine outside, would have difficulty seeing anyone inside the lounge until their eyes adjusted to the dim conditions. These surreptitious conditions appealed to Tiny who was somewhat apprehensive that someone he knew might see him in furtive discussion with two cops.

'I suppose I'm really in the doghouse now,' Tiny said as he nervously played with a drink coaster. 'As they say, if you're up to your neck in shit, keep your mouth shut. And here I am talkin' to you blokes.'

Simon frowned and shook his head. 'Yeah, well that may be the case, but unless you tell us of your involvement with our waterlogged body, we can always provide Andrew Glover with some information, like where you're living at the moment. But to be honest, Tiny, I think you'd rather talk to us than Mr Glover, don't you? Now, I think we would all agree you really are in the poo, but at the moment we don't quite know how deep you've sunk. Trouble is, Tiny, we've heard you did a little job for our Mr Glover. Unfortunately, and by sheer bloody coincidence, it seems the timing of this little job just happened to be around the time we recovered a body from Rushcutters Bay.'

'Yeah, I know,' replied Tiny. 'When I found out you were looking for me, I knew what it was about. And when I heard Andrew Glover was also looking for me, I knew what he wanted me for, and I don't think it was to pay me a bonus.'

'Okay, Tiny,' said Simon, 'I'll get another round of drinks and then you can tell us the story, from the beginning.'

On Simon's return, Tiny leaned forward, his folded arms resting on the table, his head down. After a moment he looked up at Simon. 'From the beginning?'

'Yep,' replied Simon, 'From the beginning.'

'All right. I've known Andrew Glover for several years now, not that I would call him a friend. I can't remember how we met although I seem to think it was when I was clearing out some rubbish for an old bloke in Drummoyne. See, I have a four-wheel drive and a trailer. At the time, Mr Glover was looking over potential properties to purchase. He'd buy up old houses and wait until the council rezoned the area for high density housing. He'd then sell the property on to developers who were willing to pay anything to get what they wanted.

'Anyway, he started to give me some work removing rubbish and stuff. It wasn't regular, but he always paid in cash up front, which was handy as I'm usually unemployed. About a month ago he asked if I could do a special job that would need my boat. I've got a little tinny fitted with an outboard as I like to go fishing. Anyway, he said he was going to play a trick on his nephew who owns a boat over in Rushcutters Bay. He wanted me to attach a load of garbage to the anchor of this boat, which seemed a bit stupid, but as he was willing to pay heaps, I agreed.'

'Do you remember the name of this boat?' asked Noel.

'No, it had some strange name that I couldn't remember. Mr Glover told me it had something to do with the star sign Gemini. You know, we've all got our star sign and women love reading them in the paper or magazine. I can remember that name Gemini 'cause I'm a Gemini.'

'And could the name of this boat have been "Mithuna", Noel asked, his eyebrows raised in anticipation.

Tiny clicked his fingers. 'Yes, that's the name. Buggered if I could remember it. It's not an everyday sort of name, is it? Who's going to look up their stars in the paper and read Mithuna instead of Gemini? Anyway, he told me to meet him one night at a launching ramp over in Five Dock Bay, which I did. Seeing it was night time I rigged up some navigation lights on my boat as it's quite a way over to Rushcutters and it's illegal not to have them, the lights I mean. Before I launched the boat he took the garbage out of the boot of his car and loaded it into the boat, with a lot of difficulty, might I add. I asked if he wanted any help, but he got quite narky and said he could manage.'

'And you had no idea as to the nature of the garbage?' as Simon.

'No, not until I got to where I was going,' replied Tiny, nudging his schooner glass towards Simon who nudged it towards Noel who took the hint and did the honours.

'After the garbage was loaded, I left Mr Glover and putted off down the harbour to Rushcutters Bay where I started to look for this particular boat to hook up the garbage. Problem was, stuffed if I could remember the name of the stupid thing. Eventually I came across one called the "Gemini" so I thought that had to be close enough. It wasn't until I was in the process of attaching the garbage to the anchor that I had a strange feeling the garbage just might not be the type of garbage I thought it was, you know, the shape of things.'

'So, the garbage was wrapped up in something?' asked Simon.

'Yes, I think it must have been a bed sheet, or something like that.'

'You didn't take a peek at the garbage before you attached it to the anchor?' Simon asked hopefully.

'No, I didn't take a peek at the garbage before I attached it to the anchor,' mimicked Tiny mockingly. 'What do you think I am, some sort of nut who likes to take a peek at other people's garbage? Really, Chief Inspector, do you take a peek inside other people's wrapped up garbage before you drop yours in the garbage bin? Anyway, I didn't need to take a peek, as you put it. Though the sheet was secured with some rope, there was a small gap on one side. As I was putting the bundle on the anchor, a hand flopped out. Well, it didn't just flop out, there was an arm attached to it. As Mr Glover had already paid me, I didn't want to know anything about the so-called garbage so I just finished the job, heaved the anchor back over the side and took off. Mr Glover used to get rid of garbage from places he bought and I wasn't going to ask him who the owner of this garbage was. The whole job didn't take more than a few minutes once I had the right boat, or at least one close enough to being the right boat.'

Simon pursed his lips, gave a sigh and looked at Noel. Noel shrugged in reply, both detectives conveying a tacit acknowledgement that Tiny was definitely in the poo, but neither detective could give any indication as to just how far. 'So Tiny, at no time did Mr Glover give you any hint the garbage you were disposing of was, in fact, the body of a very dead person?' asked Simon before gulping down the last of his schooner.

'Crikey, no. Sure, I needed the money, but it's pretty hard to spend up big if you're locked up in Long Bay Gaol,' replied Tiny, appalled that Mr Glover had both misled and taken advantage of him regarding the nature of the garbage he had been asked to dispose of. 'Okay, maybe I should have gone to the police as soon as I found out it was a body in the bag, but it seemed a bit late by then. It's for sure the bloke in the bag wasn't going to get too upset if I went to the police or not.'

Simon shook his head in wonder. 'Tiny, Tiny, Tiny. By not going to the police straight away means you've committed a number of offences against the Crimes Act and probably a dozen other acts. The ones we're concerned with relate to the illegal disposal of a body, your knowledge that a homicide had been perpetrated, and the impeding of a police investigation, quite apart from your involvement in the murder.'

'Hey, hang on a bit. I had nothing to do with any murder. And how do you know the body in the bag didn't die of old age, or a suicide, or was run over by a truck. Mr Glover was just getting rid of someone's garbage,' responded Tiny, getting a bit agitated by Simon's innuendoes.

'Sorry Tiny', said Simon trying to placate the situation. 'But the garbage just happened to be Mr Glover's nephew and the nephew just happened to have the back of his head bashed in. Do you know the nephews of Glover at all?'

'No,' Tiny replied. 'I've never met them in my life. How many nephews are there?'

'Well, there were two, Bruce and Paul, until someone did the nasty on Paul and you dumped his body in the harbour.' replied Noel.

'Yeah, and I bet it was his uncle who did him in,' responded Tiny, his voice edged with a touch of anger. 'After all, it's a bloody big coincidence, Andrew Glover driving around with Paul Glover dead as a door nail in the boot of his car. Now you know why I don't really care if Andrew Glover does get hit by a truck. Come to think of it, that would be most convenient.'

'Now, Tiny, no need to be like that,' said Simon. 'Just because Andrew Glover had the very dead body of his nephew in the boot of his car, and having paid you a substantial amount of money to get rid of it, doesn't mean to say he's the murderer. I agree with you that it does seem a teeny bit of a coincidence and he does appear to be on pretty shaky ground. But, at the same time, there doesn't appear to be any motive. And why did he want you to put the body on Bruce Glover's anchor?'

'Humph,' snorted Tiny. 'As I said, Andrew Glover told me he wanted to play a joke on this Bruce Glover bloke, if he's the owner of the boat I should have attached the body to.'

'Yeah, some joke,' responded Noel as he got up and headed towards the bar for more beers.

Simon sighed and scratched his right ear, his left hand on his hip. 'So, to summarise, Tiny, this bloke Andrew Glover asked you to dispose of some garbage and for doing so he paid you a heap of money. You were supposed to attach the garbage to Bruce Glover's boat, the "Mithuna", but as you couldn't remember the name, you did the next best thing and attached to a boat called the "Gemini". It wasn't until you were in the process of baiting the hook, so to speak, that you became aware that the garbage was a dead body, later identified as Paul Glover, the nephew of Andrew Glover and brother of Bruce Glover. Since then, your conscience has got the better of you and you've gone into hiding from both the police and Andrew Glover. Right?'

'Sounds a bit iffy, doesn't it?' replied Tiny, an apprehensive look on his face. 'Are you going to arrest me now?'

'Tiny, right at the moment I wouldn't know what to arrest you for. Sure there's a few charges against the Crimes Act we could haul you in for, but I doubt that would help the situation at all. No, there's a lot more work to be done on this case. Provided we know where to find you, it's probably easier for all concerned to continue our investigation without charging you. As I said, I haven't a clue what we'd charge you with and it's for sure whatever it is isn't going to change the outcome of the case one iota. Here's my card,' Simon said as he withdrew a business card from his coat pocket. 'Just let us know if you change your address, or if you want to get in touch with either Noel or myself. And thanks, Tiny, you've been a great help.' With that, the two detectives left the Paddington Green Hotel.

CHAPTER 23

*B*ack at Day Street, Simon and Noel took the stairs to their office located on the third floor. There had been very little said between the two detectives as they drove back through the heavy city traffic of Oxford Street, both men choosing to reflect on the meeting with Tiny Timmins. Once settled, Noel lent forward, his arms folded, and looked at Simon with a confused look on his face.

'Boss, I have the funny feeling you're not going to crucify Tiny. From where I stand, I get the idea you'll do a Jacko on the bloke and let him off, even if he's as guilty as Jacko was when he tried to rob that pub in George Street. If you are thinking of letting him off, I hope you haven't already mentioned his name to Hayes.'

Simon rocked back on his dilapidated swivel office chair and clasped his hands behind his head. 'Okay Noel, just put yourself in Tiny's shoes for a moment. Here's a bloke who's never had more than a few dollars in his pocket. Sure, he owns a four-wheel drive, a trailer and a boat. The four-wheel drive is lucky to be registered as it's a heap of junk, as is the trailer. As for the boat, I think it's a disaster waiting to happen. He probably retrieved it from someone's garbage.

'Now along comes Andrew Glover who offers him a heap of money to do no more than play a trick on his nephew by dumping some garbage on his boat; a very simple request and nothing illegal about it, criminally at least. Unfortunately, Tiny isn't endowed with the brightest intellect and I've no doubt he never stopped to ask any questions; he just wanted the money. However, I consider Tiny to be one of the good guys who wouldn't hurt a fly, and certainly wouldn't be consciously involved in the disposal of a murder victim. When Tiny eventually found out it was a body he was dealing with, you can bet he would have had a fit. I think it's fortunate for him he ran into Jacko as I think they both came out of the same pod. After talking to Jacko at the Spinning Wheel, Jacko realised Tiny was in a lot of trouble. You can bet dollars to doughnuts Tiny didn't stop to think of the problems he had created for himself, not at that stage anyway.'

'Yes, I can see that and I now have a better perspective of your policing technique. While I totally agree with you, I can appreciate how you came into such conflict with Chief Inspector Rose, God rest his sole. He thought nothing of castigating anyone he could get his hands on, including Jacko who didn't have a clue as to what he was doing. I only hope Superintendent Hayes doesn't follow Rosie's philosophy. And what about the man himself, Superintendent Hayes I mean? Tiny's name is bound to come up sooner or later.'

'Yes, I know and I'm not looking forward to that. I've no doubt Tiny will testify on our behalf, as long as we handle him with kid gloves and we're able to keep him onside, that is. Just right now I have the idea we're putting the cart just a little bit in front of the horse as we still haven't a clue who'll be convicted, apart from possibly Andrew Glover. I'll go and see if Chief Superintendent Paxton can come up with any suggestions. He's aware of our aversion to nailing petty crims to the wall, not that I think Tiny could even be regarded as a petty crim, yet. People like Tiny and Jacko are handy friends to have and we certainly don't need them locked away.'

'So, apart from seeing Paxton, where do we go from here?' Noel asked as he crumpled a piece of paper into a ball and had another three point shot at the waste paper bin at the end of the office – and missed – again.

'I've been thinking about that,' replied Simon as he retrieved the ball of paper and completed the shot. 'I would like to have another chat with Bruce Glover, although I haven't worked out what questions I want to ask, or the anticipated answers. I can't see why Andrew Glover would want to do away with Paul unless it is a case of a sort of tontine. Problem is, Bruce doesn't appear to be ruffled by the fact that he could be next in line for a tap on the head.'

'You think there may be a conspiracy?' Noel asked, his interest aroused by the novel theory.

'Well, we haven't stood back and had a look at the overall picture, which is a failing on our part. We always had it in mind that Andrew Glover was the guilty bugger and all we had to do was to wait for the evidence and convict him. Unfortunately, that evidence hasn't been forthcoming in its q-squared format.'

Noel looked baffled. 'Pardon my ignorance, boss, but what's this "q-squared stuff?

Simon smiled. 'In this case it's evidence in its quantity, quality and quickness format.'

Noel scowled, rolled his eyes and shook his head, but made no comment. 'Okay, boss. Now, as I was saying, what's our next step?'

'I think we should have a chat to the other two beneficiaries, the two little old ladies.' Simon flicked through his notebook for a moment. 'Yes, here we are. Vicki Agnew and Debbie Grimes. They both live in Elizabeth Bay, which makes it handy. I'd also like you to have a talk to the solicitor who handled her affairs. Find out if there were any little quirks Joyce Glover may have included in her will. Oh yes, I nearly forgot. I received a snippet of info from Inspector Crawford over at drug squad. Nothing earth-shattering, but maybe worth remembering,' Simon said and passed a hastily scrawled note to Noel.

The lady who opened the door to the house located only two doors away from "The Grovel" was probably in her early fifties and, though possibly having accumulated a bit of additional weight with the passing of time, still presented a curvaceous figure most women, irrespective of age, would be proud of. Vicki Agnew was of medium height, dark short hair and wore a bright red lipstick that accentuated the broad smile she gave the two detectives. She was wearing a pair of faded blue denim jeans and a black jumper, together with a pair of bright pink slippers which, to Noel's initial impression, suggested Vicki had something of a broad sense of humour.

After the general introductions, Vicki Agnew said, 'Oh yes, gentlemen, do come in, please. Teddy, my husband, is at work at the moment but I'll be happy to answer any questions you have. I suppose it has something to do with the death of poor Paul?'

'Yes,' replied Simon as he wiped his feet on the doormat before entering the house which, on external structural appearances, resembled "The Grovel". The major difference between the two mansions was that this mansion, with its tended garden, stood bright and shiny with an air of homeliness and warm comfort. "The Grovel", in contrast, exuded all the charm of the city morgue. 'We were hoping you may be able to give us a bit of family background as we're finding the case a trifle baffling.'

'Oh, pleased to help. Just take a seat,' Vicki said and indicated to a comfortable and sunny living room. 'Coffee?' she asked as if she had already made up her mind the two gentlemen were going to have her coffee.

'White with one,' replied Simon.

'Black and none,' replied Noel.

Within a few minutes Vicki had returned with three mugs which she set down on the coffee table. 'Now gentlemen, how may I be of assistance?'

On returning to their car, Noel inserted the ignition key but didn't turn it. Instead he sat back and folded his arms, a look of consternation furrowing his face. 'Boss, I must be thick or something, but am I missing something here? Everything is pointing to Andrew Glover being guilty of bashing Paul's brains in and then hiring Tiny to dispose of the body. Yet from what Vicki tells us, and though Andrew might be a bit of a bugger, it sounds like he and his brother got on pretty well, despite the tiff they had. I had the impression she viewed Bruce's comments relating to Uncle Andy were a bit over the top and that she considered Andrew might not be nearly as bad as Bruce makes out.'

'Yes', replied Simon. 'It appears the alleged animosity started with the nephews as soon as Tom Glover threw in the towel. At least Vicki confirmed what Bruce said about Uncle Andrew trying to weasel his way into the family fortune. But then again, I s'pose she would have no reason not to believe anything either of the nephews, or Joyce Glover, may have told her. I suppose we should be more concerned with what went on in the family after Thomas's death and the wheeling and dealing that went on in anticipation of Joyce's demise, whenever that was going to happen. By the way, did you pick up on the comment she made about Paul's girl friend, or should I say ex girl friend, Cheryl something or rather?'

'Oh, you mean Cheryl Drake. Yes,' replied Noel, 'I did think it rather odd that she should mention her, if only to say she saw her entering Bruce's house. I suppose she had a very good reason to go and see him and I'm not trying to read too much into it. After all, she was by all accounts pretty close to the family, at least close to Paul. She would want to know what the funeral arrangements were, even if she and Paul did have a raging argument.'

'Yeah, well you can bet your booties she and Bruce don't get on too well, she's the wrong gender for his liking. But Vicki said she saw her running away from the house just a couple of minutes after arriving, and that was only a few days ago. I wonder what prompted Drake to do that.

'Anyway, let's get back to Day Street and see if anything else has turned up,' Simon said without any enthusiasm. 'I can't help thinking Superintendent Hayes will be lining me up for a bollocking in the not too distant future, unless we come up with something. I'd like you to have a look at the will that didn't will Andrew a nickel, just to see if it is as simple as it sounds. With so much money at stake you'd have thought there would be some clauses in it that didn't make sense, or needed a barrister to decipher. And for all our chasing around we've done, I still can't see a valid motive to do away with Paul Glover.'

Noel frowned. 'Pardon my ignorance, boss, but a person makes a will stating who will be beneficiaries and how much of the pie each will get. In Joyce Glovers case, it seems like she should have made both a will, and a won't, a sort of thing that specifically excludes greedy people from the will, if you get my drift.'

Simon sighed and shook his head.

CHAPTER 24

$\mathcal{T}$he back lawn of the bungalow of 24 West Bank Lane, Collaroy, was generally used as the venue for many informal discussions ranging from politics or, to be more precise, the denigration of politicians, to murder and bank robbery. Where it may be expected such topics would be addressed from a policing point of view, in reality it was quite the opposite with the actions of some, if not all of those sitting in a circle sipping wine or beer, either guilty of offences under the Crimes Act, or at least conspiring to conduct offences under the said Act. Simon, during the last thirty minutes, had explained to the group of expectant listeners the progress of the investigation and the details of the interviews conducted with Tiny Timmins and Vicki Agnew.

Graham Lee reached forward and took a handful of peanuts from the bowel located on a small white metal table with a hole in the centre. The hole was for the sun umbrella but now, though a cloudless Saturday afternoon, a cool southerly breeze negated any need for refuge from the sun. 'So, you've finally established that our Anchor Man, Paul Glover, wasn't supposed to be stowed-away on the "Gemini". I must say that is refreshing, but I would still like to know why he was where he was in the first place?'

'Fair question, but we do have an answer, at last. We even know who put it there, the body I mean,' replied Simon wrestling with the decision whether to open another can of beer. He tossed his empty can into the metal garbage bin with a clunk and reached for the Esky. 'It's a bit of a long story so I'll just give you the abridged version. We know the body on the end of your anchor belonged to Paul Glover. We also know that the family of the dead man made a bundle out of property development, that the brother of the dead man, Bruce, is as camp as a row of tents and the uncle of the dead man, Andrew Glover, is something of a weasel. The matriarch, when she snuffed it, left the family fortune to the two sons, Paul and Bruce, and Bruce went and bought himself a boat, the "Mithuna".

'This bloke, Tiny, is the bloke who attached the bundle to the anchor. Uncle Andrew sucked Tiny into thinking he was playing a practical joke on Bruce and that the bundle contained nothing but garbage. It wasn't until he was actually in the process of attaching the bundle to the anchor that a hand with an arm attached flopped out and he realised he was in deep trouble. Problem is, Tiny, who no doubt works on the belief money overcomes all evil, probably considered it too late to renege on the job anyway.'

'So it appears Uncle Andrew is the murderer,' said Georgie simplistically.

'Well, maybe, but not necessarily as appearances can be deceptive. There's a lot missing, like, where was Paul initially murdered and what was, and where is the murder weapon. Obviously Andrew Glover is involved but we need to come up with more than just a motive, so our work isn't quite over yet,' returned Simon.

Noel, having listened intently to Simon, couldn't constrain himself after being presented with such an opportunity. 'So, Simon, you just stated that we don't know where Paul was initially murdered. Does that mean after his initial murder he was removed to another location where he underwent a subsequent murder? To say he was initially murdered suggests he underwent subsequent murders, maybe even a few subsequent murders.'

Simon closed his eyes, and slowly shook his head. 'Touché, smarty-pants, point taken.'

Louisa looked intently at her half empty glass of wine. 'Pardon my stupidity, Simon, but isn't the murderer usually known to the victim and, in many cases, turns out to be a member of the family.'

'Yep. So?'

'Okay. That narrows the field down considerably I'd say,' responded Louisa as she contemplated whether her glass was half empty as opposed to half full and in need of a refill. 'Seeing Paul Stack has been eliminated from your enquiry, along with any unscrupulous criminal group trying to send Graham a message, all you have to do is establish the motive and you'll have the murderer.'

'Yeah, simple. What the bloody hell do you think we've been trying to do?' replied Simon good naturedly.

As the tete-a-tete between Louisa and Simon continued, Sue, Georgie and Judy, were quietly discussing the murder. Judy, having ensconced herself comfortably in the bungalow next door at 26 West Bank Lane, had established a harmonious relationship with the other two girls, and appeared to be developing more than a friendly acquaintanceship with Ron Lange. Both Georgie and Sue appeared to take some fiendish delight in the manner Judy had acquired the premises following the tragic and synchronized deaths of two people, both of whom probably held a greater legal right to the property.

That the deaths were considered to have been "synchronized" only came to public knowledge following the release from hospital of the Long Reef Golf Course green keeper, Mr Grey, when he let it be known that he believed the deaths of the two concerned couldn't have been choreographed better. Being witness to a person providing a hefty prod on the bum with a fishing rod to an unsuspecting victim, and the subsequent fatal flight of the victim over the cliff to the wave-swept rocks below, are not events often witnessed by anyone, let alone a golf course green keeper.

In addition to this particular macabre spectacle, Mr Grey, already somewhat mentally unhinged having witnessed a traumatic and gruesome murder, was fortunate enough to see the nudger, standing on the cliff top with fishing rod in hand, admiring the success of their handiwork, reduced to a pile of smoldering ashes having been struck down by a bolt of lightning. In retrospect, and notwithstanding the serious nature of the incident, Grey, now convalescing at home after his hospitalization for severe psychological shock, now appeared to have adopted a somewhat philosophical approach and could even see some humorous features of the whole event.

The women were, as usual, quite chatty and becoming chattier with each glass of Chardonnay. Without exception, the four girls firmly believed women's logical, but probably unorthodox, approach to an investigation into the modus operandi of some raving homicidal psychopath would, in most cases, be far more productive than the time wasting meticulous and assiduous approach of mere males. 'So at the moment they still have only one suspect with no apparent motive?' Sue asked, consciously refraining from seeking confirmation from Noel.

'That's right,' replied Georgie, as she worked the cork from another bottle of Chardonnay. After refilling Louisa's glass, she topped up the other three glasses and said, 'The whole thing sucks and something's not right. The bloke they suspect just happens to be the property developer, but it seems he's short on motive. Apparently the boys still have no other contenders identified as a potential homicidal maniac, so they're running around trying to find anyone who might have something to resemble a motive. And I'll tell you something else. The first person I'd have a talk to would be this woman, Cheryl Drake. I bet she's involved somewhere along the line.'

'Why her?' queried Noel who was trying to listen to two conversations at once.

'Well, what do you know about her?' replied Georgie, with a shrug of the shoulders.

'Nothing, I s'pose. But why should we?' responded Noel, at a total loss as to why, or how, Cheryl Drake could be involved in the murder and subsequent drowning of her boyfriend, or ex boyfriend.

'Noel, the one attribute both you and Simon lack, and will never have, is a woman's way of thinking,' replied Georgie. 'So, just take it from me, this Cheryl Drake is involved.' Both conversations came to an abrupt halt as the sound of the side gate banged shut. A couple of seconds later Ron Lange struggled around the side of the house with a six pack of beer in one hand and two bottles of Chardonnay in the other.

'Sorry I'm late; I got caught up with The Spit Bridge. Bloody thing holds up fifty zillion cars so one or two show-offs can drive their dinky little boats up the harbour. At least there are some people who drive sensible boats without the big pole sticking up in the middle and causing so much congestion,' said Ron and smiled broadly at Graham. 'Now, what have I missed?'

he said as he settled himself onto a director's chair and peeled the top of a beer.

'Well,' replied Simon, 'that depends on who you want to listen to. I think we're doing okay, the girls think we haven't a clue and Superintendent Hayes has this idea we're as useless as a sunroof on a submarine. I can't say we're actually rocketing along, but I don't think we're doing quite as bad as some people make out.'

'Yeah, well it seems Bruce Glover ain't jumpin' for joy at the moment. The word I have from the haunts around Darlinghurst is that he's dropped out of the scene. He's been up there a couple of times but apparently he's not the bright and bubbly Bruce since the death of his brother. Some say he's not the same Bruce since his brother died.'

'I can understand that,' said Noel. 'It's only to be expected, even if he has got a new boat to play around with.'

Graham washed another handful of peanuts down with his beer then shrugged. 'So, if I was all morose and sad, I'd spend a lot more time on "Gemini". Gossip down at the marina is that Bruce hasn't used the "Mithuna" since he bought it. Maybe he's lost interest with his new toy.'

Simon reached for a potato chip and appeared to study it with intense concentration deciding whether to eat it or not. 'Ah, what foods these morsels be,' he pronounced before devouring the chip.

Ron shook his head. 'You know, Simon, your Shakespeare hasn't improved one iota since I've known you.'

'So who cares,' he replied and washed the chip down with a beer. 'Still tastes good. Anyway, now we're all here, I want some ideas as to who killed Paul Glover and what our next step should be.'

Georgie frowned and shook her head. 'Not wishing to tell

you how to suck eggs, my sweet, but there are gaping holes in the investigation that need to be addressed.'

'Well, bugger me and cherche la femme. Okay Georgie, as I'm not wanting a domestic in front of all our friends, would you care to be a bit more explicit?'

'Okay. Judy's new to the scene so she can kick off with the first suggestion. Judy?'

'Just one second,' she replied as she drained the last of the Chardonnay from the bottle into her glass. 'Right. As the family made its fortune in real estate, it's probably all they know. The first thing I would do is have a look at the will to see if there are any specific clauses or covenants relating to Bruce's house, like, can he sell it or does he have to live in it for a prescribed time.'

'Yeah well, we were going to do that. I've already scheduled an appointment with the Public Trustee who was the executor of the estate,' interjected Noel on behalf of his boss.

'Sue, your turn,' said Georgie.

'Well, I'm with Georgie. Paul's girl friend knows something but I don't know what that something is. I'd make a point of speaking to her.'

'Oh great,' chided Simon. 'There goes my principle of never asking a question unless you have a pretty good idea of what the answer's going to be. And now, Louisa, can we hear your little pearl of wisdom?'

'Certainly. I would like to know what the real relationship between Andrew Glover and Bruce Glover is, apart from the uncle and nephew aspect. You already have some conflicting reports on this and, as Andrew and Paul Glover were involved in trying to develop "The Grovel", I think Andrew would be a trifle upset at Paul for having opted out of the scheme. When I say opted, he probably didn't have too much to say on the matter being dead and all. As this leaves only Bruce and the floozy whatsaname left, I for one would include both on my list of suspects; in fact I think it would be rather stupid not to include them on your list. However, there is one slight problem. Bruce had no motive, well none that we're aware of, for killing his brother.'

Ron pursed his lips, looked at Simon and raised his eyebrows. 'I'm sorry, Simon, but I think Louisa has something there. If you address the points the girls have made, I believe you'd be well on the way of solving the problem. I think the girls have come up with some questions that thoroughly deserve another beer, or two, at least.'

CHAPTER 25

'So, what did the Public Trustee have to say about poor Joyce's will?' queried Simon as soon as Noel had settled himself behind his desk.

'Nothing much,' replied Noel. 'They certainly weren't the font of knowledge I expected them to be. Apart from the monetary assets, which were equally divided, the house was left to the two sons who could do what they liked with it, provided there was mutual agreement. It seems to be common knowledge Paul was very keen to get rid of the place, and Bruce wants "The Grovel" to stay in the family for as long as there's a Glover left alive.'

'Well, that supports the idea both Paul, and Bruce to a lesser extent, had a motive for doing away with the other, and Andrew still has a motive for doing away with Bruce,' suggested Simon. 'But Bruce has always held all the aces. As long as Bruce remains recalcitrant, the status quo remains. We're no better off than what we were at the start of this debacle; Paul had a far greater motive for killing off Bruce, than Bruce had for knocking off Paul' replied Noel. 'But then it ain't Bruce who's dead – yet.'

'No, but then I can't imagine Bruce Glover killing anything, let alone anybody. As for a simple case of fratricide, you're putting the brothers in the same boat as King Claudius,' returned Simon with a touch of disdain in his voice. 'And don't forget, our prime suspect at the moment is still Andrew Glover, not some pansy in a pink shirt. I want to go back and have another chat with Bruce as there are a few things we need to talk about. In the meantime, find out who this girlfriend of Paul was and go have a chat with her. We may as well address all the suggestions the girls made. Right now I'm going to see Superintendent Hayes; I think it far better for me to see him before he wants to see me.'

'Okay, and who the hell is King Claudius?' inquired Noel as Simon headed for the door.

Simon turned and looked at Noel with a look of bemusement. 'And you dare to cast aspersions on my Shakespeare. Read Hamlet, you uneducated twit,' he replied as he left the office and made his way along the corridor. He stopped outside the Superintendent's office and knocked, with some trepidation, hoping the Superintendent was otherwise occupied. Unfortunately for Simon, he wasn't and a curt reply of 'Come' cordially invited Simon into the office.

'Ah, Simon. You must by psychic as I was about to give you a ring,' said Superintendent Hayes, sitting back behind his office desk, his dark eyes boring into Simon giving Simon the uncomfortable feeling he was about to be the recipient of a bollocking. 'I've just been speaking to Superintendent Ainsworth of the fraud squad. It seems they've become aware of our investigation into the death of Paul Glover and the possible involvement of an Andrew Glover. Can you confirm that piece of information?'

'No sir, unfortunately I can't. But by the same token, I can't see why the fraud squad would lie about it so I would assume their awareness of our investigation is correct. In fact, I'm not surprised they do know as a summary of all investigations currently in process is usually disseminated throughout the force. You never know, some other jurisdiction that has refrained from revealing their interest may have some relevant information that might be of interest to our case.'

Superintendent Hayes scowled and shook his head. 'Maybe I didn't make myself clear. What I don't need, Chief Inspector, is confirmation as to whether the fraud squad has heard of an investigation we are conducting or not; we know bloody well we're conducting an investigation. The whole bloody force knows we're doing an investigation, including the fraud squad. What I want is confirmation that Andrew Glover has come to notice in the course of the said investigation. Now, have I made myself clear enough?'

Simon smiled and nodded as the light clicked on. 'Aah yes, sir. Now I'm with you. The answer is yes, sir, he has, but only so far as he happens to be the uncle of the dead body, who we now refer to as the Anchor Man, who is, or was, Paul Glover. Why? What's the fraud squad's interest?'

'They're not saying too much but apparently he's been leaning on local government people regarding zoning. I don't know too much about who's responsible for what, but it's got something to do with housing density and rezoning. It appears all information relating to zoning and proposed rezoning is held in the strictest confidence, which I can understand. Insider trading on the stock market is bad enough, but if you had insider information relating to proposed rezoning, you could really make a bundle. An application to redevelop a property with his signature on the bottom has also been tendered to council which muddies the water somewhat.'

Simon shrugged and nodded. 'Yeah, we're aware of the application which happens to be the Glover residence. And you're right; to make money, you've got to get a little mud on your hands. I don't know if it was by illicit or fraudulent means, but the Glover family made their fortune in property development and I have the idea Andrew wants to make another fortune. I'm off to have a chat to his nephew, Bruce, later today. I'll ask him if he knows anything about his uncle's leanings, along with some questions the girls believe we should ask.'

'What girls?' asked Superintendent Hayes, his dark eyebrows meeting in the middle as he contorted his face in a menacing frown. 'Come to think of it, last time I asked that question I didn't get a reply. Now, who the bloody hell are these "girls" as you appear to place a great deal of significance on what they have to say; Miss bloody Marple and her mates?'

Cripes, reflected Simon as he gazed at the line of thick unbroken eyebrows. If you put a body on this bloke, he'd look like a Neanderthal. 'No, not quite,' returned Simon, suitably miffed. 'The girls just happen to consist of Noel's wife, my wife and Louisa Porter who is the partner of Graham Lee. There's a new girl, Judy, who's just joined us after the bloke she was living with was pushed over a cliff by a woman with a fishing rod. The woman managed to get herself zapped with a bolt of lightning as soon as she had done the deed, which made Manly CIB happy as it negated a protracted investigation. Anyway, we find it's rather refreshing to run some ideas passed the girls as they think differently to men and often view situations from a totally different perspective.'

Superintendent Hayes looked somewhat dumbfounded before his face broke into a knowing smile. 'Yeah, okay Webster. Have it your way. I don't really want to know who these women are and I couldn't give a stuff as to who you run your stupid ideas through. However, I don't mind telling you, I'm not a happy man as far as this investigation is going so I don't care if you run your bloody ideas through J Edgar Hoover. Just do us all a favour, pull your finger out and arrest someone. I don't care who it is, just make an arrest.'

~

'Oh, do come in, Chief Inspector, I was just finishing my nails. Do you like the colour?' Simon, taken aback by the question, cast his gaze hesitantly at Bruce. Despite the fact that it was the middle of the afternoon, bare footed Bruce was draped in a pale blue chenille dressing gown which, to Simon's estimation, clashed violently with the bright purple toe nails.

'Well, it is a change from the red or pink,' Simon ventured.

'Yes, that's what I thought too,' replied Bruce as he raised his foot for closer inspection of the paint job. 'Today's been such a lovely day after those awful thunderstorms. They were quite frightening, weren't they? Sorry, I do go on a bit. I suppose you have some more questions relating to Paul's death,' he said as he ushered Simon into the drawing room.

'Yes, just a bit of background stuff so we know how to approach our investigation,' replied Simon as he settled himself onto the drab drawing room settee. 'How well do you know Paul's girl friend, Cheryl Drake, and when was the last time you saw her?'

'Oh, I've spoken to her a couple of times. In fact, I don't know her that well, which isn't surprising as I do prefer the company of others. I suppose the last time I saw her was at least a month ago. Overall, I'd say I rarely saw her at all.'

'About the house, "The Grovel", I mean. The contents of your mother's will state the house was left to both you and Paul and you could do what you liked with it provided you both agreed.'

'Yes, that's right. Paul, along with Uncle Andrew, wanted to sell it, or knock it down, or do something with it. He never liked the place and didn't harbour any sentimental attachment, despite it having been in the Glover family for generations,' Bruce replied as he slipped on a pair of fluffy blue slippers.

'And you don't?'

'No. I quite like it here and it's in such a convenient location. Apart from that, I do have a sentimental attachment. After all, it was mummy's and she chose to live in it. She didn't need such a big house and could have sold it for a lot of money.'

'As far as you are aware, did Paul make any overtures to anyone regarding the sale of the house?'

'No, none that I know of. He was more interested in bulldozing the place and building something else on the land. I suppose he could have been interested in selling as I never knew what he was up to. Paul could be ever so devious when he wanted to be. I've no doubt the house will be sold eventually, but at the moment I don't need the money. And honestly, Chief Inspector, think of all the problems. If someone did buy it, they would probably knock it down and redevelop the site, if they got the necessary permission from some stuffy bureaucrat in the local council. I suppose it wouldn't be my problem, but with so many laws and council stuff to go through, that in itself would be enough for you to choose not to sell. Even allowing for all the rigmarole, to get a favourable decision to redevelop the site you'd probably still have to bribe some trumped up politician. And honestly, Chief Inspector, I find the whole idea of paying anybody for favourable decisions quite abhorrent'

'So Uncle Andrew is not the least bit interested in selling?' Simon asked.

'Well, Chief Inspector, apart from the plan he and Paul concocted to redevelop the place, I couldn't care less if he is or he isn't. With the death of Paul, the house is mine and I can choose what happens to it. So there.'

'I'm sorry, but there's no need to get all petulant about it, Bruce. But let's face it, Andrew is in the property game and he'd like to redevelop the place. Sure, it would take a lot of work, what with rezoning and council approvals, but the location would be a developer's dream with millions to be made.'

'Don't care,' pouted Bruce. 'I live here and here I'll stay.'

'Yeah, well that's terrific. But what if it turns out Andrew did murder Paul? As I've told you before, if you happen to get your brains bashed in, that would leave Andrew as the sole surviving member of the Glover family. If that were to happen, he'd have a legal claim on the house irrespective of anything you put in your will. And don't forget, you have already told us you suspect Andrew of an involvement in your brother's death.'

'Well, Chief Inspector, Andrew can do what he likes; I really couldn't give a damn.'

CHAPTER 26

*S*imon turned to the next page of the Telegraph having read of the humiliating defeat of his beloved Manly Warringah rugby league team to the Parramatta Eels; oh, the ignominy of it all. Generally, Simon's daily odyssey to the city was accompanied with Noel who would drive from Mona Vale to Collaroy. There, Noel would either pick up Simon, or Simon would drive them both to work in his car, leaving Noel's car at Collaroy. Today was one of those rare days when Simon caught the bus to the city and from Wynyard, where the bus terminated, took the underground train to Town Hall. From there it was a short walk to the coffee shop where he would take half an hour over a cappuccino and become horribly depressed while reading the daily newspaper.

'Mind if I take a seat?' came a man's voice that was a welcome interruption to Simon's gloomy reading. Simon looked up but failed to recognize the owner of the voice, which was immaterial as the voice sat down anyway. Having failed to identify the owner of the voice, he couldn't help but notice that whoever the owner was, he was scruffy, unshaven and displayed a head of thick, long matted black hair that extended over the collar of his coat. The scruffy face looked no better. Simon couldn't suppress the thought that whenever this bloke shaved again, he should stand a lot closer to the razor. The only physical attribute the voice could proclaim to possess was that his clothing perfectly suited the overall appearance; scruffy. Simon frowned. 'There's something vaguely familiar about you, but I'm sorry, you have me at a disadvantage.'

'Thank God for that. If I can fool you, I must be doin' something right. But I'm not here just to see if you can recognize me, or sponge a cup of coffee, though I'll have a flat black now you're asking,' which Simon hadn't.

Without thinking, Simon nodded to Sam who immediately approached the table. 'Sam, another cappuccino and a flat black for my friend here.' Sam regarded Simon with a jaundiced eye for a moment before she raised her eyebrows and pursed her lips in a flagrant expression of doubt as to the credibility of the "friend".

The voice settled itself into the window seat, ran its fingers through its hair and gave a sigh. 'You know, the last couple of years haven't been easy, but I suppose I've only got myself to blame for that.'

'Holy bloody hell, it's Fisher!' blurted Simon in total surprise and without any regard or respect for rank.

'For Christ sake, keep it down. I'm not Fisher, I'm Foster, Nigel Foster. Fisher no longer exists.' Fisher, or Foster, had been Detective Superintendent Nigel Fisher of Day Street until Chief Superintendent Paxton had given him a choice; go undercover or do a stint in Long Bay Gaol. The limited alternatives presented were as a direct consequence of certain misdemeanours perpetrated by the Superintendent, including the fraudulent use of his position to further both his pecuniary and carnal interests. 'I hear you're in the middle of an investigation of some sort, and as a detective chief inspector?' Foster said, more of a statement than a question as Sam delivered the two coffees.

'Yeah, Paxton promoted me into Rosey's position after he dropped dead. Not the way one likes to get promoted, but I s'pose you take what you can get. And as for the investigation, you don't have to be Einstein to have worked that out. Every man and his dog knows we're looking into the murder of Paul Glover who was fished out of the harbour by your mate, Graham Lee,' replied Simon knowing full well the amity between Lee and Fisher, or Foster.

'Yeah, well, there's something you mightn't know and I would suggest you keep it quiet for a while,' said Foster as he heaped a teaspoon of sugar into his coffee. 'You see, the drug squad has identified a person who has rocketed to the status of a person of interest by the name of Bruce Glover, brother of the said deceased Paul Glover, I believe.'

'You don't mean that little pansy who likes painting his toenails pink and is as gay as a...?'

'Yes, that's the bloke all right,' replied Foster, cutting Simon short. 'You see, this Bruce Glover lives in some great mansion over in Elizabeth Bay.'

'Yes, I know. We've been over to see him a couple of times, and you're right, it is a bloody great mansion, though I've only seen the lounge room, or the living room or whatever they call it.'

'So, even though you've been out to the house, I take it you haven't been shown around the mansion yet?'

'No, we've had no need. Look, how about you start from the beginning and fill me in on what I don't know?'

'Good idea, but it's at least a two-cup story,' replied Foster as he heaved a sigh and, again, ran his fingers through his long scruffy hair, a mannerism Simon recognized as a peculiarity to

Foster that had been absent in Fisher. Simon got the message and nodded to Sam with two fingers raised in the victory salute; the two coffees arrived shortly afterwards.

Simon listened intently with mounting doubt and scepticism to the story Foster had to relate unfolded. It wasn't until after Foster appeared to have finished his tale did Simon recognize that some of what Foster had to say did fill in some missing pieces to the jigsaw. 'And there you have it,' concluded Foster. 'As you may expect, Bruce is very popular around the Darlinghurst district and is known for handing out freebies, little gift wrapped packages,' Foster added almost as an afterthought.

'Yeah, I'll bet he's popular,' commented Simon as he savoured the spooned sugary top off his cappuccino.

'As I said, I just happened by the details while working on the bigger picture. A lot of stuff is coming in by ship from Asia. The dealers know when a ship is due so they hop in their boats and go pick up a bundle that's been thrown overboard before the ship enters The Heads.'

'Well, bugger me,' was all the response Simon could muster. 'And are you sure Bruce Glover isn't into this heavy stuff? He does own a boat, you know.'

'No, at least we don't think he is, though stranger things have happened and Bruce Glover is strange, if you get my drift.' Simon couldn't help but detect a hint of ambivalence in his ex boss's demeanour. He looked at Foster for a moment and frowned. 'Pardon me, sir, but you don't seem overly excited about Glover and his illicit exploits. Is that because you're not directly involved, or have you lost your mojo, or whatever?'

'To tell the truth, Simon, I would give anything to be able to stop playing this game and get back to being Superintendent Fisher down at Day Street. Paxton knew he had me by the short and curlies when he offered me the alternatives. He knew full well I was aware of the situation and would end up dead in Long Bay, so really there wasn't a choice at all. Sure, it was exciting for a while, but it's a game of charades where one mistake could get you killed. Obviously this is having an effect on Agnes. Fortunately she accepts she married a copper and has to take the good with the bad.'

'Is there a timeframe set on your stint in purgatory or do you go on working undercover until someone blows you away?' Simon asked.

Foster tweaked the corner of his mouth and rolled his eyes. 'Gee, thanks Simon. You know, you do have a way with words and that's one subject I'll try to ignore for a while. I just thought I'd drop in and have a chat and let you know about Bruce Glover, not to discuss my career prospects that you obviously seem to think are pretty bleak.'

'Well, I'm grateful for the information. I must say I'm a little surprised, although there are aspects that answer some unanswered questions,' said Simon appreciatively. 'If I ever get the chance, I'll let Paxton know how contrite you are for your little indiscretions and that you would really like to get back to Day Street.'

CHAPTER 27

'So how did you get on with Paul's girlfriend, Cheryl?' asked Simon, his elbows resting on the arm rests, hands clasped together on his stomach while he swiveled the chair slowly from side to side.

'Not bad,' replied Noel as he debated whether to have a shot at another three pointer. 'She works for the Shire Council and sounds like a nice girl. I only had the chance to speak to her on the phone for a moment, but she said she would be glad to meet us sometime today. She's works over in one of the council buildings in Pitt Street but every second Tuesday she works at the Town Hall. Luckily for us that just happens to be today so she suggested a cup of coffee in the Queen Victoria Building. I made an executive decision and said "yes".' Noel decided against another shot; his average running around twenty percent which was bad enough.

'No, that seems fine. I'd rather have a chat on mutual ground, at this stage anyway,' replied Simon. 'I'd really like to know what upset her so much that she fled from Bruce's house, if what Vicki says is true. Oh yes, we received a message from the coroner. It seems they're just about set to release Paul's body for burial, at long last.'

'Well, it's about time, though I had this notion they would have him cremated and his ashes sprinkled in the harbour, seeing he had such an affinity with it, that is. I presume Bruce is making all the arrangements?'

Simon shrugged and pursed his lips. 'I suppose so though I didn't think to ask. I shouldn't think Andrew would want to. And what time did you say we were having coffee with Cheryl whoever?'

'I didn't, but it's at eleven, and her name's Drake. I said we'd meet her at the Druitt and George Street entrance to the QVB, opposite the Town Hall. She'll be wearing a grey suit with a pink carnation in the lapel and a dark grey trilby pulled down low over the eyes.'

'Oh yeah. And the man with the poisoned umbrella tip will accidently stab her in the leg so she won't be able to reveal the identity of the killer,' replied Simon cynically. 'Don't forget, I saw that movie too. Anyway, we'd better get going. By the time we stroll up to George Street it will be close to eleven.'

Cheryl Drake, impeccably dressed in a dark grey suit and high heel shoes, could easily have been mistaken for a business executive of a private company rather than a public servant. In fact, it was she who readily identified the two policemen as they crossed the busy intersection of George and Druitt, notwithstanding that both men were dressed in mufti.

Noel spied the tall, good looking brunette standing by the entrance of the Queen Victoria Building as she overtly regarded the two men with a look of recognition. 'Excuse me, Cheryl Drake?' Noel asked in anticipation as he approached.

'Yes. You must be Detective Sergeant Elliott.'

'That's right, and this is my boss, Detective Chief Inspector Webster.'

Simon nodded and extended his hand. 'Glad to meet you Mrs Drake. How about we get out of the way of all these people and go have a coffee somewhere. There's a quiet coffee shop down the other end of the building, if that's okay with you?'

'Yes, fine. And it's Ms Drake. I expected you to get in touch with me, though I did think it might have been a bit sooner.'

'Yes, well, we did try to leave it for as long as possible as we appreciate the events must have been very upsetting for you,' replied Simon. 'But let's get over and have that brew before we discuss the matter.'

Once seated, it was Simon who initiated discussion. 'Okay Ms Drake, let's not beat around the bush pretending we don't know anything. We have a good idea of what's going on and who killed your boyfriend, but we'd like to hear your side of the story.' Noel, having ordered one flat black and two cappuccinos, was more than surprised to hear Simon's opening gambit. To be confrontational was not like Simon, and to say they were aware of what's going on was, to Noel's knowledge at least, stretching the truth considerably.

Before Cheryl Drake could reply, the waitress arrived with the coffees, which was probably good timing as it gave Ms Drake a couple of seconds to recover her thoughts. If she had expected to be shown any degree of sympathy in light of her tragic bereavement, Cheryl Drake was to be sadly disappointed. Even before having time to drink her coffee, an irate detective chief inspector had virtually accused her of the willful murder of her adoring, thoughtful and ever-loving boyfriend, Paul Glover. 'Well, I'm terribly sorry to disappoint you, Chief Inspector, but I had nothing to do with Paul's murder. However, the way things are, if you stick around for much longer, you'll probably have another murder to investigate.'

'Oh yeah. And whose murder is that likely to be?' question Simon, retaining the bad tempered image.

'Mine,' Cheryl calmly replied as she slowly tipped the sugar from a spoon into her coffee.

'Why you?' asked Noel before Simon could say anything. 'Why you, what for, and who's going to do the killing?'

'Look, I'd better start at the beginning if you can get your boss to relax for a moment,' Cheryl said to Noel. 'He's having a bad day, isn't he?'

Noel smiled and nodded. 'He's not usually like this. Generally he's as meek as a kitten but...'

'Okay, I apologise Ms Drake,' Simon acknowledged with a touch of contrition. 'Forgive my brashness, and please, call me Simon, and this is Noel. In view of the circumstances, it might be an idea to try and keep everything as amicable as possible. It's just that I hate asking questions of anyone when I haven't a fair idea of what the answers are going to be, or should be. In your case, it was all bluff as I haven't a clue what questions I need to ask so I can't anticipate the answers, if you can understand that.'

Cheryl looked at Noel and slowly shook her head in sympathy. 'As I said, I'll start at the beginning with the whole episode revolving around the idea of redeveloping "The Grovel". I suppose it started a lot earlier than that when Paul made a call at the council offices about six months ago. That's where we met; he chatted me up, made an impression, and we became an item. The current debacle started about a month ago, one Saturday night, in fact. You see, I had this weird idea Paul and I had a future together. We were living our separate lives, me in my flat at Bondi and he at Potts Point. Obviously there were times when we shacked up together, but there were also times when we might not see each other for a week or so. Under the circumstances, it was not unusual if I didn't hear from him for a while.

'Anyway, I called at his flat on this particular night but he wasn't there so I decided to try "The Grovel" thinking he might have gone over to see his brother, Bruce. As it happened, he was there, as was Uncle Andrew. It seemed like I had interrupted the three in a somewhat heated discussion, the topic being the proposed redevelopment of the place. Paul asked me how I thought the application would be viewed by council. I told him that once it was received, my role was solely to check that there was no impediment to its progressing along the bureaucratic chain, you know, heritage listed, National Trust, The Historical Society, and stuff like that. Though he had all but ordered me to ensure a favourable decision, I told him it had nothing to do with me.

'Well, that's when all hell broke loose and I found the relationship had been a complete sham; he'd been using me as he thought I had some influence over the council decision, which of course, I don't. I could have killed the bugger as I had this stupid idea everything was hunky-dory between us. He'd previously told me he was in the process of buying a home unit for the two of us over on the north side, somewhere around Mosman, and that the redevelopment scheme would pay for both the unit and a honeymoon to Europe. What a load of crap that was, and I believed the rotten bugger. How bloody stupid was I?'

'And did you?' asked Noel in a somewhat abstract manner.

'Do what?' replied Cheryl, a little confused by the question.

'Kill him, of course.'

Cheryl scowled then looked at Simon with a look of derision. 'Good God, and here I was thinking he was a bright young sergeant. Chief Inspector, I can tell you, I've read a lot of murder mysteries and watched a lot of crime movies and that has to be the dumbest bloody question a policeman can ask. What on God's earth do you expect me to say; yes I killed the turkey with a cricket bat then fed him to the sharks. When I say I could have killed the bugger, I mean that figuratively, though I suppose if I had gun in my hand at the time, I would have blown the little weasel's brains out.

'After Paul's little revelation, any idea of a social evening I may have had was totally demolished. As the situation had degenerated into a slinging match, I stormed off in a huff leaving the three of them to get on with whatever they wanted to get on with. No, Sergeant, I didn't kill him,' Cheryl said shaking her head, with almost a smile on her face. 'Mind you, he deserved whatever he got, the cretin.'

Noel shifted uncomfortably on his chair; his embarrassment evident. 'And how is it that you believe you're a candidate to be murdered?'

Before answering, Cheryl finished her coffee, and nudged the cup and saucer away in a gesture of finality. 'I had gone over to see Bruce about the funeral arrangements following Paul's death.'

Noel, despite his floundering credibility, couldn't restrain himself. 'Cheryl, if you had gone over to see Bruce about the funeral arrangements before Paul's death, our perception of your involvement in this matter may have been quite different.'

'God, Noel, just shut up and let the girl get on with it,' came the not unexpected rebuke from Simon.

'Thanks, Chief Inspector,' said Cheryl. 'When I got to "The Grovel", I was about to ring the doorbell when I overheard voices from inside that sounded very much like an argument going on. Naturally, I stopped to listen, which one does when you hear an argument taking place. I wasn't sure who the two conducting the conversation were, but naturally I thought it had to be Bruce and that obnoxious uncle, Andrew. It was when I heard someone say that she'll have to be dead by the time of the funeral, I realised I may not be welcome in the place so I made a quick exit and took off down the street. You see, as I'm the only "she" around the family, I didn't stick around to confirm which "she" they were talking about. Whoever the "she" is, and I have this horrible feeling it's me, the conversation didn't bode well for the "she's" longevity.'

Simon looked at Noel then turned to Cheryl and said, 'Could that have been the day Vicki Agnew spied you running off down the street?'

'Probably. Look, on the last two trips to "The Grovel" I find, on the first trip, that the boyfriend is a contemptible swine using me for nothing more than a means to an end. On the second trip I find the family wants me dead. Given the same situation, I think Vicki Agnew would have spied you running off down the street if you thought they had been talking about you. For me, the safest thing to happen would be for the entire Glover family to be belted on the head and fed to the sharks. Seeing Paul was the first member of the family to get the chop, and hopefully not the last, I want to make sure he's well and truly dead and buried, the deeper the better.'

Simon nodded, appreciating Cheryl's obvious antipathy towards the whole Glover family. Although there were now only two members of it remaining, he viewed the desire for the extermination of the entire clan a teensy bit drastic. 'Of course, it's only natural you should harbour such extreme sentiments, especially once the true nature of your relationship with Paul became known. Unfortunately for you, that in itself presented both yourself and Paul with a motive for doing away with each other, and it wasn't you fished out of the harbour. But if what you say is the truth and you didn't kill Paul, there must be a reason as to why Bruce and Andrew want to get rid of you, not that I can see any motive?'

'No, neither can I. And that's one of the things I can't figure out. I thought Bruce was a really nice guy. Okay, so he's gay. But he never advertised the fact overtly and really worked hard on maintaining a low profile. Sure, he frequents the haunts up around Darlinghurst, but that's where a lot of friends hang out. When I overheard Bruce and Andrew talking about getting rid of "her", I was totally mortified as I always thought Bruce and I were good mates. As far as plutonic relationships go, I believed we got on really well and I felt really comfortable in Bruce's company. Obviously I'm a very poor judge of character.'

'And when did you learn of Paul's death?' Simon asked.

'I'm not sure exactly, but it was Uncle Andrew who rang and told me his body had been recovered from the harbour.'

'Can you recall if the phone call was before or after those huge thunderstorms we had?' Noel asked.

'Before,' replied Cheryl with certainty. 'I've had a leaky ceiling since, so I remember the storms.'

'Noel, more coffee and you better order some sandwiches. This could take some time.'

*T*hat afternoon the whiteboard, so long a piece of useless office equipment, received a good cleaning followed by a torrid work-out with both Simon and Noel contributing a lot of scribble, arrows, names and places. In fact, after about an hour of activity, Simon stood back to admire the progress and assess the situation. He couldn't help suppress a cynical smile as he recalled the blot on a politician's reputation when it was discovered the allocation of Government funds had been based solely on the extensive use of a whiteboard. 'I can't think of anything else as we seem to have covered all the bases. You see anything we've missed?'

'Now that sounds like the sort of question a bank teller I once knew would ask,' replied Noel. 'If I could see anything we've missed, we wouldn't have missed it as it would be there for me to see. Now, maybe if you said something like "is there anything you can't see that we should be able to see," it would be a different matter.'

'Oh, shut up for Christ sake or you'll be a constable plodding the beat,' responded Simon, good naturedly.

'In that case, the answer is no, I think it's pretty clear, despite the mess. I hope to hell you're right as Superintendent Hayes will be a little more than upset if you're wrong,' said Noel with a hint of caution.

'What do you mean, "you hope I'm right"? This is supposed to be a team effort. If I sink, you sink, Sergeant, and that's an order.'

'Okay boss, keep your knickers on,' replied Noel, fully appreciative of the fact that he and Simon had always worked as a team and would continue to do so with their somewhat unconventional method of investigation. 'Do you propose to interview Andrew before the circus begins?'

'No. I figure we'll have him brought in without any preliminaries. I think he'll be a bit put out when he meets some of the other guests,' replied Simon as he looked at the whiteboard and scratched his earlobe. 'Let's sit down and make a list so we can get the invitations printed up, not that I expect too many acceptances.'

Noel suddenly looked worried. 'I take it you're not really going to send out invitations, are you?'

'Of course not, you idiot. I just want to make sure we have all the right people. It will be difficult enough to get anyone, let alone everyone we want where we want at the time we want.'

'And where do we want them all to be at the same time,' Noel asked as he became a trifle skeptical of the planning arrangements Simon was undertaking.

Simon smiled, anticipating the question. 'Yes, I thought about that, but as "The Grovel" appears to be at the centre of this crime, I thought it appropriate we hold the circus there. That reminds me, I must ask Bruce if he'll be happy to host the party.'

'You plan to invite Superintendent Hayes?' Noel asked, not sure if he should have asked the question.

'And why not? As they say, in for a penny, in for a pound. If I'm right he'll love us, and if I'm wrong...Well, we won't think about that because we're right, at least I hope we're right.'

'And what about Ron?'

'No, not Ron,' Simon replied with a shake of the head. 'If anyone at this little meeting finally gets to do a stint in Long Bay, the last thing we'd want is for them to identify Ron as a police informer.'

'Cripes, I didn't think of that. Of course, our Ms Drake will be there?'

'Definitely,' said Simon, 'Or at least I hope so. She's a major player whether she knows it or not.'

'Yeah, well I think it was a bloody good thing you filled her in on your ideas,' remarked Noel. 'I still don't know if she's just naïve or does she really know what she's got herself into?'

Simon shrugged and drew a circle around her name on the whiteboard. 'I think we'll just have to wait and see what happens. I'd be very surprised if she was involved in the murder of her boyfriend, but what do I know about a woman's logic and how they think? After she found out Paul was just using her, she had motive to kill him. But then Andrew rings her up and tells her Paul's already dead. I wonder how she felt then; either mortified or deliriously happy, I'd say.'

Noel rested his chin on the palm of his hand, his elbow resting on the table. 'And when is all this going to take place?'

'I'll let you know, but at the moment I haven't a clue. Before it does, we'll have a chat about the actual get together. If it turns out as hoped, the investigation into the death of our Anchor Man will be wrapped up.'

CHAPTER 29

$\mathcal{I}$f Simon had found "The Grovel" disconcerting in broad daylight, by eight thirty at night it looked dangerously forbidding, the meager internal lighting doing nothing to temper the grim atmosphere that cloaked the mansion. The scene within the drawing room could have been taken from the climax of an Agatha Christie movie with Hercule Poirot puffing away on a Small Panetela ready to reveal the identity of the murderer; but then again, Detective Chief Inspector Simon Webster didn't smoke.

On the drabby settee sat a very reluctant Tiny Timmins, whose attendance at the party could only be attributed to the persistent cajoling of Jacko and Simon. Next to him sat two other men, Superintendent Michael Hayes, dressed in a dark grey suit, and a tall thin gentleman, dressed in a pair of blue jeans, a brown sports coat over a white shirt and light blue tie that hung loosely around his collar. Simon's first impression of Andrew Glover was not overwhelming, he taking an immediate dislike to the man. According to Simon, Glover looked like a sleaze, so therefore was a sleaze. The fact that Glover had taken full advantage of Tiny Timmins, a man Simon regarded as salt of the earth, despite his apparent lack of insight into the malevolent working of the criminal mind, only added to Simon's intense hostility towards Andrew Glover.

Sitting on one of the lounge chairs was Bruce Glover wearing a pair of faded blue jeans and a gold smoking jacked wrapped around him. Stuffed into the top of the jacket was a dark blue cravat, neatly tied around his neck making Bruce look like the epitome of the Hollywood movie producer. Simon, wearing mufti consisting of dark brown slacks and a light brown sports jacket, stood warming himself in front of the unlit open fireplace, his arms folded. Having disposed of the tedious job of introductions, he decided it was time to get down to the nuts and bolts of the evening's little get together, notwithstanding the fact that two of the guests were yet to arrive.

'Right, gentlemen, though we are short a couple of guests, I expect them at any moment so we may as well get started. I don't propose to bore you with the details of events that we are all too well aware of. Tonight we will enter into the realm of the "who did what", not the events of what the who did because, as I said, we all know what the who did, we just have to reveal who the who is.

'As there are three Glovers involved in this case, and to help avoid any misunderstanding as to who the who I am referring to really is, I shall refer to christian names. To me the case presents two major issues and I propose to deal with these separately. The first is the murder of a member of the Glover family and the second is the disposal of the body. Okay, so let's look at the murder of Paul Glover, and there's no doubt it was a case of murder.

'From the outset we had the three Glover family members, Bruce, Paul and Andrew all vying for the honour of winning the coveted prize of doing away with the other two before they themselves were done away with. Of course, whether Paul wanted to do away with the other two members of the family is open to speculation as he was, surprisingly, unavailable for questioning. Unfortunately it was Paul who drew the short straw so he just happened to be the first, and hopefully the last, cab off the rank.'

'What do you mean, first cab off the rank? And what's this idea of everyone trying to knock each other off? The whole idea is absurd. And to liken the murder of my brother to taking a trip in a taxi is insulting. What do you think we're doing, waiting around for a Bondi bus driven by the Grim bloody Reaper, or something?' Bruce riled, a little disconcerted at the possibility there may be others, including himself, in danger of a gruesome death.

'No, not at all,' came Simon's quick reply, fully appreciating Bruce's alarm at the prospect of finding himself the second Glover to pollute the bottom of the harbour. 'But let's face it, Bruce, both you and Paul inherited a lot of money from your mummy while poor old Andrew here, despite his expectations, didn't get a dime. Well, okay, he reaped a couple of dollars, which was worse than nothing. That could have made Andrew one very annoyed uncle.'

'Well, I'm not, not now anyway. Sure, I may have been a little peeved at first, but I soon got over that,' responded Andrew indignantly. 'I'm doing quite well financially at the moment, thank you very much.'

Simon nodded in acceptance of the rebuttal. 'Well, it's not like greed might be your only motive. The way I see it, you had at least three motives for doing away with Paul, and you have at least three motives for doing away with Bruce. I'll admit that two of your motives are the same for both Paul and Bruce, the first originating from when you left the real estate company following a dispute with your brother, Thomas. That dispute, despite it having happened years ago, left nothing but bad blood within the family. The second motive, the handling of Joyce Glover's will, didn't do anything to help patch up reasons for the first motive. In fact, it gave you even more reason to reap your vengeance on the family.

'The third motive for doing away with Paul stems the fact that you and Paul wanted to develop "The Grovel" property. If you were to become the sole remaining Glover left alive, you would get to inherit the entire Glover family fortune, together with all the profits from your redevelopment scheme. Of course, this little scenario calls for the elimination of Bruce. So there you have it; three pretty good motives for killing off Paul, and Bruce

'Holy hell, where'd you dream us this little brain wave?' came Andrew's response from the drabby settee. 'Sure, what I expected and what I got from the will may have left a lot to be desired, but Paul and I were working on a pretty lucrative scheme anyway. There's no way I wanted to see Paul dead. And as for Bruce here, why would I want him dead?'

'Ah yes, this little lucrative scheme. For those who aren't aware, under terms of their mother's will, both Paul and Bruce had to agree to sell, or do whatever, with "The Grovel". Paul wanted to have the place demolished and the site redeveloped with the help of Andrew, after they had come to an agreement to split the profits. On the other hand, Bruce wants the place left as it is. By just selling the place, that is if Bruce ever decided to change his mind, Bruce and Paul would probably pocket around a million dollars each and Andrew wouldn't get a nickel, again. By redeveloping the place, the three Glovers stood to rake in around two million each, but as Bruce wouldn't agree, Andrew and Paul had to think of an alternative. To comply with council regulations, they needed Bruce's signature on the development application as his name appears on the title deed to the property,' Simon explained, indirectly requesting some sort of clarification from Andrew.

Andrew sneered and shook his head. 'Hell, that was easy to get around. Paul just signed Bruce's signature. No-one ever checks that sort of stuff, not public servants anyway.'

Simon cast a glance at Bruce who seemed totally unruffled by the revelation. 'Bruce, this doesn't upset you at all?'

'Of course it does,' Bruce responded as if the question was puerile. 'But apart from going to the police and having both my uncle and brother arrested for forgery, there's not much I can do about it, especially as far as Paul is concerned anyway as he's dead.'

'Yes, we're aware of that little fact, but it's odd, isn't it? If anyone was in line to be murdered, I would have thought it would have been you, Bruce, seeing you didn't want anything to do with the redevelopment.' Simon ceased his pacing in front of the fireplace, folded his arms and looked at the ceiling, a look of deep concentration on his face. 'Look, I'm sorry, but I think I've lost the plot here as there are some things I just don't understand. Surely, with the forged application at council, Paul would be the last person you'd expect to find dead.

'The thing is, once having decided it was Paul who was dead, I started thinking about motives. The first thing to come to mind was the idea Andrew might take his obvious malevolent and spiteful revenge on the Glover family by murdering both his nephews. But that would mean doing away with you as well, Bruce, and you ain't dead, yet.

'As I've said, if anyone was to be murdered, I thought it would have been you, Bruce, what with your intransigence to Paul and Andrew's redevelopment scheme. Greed is a good motive for murder and you stood in the way of Andrew and Paul making a lot of money.'

Bruce looked at Andrew, smiled and shook his head. 'Good grief, Paul was my brother, for heaven's sake. No, he mightn't have liked my decision, but he would never have gone so far as to kill me. Neither would Andrew, even if he was involved in a bit of forgery with Paul. After all, we were all family and could have work around any problems we may have had. There was no need for anyone to kill Paul.'

Simon shrugged his shoulders, took a deep breath and put his hands in his trouser pockets. 'Okay, Bruce, but as I said, greed has proved to be a very strong motive for murder in the past. Anyway, the thing here is Andrew's a greedy bugger and he needed you to either change your mind or be moved on, so to speak, so he and Paul could continue to work their scheme. Andrew needed Paul alive, at least until the redevelopment was going ahead, not you. To my way of thinking, and as you're not dead, that lets Andrew off the hook for killing Paul, unless of course, you do end up dead.'

'Now, listen here, Chief Inspector Webster,' suddenly interjected Superintendent Hayes, a look of annoyance on his face. 'We've come along to this little get together for your disclosures and revelations that I hoped would put an end to the case. So far the only bit of useful information you've given us is the name of the person who isn't the murdering reprobate.'

Simon raised a hand in a gesture of compliance. 'Yes, I know that, sir, but I believe in so doing I will paint a more complete picture of events thus eliminating the need for a lot of stupid bloody questions when I'm finished. You see, the whole investigation was predicated on the basis of Bruce's identification of the body as that of Paul. Bruce here identified the body as probably being that of his brother Paul and, as the DNA didn't give us the names of the persons from whom the respective DNA samples were taken, we took it for granted Bruce's identification of Paul, was correct. DNA samples taken from both the body and from Bruce confirmed they were related so we accepted Bruce's ID on face value. As a consequence, we were totally flummoxed as nothing made any sense.

'While we had quite sufficient motives for Andrew to do away with the entire Glover clan, we had the wrong body for him to tick all the boxes to be the guilty party. Our investigation has uncovered quite sufficient evidence to convict Andrew of his involvement, but it doesn't add up to him being the actual murderer. No, Superintendent, we've been had, and something smells rotten in the state of Norway.'

Superintendent Hayes looked annoyed. If my chief inspector has lost the plot, where the bloody hell am I, he thought as he settled back on the settee.

~

Before Simon could continue with his exposé of the case, there was a knock on the door. 'Oh, that must be our latecomers,' Simon said as the door to the living room opened. The latecomers included a man dressed in a dark suit, a woman wearing high heeled shoes, an electric blue skirt and tight fitting white polo neck jumper, followed by a uniformed policeman.

'Ah Noel, at last.' Turning to the men already seated, he said, 'Gentlemen, may I introduce Cheryl Drake, whom I think is already known, at least to the Glover family. The other person is Detective Sergeant Noel Elliott.'

If Bruce and Andrew Glover had felt at ease before Cheryl Drake entered the room, they now appeared downright disconcerted. On the other hand, Cheryl just stood in the centre of the room, her gaze fixed on Bruce Glover. Simon watched on in anticipation, the silence becoming more silent, the gaze becoming more hostile with each passing second. It was clear something had upset Cheryl Drake who was now in the process of stoking a rage of monumental proportions.

Finally, Cheryl appeared to come to terms with the turmoil she was undergoing. 'Well, well, well. Just look what we have here; a real live and kicking dead body, and without a scratch on it. Whoever did the autopsy was either really neat or very clever, if I remember my biology classes. Anyway Paul, I really do hope you're feeling a little better now. From what I've seen of it, the morgue isn't the most restful place to repose, if you're still alive that is.'

Andrew slumped back on the settee, closed his eyes and, with a hand to his forehead, slowly shook his head in despair. 'Oh, bugger.'

Detective Superintendent Hayes looked at Cheryl, then Paul before casting a searching glance to Simon. It was clear to both Simon and Noel that the good Superintendent Hayes hadn't lost the plot; he never had it to lose in the first place. While Andrew was in the process of giving everyone the impression the game was up, Paul's eyes were darting around the room without fixing his gaze on anyone or anything.

Having completed the delicate task of re-establishing the fragile acquaintanceship with the weasel, or ex-lover, Cheryl made a beeline straight for a cocktail cabinet, previously un-noticed by Simon. 'Yeah, go right ahead. Help yourself,' came Paul's contemptuous invitation. Cheryl chose to ignore Paul and poured herself a large Scotch whisky which was consumed in impolite haste.

Carefully, and with great resolve, she poured herself another, took a sip then slowly, and with dignified grace, strolled to a vacant lounge chair where she unceremoniously flopped without spilling so much as a drop of her potent thera-peutic beverage. All the while her eyes never left Bruce's face, or was it Paul's face? Notwithstanding Cheryl's tempestuous demeanour, to her credit she was trying to adopt techniques designed to create a feeling of quiet tranquility. Unfortunately, the techniques were failing dismally, her well endowed chest heaving in concert with her deep breathing as she fought to control her pent-up fury.

After taking a further sip of the Scotch, Cheryl's attention was drawn to the soft amber fluid filling her glass. 'You know, Paul, this has to be the best Glenfiddich I've tasted, it is smooth, smoother than the Glenfiddich I have at home. I'm glad I changed my mind after opening the bottle of wine you have on the cabinet. No doubt you can drink it later.'

For some reason Paul appeared to be overcome with a bout of fearful dismay. 'You opened the bottle of wine, the one on the cabinet?'

'Yes, you said help yourself, so I did, but I changed my mind and opened the Scotch instead.

'You bloody stupid woman, don't you know what you've done? That wine was my '62 Grange and worth a couple of thousand. And there was a bottle of Glenfiddich already open. You didn't open the other bottle, did you?'

'Yes. I didn't look for your stock of Scotch. Anyway, it doesn't matter having two bottles open as they'll both be drunk. But I must say, this is very smooth,' said Cheryl and scoffed the remaining Scotch.

'Holy hell.' Paul had gone to the cabinet and picked up the two bottles, the Grange and the Glenfiddich. The bottle of Scotch displayed the stag's head and name Glenfiddich, but under the name were the words "Rare Collection" making the contents of the bottle somewhere around the ten thousand dollar mark.

While Cheryl and Paul had cemented their mutual hatred for each other, the remaining guests were fascinated being in the presence of such august alcoholic beverages, the likes mere plebs can only imagine. Cheryl looked smug and cast a sly glance at Noel who immediately knew that Cheryl had made no unintended blunders; she had sought revenge and found it, and Paul was not happy.

Simon took up his stance in front of the fire place and folded his arms. 'For Christ sake. We're not here for a wine tasting so can we get back to the matter at hand. For the benefit of those unaware of the source of Cheryl's anger, which is probably the majority of you, I think I can give you an explanation and clear up any misconceptions you may have. To begin with, Paul, you can cut the charade of pretending you're Bruce the pansy because, unless I'm horribly wrong, and I'm sure I'm not, you're not Bruce at all, you're Paul. Bruce is dead, as you well know having bashed him over the head in this very room with the fire poker. And I don't think you'll be around much longer to enjoy your booze.

'Police forensics have confirmed the poker we recovered on our previous visit, is the murder weapon. While we were unsure as to who did the actual bashing, we failed to find any other finger prints on the poker apart from yours, Paul. In fact, it would have been rather surprising to find Bruce's fingerprints. You see, some years ago, Bruce was done for a minor drug offence and his fingerprints were recorded by police. Surprisingly, the prints taken from our seafaring corps matched those of Bruce Glover. Now, Bruce, unless you are an exceptional example of the living dead, I'd say you had to be Paul Glover.'

Bruce Glover, or was it Paul Glover, leant back in his chair, closed his eyes and slowly shook his head before turning to Superintendent Hayes. 'Superintendent, I know most of you blokes get your badges out of a Wheeties packet, but what planet did you find this one? The whole idea is preposterous.'

Superintendent Hayes frowned. The last thing Superintendent Hayes wanted was to be asked a question, any question, as he was already having trouble coming to grips with what had already been revealed. 'Ahh, yes. Chief Inspector Webster, just so we're all reading from the same book, could you please explain these allegations?'

'By all means, sir. Quite apart from the fingerprints taken from the body, Paul's fingerprints were found on the murder weapon. Now, if it was Paul who was found dead in the harbour, it tends to suggest Paul is both murderer and victim, having bashed his own brains in with an iron bar. The person here passing himself off as Bruce Glover is, in reality, Paul Glover. Obviously he is stricken with remorse over the loss of his dearly departed brother, quite apart from the fact that he's committed the heinous crime of fratricide.

'We had problems that caused some delay in coming up with the identification of the body, notwithstanding that such delay was beyond our control,' added Simon as he cast a passing glance at Superintendent Hayes. 'In fact, it wasn't until an old friend put us on to Tiny Timmins were we able to follow-up information that led us to the identification of the body. Obviously other people were well aware there had been a body retrieved from the harbour, well before we had any idea as to the identity of the body.

'But you see, Andrew had already told Cheryl that Paul had been fished out of the harbour well before we determined who the body belonged to. You remember, Andrew, you rang Cheryl before those awful thunderstorms to advise her of Paul's death. Although Paul, playing the role of Bruce, had identified the body as that of Paul Glover, we didn't receive DNA confirmation that the body was definitely a Glover until well after those storms. I can't see how you were so sure it was Paul, and not Bruce, who was fished out of the harbour, unless you and Paul had planned the whole thing.'

'But doesn't that open up a whole new can or worms?' asked

Superintendent Hayes, his interest overcome with a sense of enthusiasm that had been somewhat lacking up to now. 'If it's Bruce lying in the morgue, and not Paul, that presents both these two with motive, means and opportunity.'

'Hey, now just hang on a moment,' protested Andrew who was evidently peeved by the superintendent's comments. 'I take it you are referring to my own nephew, Paul, and his associate, Mr Timmins? Paul would never do anything like murder his own brother.' Tiny's immediate reaction to Andrew's question was a look of intense horror, though he managed to remain stoic in his reluctance to make any comment, just as he had done all night.

'No, Andrew,' replied Simon. 'The superintendent is referring to you and Paul. I've no doubt you were present when Bruce was murdered, and even if it wasn't you who did the actual liquidating, you immediately volunteered to dispose of the body. Evidence suggests you initially dumped the body in the back of your Mercedes as forensics have matched the tyre treads of your car to those found out in the yard, along with traces of Bruce's blood in the boot of your car. Quite apart from that, I have my doubts Tiny has ever met Paul before tonight's proceedings. Isn't that right, Tiny?'

Tiny shook his head in categorical denial. 'No, I've never met the man in my life before tonight. I did meet his brother, whoever it was, but he was already dead by then.'

'Ah, get off the grass, Mr Policeman. Who are you trying to kid? Whose body was I trying to get rid of and why would I want to get rid of it anyway? That would be against the law,' responded Andrew with righteous indignation.

Simon folded his arms, gazed fixedly at the floor and slowly shook his head in wonder. 'Look, Andrew, Tiny has already provided us with a written statement. He says you pulled a shoofty on him when you paid him to dispose of a bag of garbage on Bruce's boat. Tiny thought the idea pretty stupid, but he needed the money, so he didn't ask any questions. Poor old Tiny had no idea what he was actually doing until he found the bag of garbage was really a bag of body. He had nothing to do with the murder, apart from earning a few bob from you. But if you're so keen to talk about the disposal of the body, let's talk about the disposal of the body.'

Simon pursed his lips, clasped his hands behind his back and shrugged his shoulders. 'I must admit, the actual method of disposal was quite intriguing. To be left hooked to the anchor of a boat moored in the harbour could suggest the body was the victim of a drowning, or maybe even a suicide, which was definitely not the case. The body was quite dead before it hit the water, a condition Tiny has already confirmed in his statement. The pathologist supports this as he found Bruce Glover had been killed by a blow to the back of his skull prior to him entering the water.

'At the time, Andrew's method of disposal was totally immaterial to Paul. But Andrew was thinking outside the box. Knowing Tiny would do anything for a buck, he conned Tiny into believing he was playing a trick on Bruce. In reality, he got Tiny to do the dirty work of actually hooking Bruce's body up to the "Mithuna", not that Tiny was aware it was a body, at that stage anyway. Andrew told Tiny the name of the boat and where it was parked. He also had to vent his knowledge of astrology by giving Tiny a lecture on the history of Mithuna which, of course, is the Sanskrit name for Gemini. Unfortunately, by the time Tiny reached Rushcutters Bay, he couldn't remember the name of the boat so he did what he believed to be the next best thing; he attached it to a "Gemini" owned by Graham Lee, not that Tiny had any idea who the owner was.'

'But why dispose of Bruce on his own boat in the first place?' interjected Superintendent Hayes.

'Paul never stopped to think about the deed he had perpetrated or the repercussions it would cause. He just thought the first priority was to get rid of the body and everything would be hunky-dory. Andrew, on the other hand, had a few more clues and realised that if he disposed of the body where it wouldn't be discovered, there would be no death certificate issued for another seven years and this certificate was an essential requirement to their money making scheme.

'Sure, it was easy enough to forge Bruce's signature, but without a death certificate, the deeds to the property would remain in joint names thus making the long term project of Andrew and Paul difficult, if not unmanageable. Andrew knew Bruce's body had to be found eventually in order for a death certificate to be issued. Another point of disposing of the body in the manner it was is the fact that by the time it was discovered, identification by any means other than DNA would have been impossible, along with the hope that the murderer's trail might have gone cold. Maybe Andrew hoped the sharks would make a complete meal of Bruce, provided they left sufficient identifiable evidence for a death certificate to be issued.

'Ahh so,' exclaimed Superintendent Hayes, suddenly catching up with at least one aspect of the Anchor Man murder case. 'Andrew stashed the body away in a place where it would eventually be found?'

Simon placed his left fist on his hip and with the thumb and forefinger of his right hand squeezed the bridge of his nose. 'Well, sort of, sir. Andrew had told Tiny to dump the garbage on Bruce's boat, not Graham Lee's. If Tiny had got it right, Bruce would still be feeding the fishes while hanging off his own boat's anchor. An abandoned car will eventually draw attention whereas it will take a lot more time for an abandoned boat moored in the middle of Rushcutters Bay to come to someone's attention. Sure, it would be found eventually, and in a lot less time than seven years, probably when the annual mooring fees became payable.

'You see, Andrew never told Paul just where he was going to dump the body. Andrew knew that Paul couldn't care less about some insignificant little boat Bruce had purchased; he had no interest in boats whatsoever. As a consequence, no-one was going to raise the "Mithuna" anchor in the foreseeable future, and Andrew knew this. All in all, it made a perfect hiding place for the body which would either decompose or be eaten away by the marine life, thus making identification difficult, but not impossible. Paul, acting as Bruce, was able to establish the DNA relationship with the dead body and claim the body was Paul's. Unfortunately for Paul and Andrew, with Tiny using the wrong anchor, the body was recovered much sooner than anticipated.

'Irrespective of Bruce's murder, I somehow think Andrew was out to seek revenge on the rest of the family, and that meant the elimination of both his nephews. It's just that he was happy to bide his time, recognising "The Grovel" was worth a fortune in itself. He therefore came up with the redevelopment idea and when Paul did away with Bruce, Andrew must have thought all his Sundays had come at once.'

Paul looked at Andrew, his forehead furrowed, his eyes reduced to mere slits of anger. 'So, you bloody washed up, two-bit lord of the manor, you wanted the lot for yourself. No way in the world would I let you get away with it.'

'Ahh, get stuffed,' came Andrew's impatient response. 'The whole thing is a load of crap. Since when did you start believing what the police have to say?'

Simon smiled and shook his head. 'Paul, you just don't get it, do you?' Andrew was quite happy when you murdered your brother as that accounted for half the Glover family and moved him a lot closer to the family fortune.' Simon turned to Tiny who had continued to maintain the low profile throughout the evening's revelations. 'Tiny, you were aware that there was gossip around the traps that Andrew Glover was looking for you?'

Tiny looked uncomfortable and it was fairly obvious he would have preferred to have been anywhere else. 'Yes, I'd been told by a few people that he was looking for me, but so were you. I could understand why you were after me as I had disposed of a body and something told me that that might not be quite kosher. Unfortunately, I had this funny feeling if Andrew Glover found me I wouldn't get to do too much fishing in the future.'

'What a load of crap,' exploded Andrew Glover as he lurched out of his chair and made a beeline for the cocktail cabinet. After pouring himself a good size glass of whisky and throwing the contents down his throat, he turned to Simon. 'Yes, Tiny's right, I was looking for him, but not to kill the bugger, but to offer him another job.'

'And we can assume Tiny would have had previous experience in the job you had in mind?' enquired Noel who was quite enjoying the spectacle of seeing the Glovers squirm.

'Well, whatever you assume is your business,' snarled Andrew, now becoming irritable with the innuendos pointed in his direction. 'As far as I'm concerned, you can bloody well think whatever you like. I had nothin' to do with Paul's death. That night after Cheryl left, Paul asked Bruce for the last time if he would change his mind. When he said "no" Paul flew off the handle, picked up the poker and bludgeoned Bruce to death. We hadn't planned on killing him then, it was just a spur of the moment sort of thing.'

'Ah-ha,' Simon exclaimed as he clasped his hands behind his back and started his pacing back and forward in front of the fireplace. 'So, you two had conspired to do away with Bruce. It just worked out that Paul got carried away and belted Bruce at that particular moment, not later as planned. Andrew, you must have viewed Paul's action as a most fortuitous act, irrespective of when Paul bludgeoned Bruce. With Bruce's death you suddenly saw that, with a little luck, or ingenuity on your part, you could end up being the sole Glover left alive and the family fortune would be yours, along with the fortune the property development would make. It was very nearly a case of a tontine coming to fruition.' Simon stopped his pacing and looked at Paul. 'And you, Paul, you had no idea Andrew was planning to do away with you?'

Paul looked aghast. 'What the bloody hell do you mean, "do away with me"? Why should he?'

Simon frowned and shook his head. 'Money, you idiot. You may have had this idea you and Andrew were all pally and friendly, but Andrew would quite happily slit your throat. Ah, for goodness sake, do I have to spell it out for you? Uncle Andrew over there planned to eliminate you, just as you planned to eliminate both Andrew and Cheryl, Andrew because you're just as greedy as he is and, on top of that, he knew you had murdered Bruce, knowledge he may have used further down the track. You planned to do away with Cheryl because she could destroy the whole scheme and give the police a very interesting story. Really, the only beneficiary in all this would have been Tiny who would make a fortune disposing of dead bodies, though I s'pose it would have been a race to see who kills who first, not that I think Cheryl was about to kill anybody.'

The superintendent still had a somewhat confused look on his face. 'Okay, I can see why Bruce's dead. But what has Cheryl got to do with all this? And why on earth did she hook into the boyfriend? I thought she would have been glad to see he was still alive.'

Simon turned to Paul and asked, 'Do you want to tell Superintendent Hayes of your fiendish little plot or shall we ask Cheryl to explain?'

Paul had removed the smoking jacket and cravat to reveal a dark grey T-shirt with the picture of a naked woman sitting astride a Harley Davidson. 'No, you seem to have all the answers, even if the whole thing is ridiculous,' replied Paul with a look of total boredom. 'As far as I'm concerned you can ask whoever you like.'

'Cheryl?'

'Delighted, Chief Inspector,' returned Cheryl Drake, as she sat down after having helped herself to another somewhat substantial Scotch from the rapidly depleting expensive bottle. Having regained her composure and, though still visibly annoyed, she was glad of the opportunity to tie the rope tightly around her former boyfriend's neck. 'I'll cut to the chase without all the crap relating to the nature of our relationship, which was a total sham and a complete waste of time and effort. I must admit, Paul led me up the garden path well and truly and if I can help the police hang the bastard, I'm happy to do so, after I drink his grog.

'Obviously Paul started his homework early on in the process and had convinced me of his sincerity well before any redevelopment paperwork hit council. Unfortunately for me, the sod won me over for the sole reason he believed my position within council could influence the decision regarding the application. He had asked me, in a not so round about sort of way, that I should ensure any application for the redevelopment of the property received favourable consideration. God knows exactly what techniques I was supposed to use to gain this "favourable consideration" from a bunch of bureaucratic non-events, but I can hazard a guess. I made it very clear to Paul that I was never, nor would be, in any position to influence a decision, irrespective of what techniques were available. I can now see that's all I was to Paul; someone to push any application he made into the right basket.'

Noel, having listened to proceedings with interest, and in light of Cheryl's tale of manipulation and exploitation, had a question. 'Cheryl, as Paul had conned you into a contrived relationship, how do you think he would have ended it? After all, you were going to bump into him at some point in time, and that would blow the whole thing wide open.'

'Harrumph,' exclaimed Cheryl. 'I know bloody well how he intended to end it. So does Andrew. You see, you two rotten bastards, I overheard your little conversation about having to get rid of "her" before whoever's funeral, which would probably have been the first opportunity I'd have to see Bruce, or Paul. I've no doubt I'm the "her" to whom you were referring. Naturally I thought I would be seeing Bruce at the funeral where in reality I would bump into lover boy here. You're absolutely right, Sergeant Elliott, they had to get rid of me as their whole scheme depended on Paul appearing to be dead while the harmless Bruce, God rest his sole, was alive and kicking. And if you want any more proof that this yobbo is Paul, I can tell you he has a mole...'

'Just shut up,' roared Paul, or Bruce. 'You don't have to go there.'

'Ooh, tetchy, isn't he,' chided Cheryl. 'Anyway, Bruce never did get on with Andrew and, despite his sexual inclinations, he would never have got into bed with him, metaphorically speaking that is. That left it up to Andrew and Paul to work out a solution. Maybe Andrew and Paul had already conspired to kill Bruce, but I'm pretty sure it wasn't meant to happen when it did. It must have been as Andrew described, you know, the night I was over here when Bruce refused to change his mind, obviously a bad decision on his part. Not wishing to let a little case of intransigence get in the way of money, they bashed his head in, forged his signature on the application then proceeded as if nothing had happened.

'Andrew had been buttering up council members for yonks with an aim of getting the redevelopment plan approved while Mr Prince Charming, over here, was charming me out of my knickers in the hope I would guarantee the council decision. How naive and stupid was I? Andrew's a greedy bugger and was very bitter about getting zilch from his sister-in-law's will. He saw Paul as nothing more than a means to an end of getting his hands on the Glover fortune, the idea to knock this place down and build a nest of ritzy townhouses being those means. He had no doubt Paul would be all for it, while suspecting Bruce would never agree. Andrew was right on both counts as Paul was just as greedy as Andrew, and Bruce was never going to alter his decision. What I didn't know was who the actual killer was. Obviously I believed it was Paul who was dead, but then again, it is difficult to kill a weasel. It certainly becomes a lot clearer now we know it is Bruce who's dead as he was the stumbling block to Andrew and Paul's scheme to make millions. So the two of them got together and killed Bruce?'

Simon smiled and nodded. 'Yes, I think it probably worked out as Andrew has described. The only difference I'd make is to point out to Andrew that although he may not have done the actual killing, he'll still be charged with murder.'

'Now you just hang on a minute. Even if Andrew has told you what he thinks happened, and my finger prints are all over the poker, and considering Bruce really got up my nose for not going along with our scheme, it's all circumstantial. You've no real evidence against Andrew or me, apart from the fact that Andrew hired Tiny to dispose of a body,' remonstrated Paul, sounding almost aggrieved by Simon's statement. 'It could have been anybody's body.'

'Circumstantial, my bloody eye. We know it wasn't just

anybody's body, it was your brother, Bruce,' interjected Cheryl as she made her way back from the cocktail cabinet with another large Scotch. 'Oh oh, here constable, hold this for a second' she said to the uniformed policeman who was standing next to the door. 'Don't anybody say another word until I get back as I want to know what the hell's going on. I'll only be a moment, but I need to go to the loo; all this alcohol.'

Whether it gave the men sitting around the drawing room time to gather their thoughts, or to reflect on the evening's disclosures, silence prevailed, which was quite remarkable in view of the allegations currently being bandied around. Within two minutes Cheryl Drake returned looking far more composed and, after taking her drink back from the constable, who had furtively sneaked a sip of the single malt nectar, she relaxed back in the lounge chair she had been previously occupying. 'Now, that's much better. We can get on with it now.'

CHAPTER 30

*D*etective Superintendent Michael Hayes had listened intently to the expose of events that were about to catapult his reputation within the force, but more specifically, establish his credibility with his colleagues at the Day Street CIB. There were still aspects of The Anchor Man murder mystery he didn't understand. Secretly, Hayes had admitted to himself that there were times he had incurred difficulty keeping up with Simon's "who did what" objective of the night's little soiree.

Following Cheryl Drake's return from the call of nature, Simon continued, his hands in his trouser pockets, his head down unconsciously noting the pattern on the faded rug. 'Now, where were we before that brief interruption? Ah yes, the dead body, and yes I know, most bodies are dead for all you pedantic know-alls. The whole scheme was meticulously worked out between Andrew and Paul, even to the extent Paul had been in the process of stealing Bruce's identity and developing Bruce's persona, as we have all borne witness to. In fact, Paul carried off the gay act to such an extent, it couldn't be real, and Cheryl here has painted us a far different picture of Bruce than that acted out by Paul.

'Obviously there was more to Paul's hostility towards Bruce than just the fact that Bruce wouldn't sell up, and that was the fact that Bruce was gay. Paul's total disdain for his brother was exemplified as he flagrantly lampooned and ridiculed Bruce who, in reality, was nothing like the person Paul made him out to be. Quite apart from your abject failure to display Bruce's true physical demeanour, Paul, what's the make of engine in the "Mithuna"?'

'How the bloody hell would I know? An engine's an engine and that stupid boat belonged to Bruce. And who cares anyway?' replied Paul in a very belligerent manner.

'Well,' responded Simon as if it was perfectly obvious, 'no matter how hard you tried to steal Bruce's physical identity, you would never have been able to steal his feelings and emotions, which included his love of boats. Eventually someone would become concerned that such a lovely boat was going to rack and ruin. You see, Paul, people who like boats regard them more than just boats; they're living entities with a heart and soul.'

Superintendent Hayes frowned, got up from the settee and made his way to the cocktail cabinet where he poured himself a Glenfiddich, a first for Hayes who was usually a Jim Beam drinker. He returned to the settee and set about trying to catch up with the unfolding events. 'One thing I'm just a bit unsure of, DCI Webster. You say Paul is the murderer, and I mean the bloke who actually did the cracking of Bruce's head. On top of that, Andrew has already stated that it was Paul who, in a fit of rage, whacked Bruce with the fire poker. As Andrew and Paul had conspired to kill Bruce, they could never have foreseen the murder being perpetrated while in a fit of rage, and not exactly according to plan. As a consequence, have we got them for actual murder or manslaughter? I could never get my head around that actus reus and mens rea stuff.'

The significance of Simon shaking his head was probably lost on the Superintendent, despite Simon's efforts to constrain the thought that the senior police officer must have been kidding. 'Well, the act was real enough, however I suppose the mens rae stuff could be debated. Though the physical act of the killing was a trifle different to what they had originally intended, they had already conspired to do away with Bruce. If Paul had picked up a feather duster and belted Bruce with it, and Bruce subsequently had a heart attack and died, Paul might possibly go for manslaughter, in the worst case. But even in a fit of rage, one doesn't grab an iron bar and belt someone over the head in an effort to induce nothing more than a headache. Paul grabbed an iron bar that, by all accounts, could be considered a lethal weapon. Any jury would find that a person armed with such a weapon would have to know full well that to belt someone over the head with it would be a life threatening act.'

'Before you go any further, Chief Inspector,' interrupted Paul. 'If I'm Paul, how come as soon as Bruce was dead, Andrew and I didn't press council for a decision on the redevelopment straight away?'

Simon nodded before clasping his hands behind his back. 'Yes, you really played the part extremely well. As Bruce, you had to continue the charade of being opposed to the idea of redevelopment. But then again, you had to. Bruce had let every man and his dog know how he felt about the proposal. For Bruce to have a sudden change of heart would have been totally out of character and would probably have prompted some embarrassing questions. You therefore had to ease the change of heart gently over a period of time so people would be able to see

Bruce had altered his views on the matter. Mind you, I have never heard of a case where someone was trying to slow down a council application; they're quite slow enough.

'But everything hinged on Bruce's decision not to redevelop or sell or do anything to the property. Oh sure, everyone knew he would never change his mind. But why? Why was Bruce so determined to keep the place as it is? Paul?'

'The stupid ponce had this weird idea of family history, and the house was part of that history. I don't know, he just wanted to keep it in the family,' replied Paul in a belligerent tone.

'Andrew?' Simon asked.

'How the bloody hell would I know. Just to be a real nark and be a pain in the neck, I suppose.'

Simon shook his head, folded his arms and looked pensively at the floor. 'Paul, I take it you don't live here on a permanent basis?'

'Hell no. I prefer my flat up at Potts Point. I only come over here on the odd occasion. It's just coincidence you've happened to find me here when you've called.'

'So there are rooms of this mansion that you haven't entered, at least not since the death of Bruce, that is?'

'Of course there are. It's a pretty big house and I really don't give a stuff about the place.'

Simon smiled a knowing smile filled with knowing implication. 'Just to satisfy my curiosity, do you mind giving us a guided tour?'

Paul hesitated and said, 'And what the hell has a guided tour got to do with any of this.'

'Just humour me,' returned Simon. 'What's upstairs?'

'Four bedrooms and two bathrooms,' replied Paul arrogantly.

'Downstairs?'

'Kitchen, dining room, library, this room, and a couple of others at the rear of the building.'

'Well, let's go have a look at the ones at the back of the house first,' Simon said.

Everyone in the living room, including Paul, now had their interest piqued as it was evident Detective Chief Inspector Simon Webster had expectations as to the outcome of the little exercise. Superintendent Hayes gave Simon a questioning look as he took up his position in the queue, led by Paul who headed for the door.

The first room to be opened turned out to be nothing more than a storage room for a broken bed and half a dozen empty tea chests covered in dust. A small window on the external wall was covered with a blind and, as there was no light globe, the room was very dingy and squalid. Simon watched Paul attentively as he made his way to the second room and, without hesitation, opened the door.

Seven individuals filed back into the drawing room; Cheryl, Paul, Andrew and Superintendent Hayes headed for the cocktail cabinet for fortification, Noel and Tiny to their seats while Simon stood in front of the fire place and scratched his right earlobe in contemplation. The uniformed police officer, whose poker-face countenance hadn't changed all evening, took up his position by the door after having accompanied the tour of the mansion.

Once all were seated, there appeared to be no great desire for anyone to say anything, it being left to Simon to reignite proceedings. 'So Paul, you had no idea of what Bruce was up to?'

'As I said, I don't live here, this was where Bruce used to live. How the hell would I know he'd been cultivating marijuana with all that stuff. I've never been inside that room before, and that's the truth.'

'And you, Andrew. You knew nothing about it?' Simon asked knowing full well the answer he was likely to receive. He wasn't wrong.

'I know nothin' about anyone growing that stuff. What do they call it? Hydrotherapy? hydro something or other?'

'Hydroponics, you moron,' broke in Paul.

'Well, at least now you know why the lighting is so bad in this place,' Simon remarked. 'Bruce had it wired up so that his little horticultural enterprise took almost all the electricity. From what I'm led to believe, it's all very sophisticated and produces a very high quality product, not that I'm an expert in the field of marijuana cultivation. No wonder he never wanted to get rid of this place. It seems he was earning a few bob by selling it to dealers up around Darlinghurst while at the same time giving out little packets of freebies to help boost trade and win friends. No, the last thing Bruce wanted was to give up this place. And now you have the real reason as to why he would never agree with your little scheme.'

Superintendent Hayes looked lost. 'You mean, you knew about this little narcotics factory, Chief Inspector?'

Chief Inspector Webster nodded. 'Yes sir, we've known about it for some time but as we weren't investigating the supply of cannabis, we had no reason to act on that knowledge. It's probably inconsequential, but seeing it was the police drug squad who told us about it, we just let it slip.'

'You let it slip? But it's illegal.'

'Yep, but we were investigating a murder and we now have two suspects under arrest. I think two murderers over-trumps one dead marijuana grower, don't you, Noel?'

'Undoubtedly, boss.'

'So, I take it that puts a closure to the Anchor Man investigation?' said Superintendent Hayes, still not sure as to what charges would be laid against the guilty party, whoever that guilty party may be.

CHAPTER 31

The weather was perfect for an afternoon cruising around the harbour and the guests aboard the good ship "Gemini" were eager for a slightly more successful afternoon than that previously arranged by Graham Lee. Simon, Georgie, Noel and Sue, the last to arrive, completed the guest list that included Ron Lange and Judy Kemp, notwithstanding the invitation had been addressed to Ron Lange and "friend". Georgie and Sue were both delighted and somewhat surprised to see Judy, though Louisa thought it perfectly natural when Ron had walked along the marina pontoon with Judy on his arm.

'And just how long has this been going on?' demanded Georgie in a good-natured manner.

Ron looked at Judy and smiled before replying. 'The question is not so much how long it's been going on, but how long is it going to go on for, and I don't think it will be over by the end of the day.'

'Look, just leave them alone. I think it's wonderful,' interrupted Louisa. 'Now, where would you prefer to sit, in the saloon or out here on the afterdeck?' In view of the sunny conditions, it was a unanimous decision to relax outside. With everyone aboard, Graham Lee climbed to the flybridge where he and Charlie Chambers briefly discussed the day's outing and, with no anchor to be raised, he waved to Adam Vance standing on the pontoon to cast off. Graham and Charlie had already agreed that Adam would spend the day at the marina to do the various odd jobs that never seem to get done, especially when you own a boat.

'Well, glad you could all make it,' said Graham as he joined the party. 'Sorry about last time. Hopefully we'll have a little more success this time,' he said as he removed a cushion from the bench seating to reveal a cubby hole containing a very convenient refrigerator filled with an assortment of wines and beer. 'Louisa, would you grab some wine glasses from the galley, please, and while we're at it, anyone for a beer?'

Charlie slowly edged "Gemini" from the marina for the short trip to Athol Bay, an anchorage on the northern side of the harbour, and just off Taronga Park Zoo. Graham's guests were now settled on the seating that ran down both sides of the afterdeck and across the stern, save for a gap for access to the vessel's transom. A small table centered on the afterdeck was well provided with the mandatory supply of nibblies and a variety of cheeses, the subliminal enhancement to any glass of wine. As he settled himself beside Louisa, Graham Lee couldn't help thinking that "Gemini's" progress through Rushcutters Bay was an infinite improvement on the last outing.

The main topic of conversation was, as to be expected, The Anchor Man as everyone was aware of the final outcome, but not the specifics of the case. While Simon and Noel were obviously aware of the events leading up to the eventual arrest of the culprits, there were those busting to know the hows, whys, and wherefores of the case, especially as everyone present had been actively involved, to some extent at least.

'So, little Lucy Brucie wasn't the sweet little old Brucie we thought he was?' Ron remarked as he actually poured himself a glass of beer, an action that caught everyone's attention. No-one had ever seen Ron pour a beer as he usually drank the contents straight from the bottle, or can. Ron was out to impress.

'Oh, I don't know,' mused Simon. 'I think he took up the job of growing marijuana as a hobby and found he could produce a high-grade product that made him very popular with the people he associated with. Once he had it all setup at Elizabeth Bay, it was no wonder he didn't want to sell the place or have it knocked down. Obviously he wasn't in the horticultural business for the money, more the popularity he attracted.'

Graham, looking a bit perplexed, shook his head in wonder. 'Okay, Simon, but if the drug squad knew what he was up to, why didn't they bust him?'

'Ah, yes. When your old mate Superintendent Fisher, who is now known as Mr Foster but wants to become Superintendent Fisher again, told me the story, that was my immediate question too. The thing is, drugs are apparently coming in from Asia on ships. They're being dropped off outside the heads where the dealer, or dealers, run out in their little boats and pick them up. As Bruce had a boat, and was known to police for his involvement in drugs, albeit a long time ago, they were keeping an eye on him to determine if he was into the heavier drug trade, which of course, he wasn't,' replied Simon with a shrug.

'But did Paul or Andrew know of Bruce's horticultural interests?' asked Judy.

As Simon had just put a handful of peanuts into his mouth, Noel volunteered an answer. 'No, not at all. They were of the belief that Bruce's reason for not wanting to do anything with the place was based solely on family tradition, which, as we now know, was a load of hogwash. Sure, Bruce could have made a bundle if he had agreed to their scheme and he wouldn't have got himself killed. As it was, he just happened to be very content with what he had, apart from a homophobic brother. Having buckets of money couldn't buy him the prestige and celebrity status he was gaining by handing out little packets of high-quality marijuana; everyone loved him except his brother and Uncle Andrew.'

Simon clicked his tongue and shook his head. 'The stupid thing is, had Andrew and Paul been aware of what Bruce was up to with his marijuana plantation, it would have been easy enough to stab him with a needle. As the police knew of his little venture, a case of an overdose by a person known to dabble in drugs would not have come as a surprise. Andrew and Paul could have said it was accidental death and everyone would have believed them, thus negating all the trouble they went to con everybody.'

It was Georgie, currently in the middle of pouring herself a Chardonnay, who asked, 'And what about the council worker? She had no idea Paul was using her just to make sure his development plan was approved?'

'Ah, you mean the delightful Cheryl Drake,' replied Simon to a captive audience. 'No, she honestly believed the relationship would eventually end up in marital bliss. Irrespective of whatever she thought, Paul had no intention of letting the relationship develop into anything more than it was; a means to an end. The odd thing was that Cheryl was in no position within the council to influence two flies on the wall, let alone a redevelopment plan involving mega bucks.'

'So Paul intended to do away with her once he'd received the necessary approvals?' asked Georgie.

'I don't think Paul had thought that far ahead. The whole scheme fell apart when Andrew phoned Cheryl and told her

Paul, who was actually Bruce, was dead, and that was a monumental blunder. A police investigation would have determined that Cheryl knew of the death well before anyone else, apart from Andrew and Paul. In addition, somewhere down the track Cheryl was going to run into Paul, the real Paul, which would probably have been at Bruce's funeral, which was supposed to be Paul's funeral. As they couldn't let that happen, and with Cheryl's knowledge of events, they decided to do away with her before the funeral took place.'

Graham Lee lobbed his empty beer can into the bin, sat back and folded his arms. 'So even if Paul hadn't killed Bruce in a fit of rage, he and Andrew had already conspired to kill him off?'

Simon smiled and nodded. 'Oh yes. Bruce had set himself up to be murdered all right; his opposition to the redevelopment made sure of that. The redevelopment application with Bruce's forged signature, together with Joyce's covenant on the property, will be presented as evidence in the criminal court. Quite apart from the criminal aspects of this case, Bruce could have sued Paul for millions in a civil court, if he had lived that is. By killing him, it left all the decisions to Paul and saved both himself and Andrew from being sued.

'You see, After Andrew and Paul killed Bruce they realised it could be seen that they both had motive, means and opportunity to kill him. That in itself would have given the police a hefty start to their investigation, and with redevelopment plans already lodged with council in the names of Paul, Andrew and Bruce, things would have been fairly simple for the police to finalise the case. Now, with Paul's death, the motive is far more difficult to establish. As we said all along, it's was Bruce who should have been dead, not Paul. However, with the real Bruce's death, all Paul, acting as Bruce, had to do was to say he'd changed his mind and was happy for the place to be redeveloped. As a consequence, they decided the bloke they murdered had to be Paul, so Paul set about stealing Bruce's identity. After all, it was for sure Bruce no longer needed it.'

Louisa, after studying her wine glass to determine whether it needed a top-up, looked at Simon with a frown on her face, and determined to make a point. 'Simon, could you confirm Tiny's decision to anchor Bruce's body on "Gemini" was a mistake, just for us stupid women's satisfaction?'

Simon raised his eyes to Graham who happened to be sitting next to the cubby hole. 'Thanks, ta,' he said as Graham passed him another stubby of beer, the contents of which he promptly poured into a glass; all terribly refined.

'But you still haven't said why Tiny chose the wrong boat,' said Louisa with a touch of frustration.

'Sorry, but that's easy. When Andrew Glover came up with the idea of anchoring the body to Bruce's boat, he obviously knew the boat's name. When he asked Tiny to load some garbage onto the anchor, he had to expound his knowledge of the stars and what the connection was with Bruce's boat. He then proceeded to give Tiny a lesson in astrology wherein he told him what Mithuna meant, as Judy pointed out a while ago. In the middle of the night and by the time he'd puttered from one end of the harbour to the other, poor old Tiny couldn't remember the name of the boat to which he was supposed to attach the garbage. However, he could remember Andrew's little story and the name Gemini, so he put the consignment on the boat with the name that he could recall, and that was "Gemini". And okay, you girls were right from the start. I'll concede it was a mistake,' said Simon and raised his can of beer in salute.

It was Ron who diverged from the actual investigation as he turned to Simon. 'And Simon, just what was the wash-up with Detective Superintendent Hayes? Is he the man of the moment at Day Street with the reputation of a super sleuth?'

Simon was in the process of lobbing an empty beer can into

the plastic garbage bin strategically placed in the corner of the afterdeck for such lobbing. Having successfully completed the lob he turned to Ron. 'You know, Ron, Mick Hayes is a nice enough bloke and he'll get on with people at the station. I think I once said something about his predecessor; nice bloke, bad cop or bad bloke, good cop. At superintendent level you're the boss and can't be worried about what people think of you. It's the results that count and you have to let your subordinates know that you're tough enough not to be overly concerned with any ill-will or rancor that comes with the job of being boss. Unfortunately Mr Hayes tries to be Mr Nice Guy all the time and, as a consequence, he turns out to be more like Inspector Clouseau.'

'You honestly believe he's that dumb?' asked Noel.

Simon shrugged. 'No, not dumb. I think he possesses the tendency to be a little slip-shod in his eagerness for results. After all, he was hell bent on us getting someone arrested, and for the life of me, I get the idea he didn't care who it was. There were some inherent delays in this case that we had no control over and he couldn't appreciate that fact. But then again, there were moments when I think the superintendent failed to understand just what was going on. To me, the highlight of his performance was when he opened his mouth to his senior mates in the force. It seems he told them he was investigating a murder involving a gangland war for control of the casinos. I think he's trying to keep a very low profile, now it's turned out the so-called gangland murder was, in reality, nothing more than a case of a family dispute.'

'And have you spoken to Paxton since the arrests of the Glovers?' Noel asked as his attention, momentarily distracted by a passing cruiser with two women sun-bathing topless on the deck. Sue gave him an admonishing kick in the shins.

'Yes, he's very happy with the result. I did mention Superintendent Fisher, or Foster, and his wish to return to Day Street. I don't know if it did any good and I got the idea he already knew of Fisher's wishes. Who knows? Maybe we'll see him back at Day Street after he finishes his stint in exile.'

The Anchor Man conversation was interrupted by Charlie Chambers as he joined the group on the afterdeck. 'Sorry to interrupt, boss,' he said addressing Graham. 'Weather report says a southerly buster blowing in from the south with late rain and thunderstorms.'

Graham Lee nodded. 'Thanks, Charlie. Might be an idea to get us back to Rushcutters Bay and moored before it hits.'

'No problems, boss. I think we have another hour or so out here then we'll head back.'

Noel frowned. 'Graham, you know all about weather forecasts and stuff. As we all know, "southerly busters" come from the south. Seeing we don't get "busters" from any other direction, it seems to me to be an exercise in tautology to call them "southerly busters" when "busters" alone would suffice. Is there any reason then why we call them "southerly busters"?'

Noel, greeted with a chorus of convivial expletives, all different but all meaning the same thing, received another kick in the shins from Sue, together with a look of admonishment from Simon. 'Well, I suppose you're right,' replied Graham, taken aback by the question. 'After all, if it came from the north it would have to be a northerly buster, which we don't get, we only get southerly busters.'

Simon slowly shook his head in wonder and said, 'I'm sorry, Graham. I shouldn't have to make excuses for Noel. He comes up with these bloody useless little gems of stupid diatribe every now and then. I only wish Rosey was still around so Noel could drive him nuts with such idiotic questions.'

Graham smiled. 'That's okay, Simon. Everyone has their little burden to bear and I think Noel will now have his.' He turned to Noel, a serious look on his face. 'Noel, after Adam pulled the anchor up and found the body attached, we haven't had a need to pull it up as I now have a Maritime Board buoy. Seeing Adam is back at Rushcutters, would you be so kind as to go forward and heave in the anchor. Charlie isn't that au fait with what seems to come up with it and, who knows, it might be your turn to haul in the next juicy murder case.'

ABOUT THE AUTHOR

John Henderson was born in Singleton, New South Wales. The family moved to the town of Yass soon afterwards where he spent his younger days before a further move, this time, to Sydney. John went to Manly Boys' High School, represented the District in cricket and spent time surfing. He joined the Army in 1968 and toured Vietnam in 1969-70.

After a brief stint in the Commonwealth Public Service, and with his dry, cynical sense of humour, John chose to write crime satire. A Blind Eye and The Anchor Man in the Simon Webster Fiascos Series, represent an amusing and skeptical view of life and bureaucratic nonsense as viewed by the author.

twitter.com/JohnHenderson07